TRESPASSERS

BOOK 1 OF THE CHAOS SHIFT CYCLE

TR CAMERON

Happy Reading!

JR Cameron

MD PRESS

For Laurel, my love, and Dylan, my life.

Want More Fantastic Science Fiction Action and Adventure for Free? Join the Readers' Group and get *Suicide Run* as a thank you!

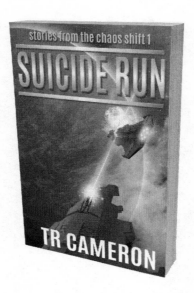

Visit www.trcameron.com/Trespassers to download it for free!

CHAPTER ONE

Lieutenant Commander Anderson Cross didn't realize that this day, this shift, would be the beginning of the end of life as he knew it. He was unaware that he would be responsible for all that was to come. For now, it was just one more night, one more patrol.

"Alter course twenty-two degrees to the north," he barked. The response wasn't as quick as he would've liked. Maybe his baritone wasn't as authoritative as he imagined.

"Aye," replied Lieutenant Erin Smythe while tapping a series of controls on the flat display in front of her. The ship responded smoothly to her touch, the course correction a hint of motion accompanied by the usual pressure-flex in the hull.

Cross was long accustomed to the second shift command, allowing him to work with the second and third shift officers, but several of his new "night" crew were still having adjustment issues. His executive officer, Lieutenant Commander Kate Flynn, glanced up from the science station and shared his look of amusement. They both remembered their own first steps toward command, which included rotations in each of the crew positions.

"Thank you, Lieutenant," Cross said. He took a moment to

appreciate the ship around him. She was a far cry from the newly-minted, gleaming warbird he always envisioned commanding. One of the final ships off the last generation's production line, UAL-2112 showed the cracks and dents that came with age and experience. The *Washington, DC* was her official name, but in practice she was routinely called the *Washington*, or the *Dee-Cee* by her crew. He was proud to be aboard, and prouder still to be in command—even if it was only command of the second shift. He was number three in the *Washington's* hierarchy, subordinate to Captain James Okoye and Commander Felix Olivas. Still, command was command.

Kate's voice cut through his musings. "Permission to leave the bridge, Lieutenant Commander Cross?"

"Granted," he said without thinking. As his brain caught up, he asked "Where are you headed?"

"Jannik and I think we've finished the sensor upgrades on our survey satellites. If it tests out, we might be able to improve the sensors in our torpedoes with the mod. I've done all I can from up here, and he wants to run a couple more simulations before he goes off-shift."

"As if he's ever off-shift." Cross nodded and injected appropriate command gravitas into his response, "Sounds like a worthy project, Lieutenant Commander Flynn. Carry on." He could never pull off a believable level of formality with Kate, a friend and on-again, off-again romantic partner since their academy days. He deliberately did not watch her leave the bridge.

TWO MORE HOURS of endless patrol passed, leaving the crew working hard to stay alert. Cross groused in his mind about the foolishness of patrolling this sector of space where only random chance would put them within sensor range of a threat—

"Contact bearing 313°, 30 low. Running analysis now." His tactical officer's voice betrayed her youth and excitement.

Cross issued the commands to set an arcing intercept course with the unknown blip as Lieutenant Claire Martin resumed speaking. "Contact is an Alliance destroyer. He's in the database, AAN *Gagarin*." Cross moved to peer over her shoulder. The tactical display streamed information about the Alliance ship.

"About our size," Cross murmured. Weapons and defense specifications scrolled past, and he acknowledged it with a grunt, clapping her on the shoulder. "Good work, Martin."

He returned to the captain's chair, sitting down and rocking to get comfortable. New ships boasted adaptive seating for the bridge crew, a luxury he had enjoyed during his rotations and missed now. "Casco, hail his captain with my regards. Politely request that they leave this sector of Union space." The communication officer followed his orders, the message taking only seconds to travel to the other ship. A reply arrived with matching speed.

"Sir, they claim that they have every right to be in this area, as it is a contested zone between our two governments. They suggest that perhaps we would like to depart forthwith."

Cross barked a short laugh. "Forthwith? Who says that? Send reply: Respectfully request that you follow your own advice and get out of United Atlantic League territory immediately." He felt the eyes of the bridge crew on him, but refused to acknowledge them. *The other ship wanted to play? Then play they would.*

"Response received, sir. I'm routing it to your display." A small screen glowed on the wide arm of his chair, and he activated the nondescript earpiece that all the ship's commanders and execs wore. Cross appreciated Ricardo Casco's sense of discretion as he played the imaginative, expletive-laden challenge to engage in anatomically impossible actions from the Gagarin's commander. His teeth flashed in a grin. *Oh, it's like that, is it?*

"Helm, plot and execute a direct-intercept path with the *Gagarin*. Weapons, open tubes and bring cannons to full power. Tactical, orient shields toward the enemy and balance them, but be ready to react. There's no predicting what he'll do." Cross tapped a command code to adjust the ship's status. "Setting battle standby throughout the ship."

The bridge crew jumped to their tasks, as the computerized voice announced the change. The thin, light panels running along each wall turned from white to orange-gold and began a repeating pattern. On every deck of the *Washington*, crew members hurried to their assigned battle stations, with those in the outermost sections of the ship climbing into vacuum suits upon arrival. The *Washington* lacked the power-assist models that were now standard issue.

His chair display registered a query from Captain Okoye. Cross quickly typed a reply outlining the situation and received a "carry on" in response. Encounters with the Alliance were common on patrol, and unless things escalated, the captain would trust him to handle it.

Cross watched the enemy ship turn to meet their approach on the main display. Lieutenant Martin confirmed the enemy's course change and reported readiness. "He has six launch tubes facing forward, covers open, plus a pair of long-range plasma cannons. His broadsides are similar to ours, with a dozen lasers mounted and half that many tubes. Aft armaments are weaker than ours. He's only got two tubes and one medium range plasma cannon."

The most frustrating thing about the quarrel with the Allied Asian Nations was that the two factions were so evenly matched. Each came from the same gravity well, expanded at roughly the same rate along only slightly different vectors, and developed technology at almost identical paces. Add in the actions of spies on both sides, and it was beyond difficult to gain a lasting technological edge over the opposition.

In his anxiousness, Cross leaned toward the main display. Forcing his nerves down, he sat back in his seat, depicting the picture of calm for his crew.

"Continue on intercept course, but be ready for evasive maneuvers when he breaks off, or when we launch, whichever comes first. Weapons, at a range of 10,000, launch a spread of torpedoes set to detonate in between our two ships, and fire a quarter power blast from our plasma cannons into his forward shields. If we're lucky, he'll get the message." The monotony of second shift command fell away, and was replaced by the anticipation of real action.

As the distance clicked down to 20,000 meters, Cross keyed the ship-wide intercom and announced, "Stand by for maneuvers. Standby. Standby." Throughout the *Washington*, crew members moved to grab the handholds present in all compartments and passageways, or secured themselves at their battle stations. On the bridge, automatic harnesses deployed from the seats at all positions, locking them into their insufficiently, padded non-adaptive chairs. He shrugged to settle his harness into place.

At a distance of 11,000, the *Gagarin* fired first. Where Cross had envisioned the encounter as a test of wills to be resolved with a show of bravado, the other ship's commander apparently saw it as a test of power that required the starship equivalent of bloodshed to determine a victor. Both plasma cannon blasts splashed against the *Washington's* forward shields. The bridge's display dimmed to compensate for the brilliance of the beam. It brightened again just in time for Cross to see the impact of six exploding torpedoes.

"Helm, evasive pattern Alpha, but circle for a broadside. Weapons, ready all around. Tactical, damage report."

"Shields holding, sir. Minor bumps and bruises to the crew, but no significant damage to the ship. One or two more dings and scrapes." Every sailor aboard took pride in the accumulated scars that the *Washington* displayed. "The *Gagarin* is circling back toward us."

Smythe announced, "Broadside position in twenty-seven seconds."

Cross fielded another question on his display and summarized the situation as, "Trading shots across the bow." There was no response. He feared that the Captain was already running toward the bridge.

"Hail from the *Gagarin*," reported Casco. "He requests cessation of hostilities and for both ships to exit this contested territory."

Cross frowned. *Arrogant bastard.* "No reply."

FIFTEEN SECONDS LATER, the two foes reached classic broadside position. Tactical officers on both ships were accomplished at their craft and angled the shields to absorb the impact of a salvo of missiles and a cannon barrage. The space between them overflowed with propellant, shrapnel, and lances of coherent-energy seeking a crevice to creep through. A laser overloaded on the *Gagarin*, catching fire and melting down to a blackened piece of slag. The *Washington* accumulated more cosmetic damage, but nothing beyond that.

"Send message to the *Gagarin*: Again, request that you depart UAL space forthwith," his earpiece crackled with the captain's voice.

"Cross, status report."

He spoke in a hushed tone, confident the earpiece's microphone would pick him up, "Trading shots with an Alliance ship still, Captain. I don't think it will go anywhere." He paused, waiting for Okoye's reply. It was not the one he wanted to hear. "En route from Engineering. ETA eight minutes. Try not to destroy my ship in the meantime."

The two ships circled in space. Casco reported, "The *Gagarin* is requesting visual comm, sir."

Cross swiveled his chair to look at the communication officer and raised an eyebrow. "Really? That's interesting. Sure, let's see what they have to say." He turned back to face front and ran a hand through his hair, an unconscious and consistent move prior to important conversations that always amused those who knew him well.

Lieutenant Ricardo Casco's hands moved across his controls, and the display split in two, with the real-time exterior view of the *Gagarin* on the left and its commander on the right. He was a veritable giant of a man, almost spilling out of the command chair.

When he spoke, his rumbling voice reminded Cross of stones

grinding together, "You damaged one of my guns, Union. An apology is in order."

Cross reclined and made a show of thinking. "I think it is more accurate to say that your gun was faulty, and failed to discharge its duty in the heat of battle. I cannot be held responsible for your gun's inadequacy."

The Alliance captain reddened slightly while Cross spoke, the only signal that his needling had hit home. His response was measured, "I believe that you are incorrect. My original statement stands. Are you prepared to apologize for this inappropriate provocation in neutral space?"

Cross straightened and locked eyes with the image on his screen. "First, we are not in neutral space. The United Atlantic League claimed this territory more than a year ago, and I have no doubt this was duly communicated to your government. Second, it was you who fired on us first, and that makes you the one guilty of 'inappropriate provocation.' Third, perhaps I used the wrong word when I described your gun as inadequate, and for that I apologize. I meant cowardly."

His bridge crew sat in stunned silence at Cross's words. The commander of the *Gagarin* was silent as well. His face stilled the way a predator's might before charging. The moment stretched as the two commanders stared at each other.

After an eternity, the Alliance officer nodded. "So be it. You have chosen your fate. I will deliver it to you." He cut the communication line, and the screen reverted to a full-size image of the Gagarin orienting for another attack on the *Washington*.

"Helm, evasive Bravo. Get some distance, minimal cross-section. Tactical, keep shields oriented toward him, extra power forward. Weapons, set up firing solutions on his engines. If we can knock those out, we can take care of him at our leisure."

Cross watched as the *Gagarin* advanced on the main display even as the *Washington* retreated.

"Setting battle stations." Orange-yellow lights turned to a red strobe, and pressure hatches closed throughout the ship.

"Casco, send to *Gagarin*: Last chance. Leave this sector now. We don't have to do this." In his heart, he hoped that they wouldn't take his offer. He knew his ship and his people were better, and he would enjoy proving it to the AAN commander. "Tactical, battle display please."

A moment later the forward screen split again, displaying a real-time camera view in one half and a three-dimensional representation of the *Washington*, the *Gagarin*, and the natural obstacles present in the area. To the benefit of both sides, there was very little space debris in this remote part of their patrol pattern.

"No response from the *Gagarin*, sir. I have the message on auto repeat."

"Excellent, thank you." The other commander wanted to mix it up. That suited him just fine.

"Standby, people. We'll let him make the first move and reveal all of his secrets." Cross saw space combat as a multilevel game of chess. The psychological played out on one board, the tactical on another. He had already achieved dominance on the first by pushing the *Gagarin's* commander into an emotional response rather than a measured action. Now he would see what opening strategy he used, and through it understand his approach. Cross didn't lose often, although his style often left few pieces standing at game's end.

Without warning, the *Gagarin* vanished in a smear of acceleration. "Tunnel jump," the officers at tactical and the helm reported as one. The response was automatic, and the helmsman activated their own tunnel drive, throwing them into the unreality that transcended time and space.

CHAPTER TWO

The tunnel drive was the backbone of modern space travel. Cross didn't understand the deep science behind it, but he knew the basics. When activated, it created a shortcut from here to there—wherever here and there might be. For short distances, such as the combat tunnel jump, the transit was virtually instantaneous. For longer spans, there was a huge mathematical equation that explained how long it would take per parsec traveled. Fortunately, computers handled that calculation effectively. All he needed to know was it was the only way to cover the vast distances between systems without growing old on the way, and using it too near a gravity well resulted in the complete destruction of the tunneling vessel.

Once the tunnel drive was available, combat applications were inevitable and immediate. But after years of use, those applications had lost their effectiveness. The "tunnel jump" repositioned a ship into an advantageous position during battle. The UAL used the tactic to great effect until the other side began to as well. Now, both sides compensated for it as a standard operation. Upon entering a new sector, the ship's helm officer set up a jump point that looked safe.

With everyone committed to this policy, the tunnel jump became at most a distraction, rather than an advantage.

Time and space bent again, ejecting first the *Gagarin* and then the *Washington* into normal reality, further apart than before the jump. The tunnel quickly fell in upon itself and disappeared. A countdown clock appeared on the display tracking the time until the drive would be reset and ready for another transit. This was also a function of distance jumped. In this case, the two ships could not jump again until about six minutes had passed.

Cross failed to understand the science behind this as well, but was aware collecting microscopic reaction mass was somehow pivotal. All he knew for sure was that for the next five minutes and fifty-two seconds, both ships were restricted to operations that occurred within the normal confines of reality.

"He's closing at 80% max, and angling to come at us from below." Claire Martin's voice was matter-of-fact, but Cross heard the slight tremor underneath the words. It occurred to Cross that like Martin, several other officers may not have had any non-simulated battle experience. When the new officers arrived under his command during their last base visit, he had reviewed each of their jackets. Many of them were newly minted and still going through the rotations process to hone their skillsets. He would need to check in with each of them once this altercation was over to make sure they handled actual combat without problems.

The rest of his crew were officers content to be masters of a single position on a succession of ships, like his weapons officer, who lived to shoot things.

Martin's voice was slightly less deadpan as she reported, "Six torpedoes inbound on a direct path. Computer suggests high probability they are standard explosive. Bow shields reinforced."

"Very good, Lieutenant Martin. Helm, we'll make our first pass to their starboard side. Weapons, prepare our port broadside. When we reach 5000, launch forward tubes, and set torpedoes to circle behind to strike his engines. Once in broadside position, fire at will. Tactical, don't neglect the other areas of the ship as you shift shields. That devious bastard may have up some surprises up his sleeve." His officers confirmed his orders.

"Comm, verify the tunnel beacons are recording." Inspired by the black boxes used on airplanes in days long gone by, the beacon was a small tunnel drive with a recording chip in it. That chip contained recordings of all the ship's data up to the second. It also held updated information on the location of the nearest friendly ship or base. Individual beacons could be launched manually, and all would launch automatically if the ship's condition deteriorated to a point where the computer calculated destruction was imminent. After detaching from the ship, the beacons were programmed to tunnel to the closest ally and communicate its data in the hope that any survivors might be rescued.

"Verified, sir."

Both ships closed, and the officers obeyed their instructions. Vibration thrummed with the launch of the *Washington's* torpedoes, and a moment later the enemy's missiles slammed into the *Washington's* forward shields. The humans were knocked around just enough to slow their reaction time, but the computer executed its pre-planned operations without flaw. A broadside of energy weapons and torpedoes slammed against the shields of the *Gagarin*. He responded in kind, opening up with everything in his starboard broadside. Both emerged unscathed from the exchange and traded launches and blasts from their aft armaments as they sought separate corners.

"Well, that was inconclusive," Cross said. "Okay people, time to try something a little different. One thing this old girl has going for her is ridiculously overpowered maneuvering thrusters. Let's use those. Helm, set up for a pass on his starboard side again. This time, do an old-fashioned barrel roll alongside him, cutting our velocity to keep us in contact as long as possible. Weapons, program a sequence to match the helm's actions and fire every weapon on the ship as it comes into alignment with the *Gagarin*. Instead of a single broadside, we'll hit him with everything we've got. Tactical, plot the rotation to have our shields angled throughout the roll."

Cross waited as the bridge crew—his bridge crew—worked to fulfill the tasks he had set for them. Time acted oddly in moments like these, simultaneously compressing and stretching. Eons passed during the short seconds as he watched them calculate navigation, offense, and defense. One by one, stations reported ready. He took a deep breath, smiled at his people, and bared his teeth at his distant enemy. "Execute."

The *Gagarin* was already in motion as the *Washington's* engines pushed her ahead, and the distance between the ships evaporated. The enemy commander showed he was also capable of clever tactics, and launched torpedoes from all his ports at a distance. Their flight patterns revealed they would curve in and strike the *Washington* from multiple angles at once.

"Countermeasures," Cross commanded.

"Countermeasures, aye" the tactical officer said, and a flurry of small projectiles ejected from defensive emplacements spotting the hull, quickly lighting up with the blooms of engaging thrusters. These miniature rockets were all engine behind an explosive nose, and they moved at twice the velocity of the incoming barrage. Impact crushed the triggers within the warheads, setting off shaped charges that detonated their targets, eliminating the majority of them. The ones that remained could not get through the *Washington's* shields.

"Countermeasures successful," Martin reported.

Upon reaching broadside position, the *Gagarin* unloaded a torrent of energy that spread across the strengthened shields and dissipated, failing to find a breach to exploit. The *Washington's* first broadside did the same. Then she rolled and brought her second broadside to bear on the aft portion of the *Gagarin's* starboard defenses. His shields were still recovering, and the additional onslaught penetrated, scouring gun emplacements from the hull and sending flames into the missile tubes. A chain of explosions began within the magazines for the starboard launchers, and sections of the ship blew out into space.

The *Gagarin's* shields flickered, and Cross seized the opportunity to clear the board. "Weapons, target his engines. Fire all aft torpedoes, then add the plasma cannon right as they hit."

Cross watched as the missiles leapt from their tubes, the main display now segmented by one of his crew into forward and aft views. Time stretched again, and it seemed a lifetime until the projectiles met and battered the unstable shields of the enemy ship. The cannon pierced the compromised defenses, its beam of coherent energy drilling deeply into the engine housing. An explosion rocked the *Gagarin* as it lost half of its power. Cheers erupted around him. Cross smothered his wide grin and got back to work.

"Helm, put us at a safe distance. Comm, message to the *Gagarin*: Take your remaining engine off-line and stand down. Once you have stabilized your ship, we are ready to assist. We will tow you to the nearest UAL base, where your ship will be impounded and your crew released."

Additional explosions shook the *Gagarin*. They shrank in both size and frequency as the damage control teams on the Alliance ship fought them. Low-volume conversations began on the bridge, replaying moments of the battle. The tension that had sustained all of them through the terrifying experience of combat bled off, leaving everyone a little unsteady. Among them, only the helmsman noticed the numbers in the corner click down to zero.

The communication officer spoke up. "Lieutenant Commander Cross, the *Gagarin* requests a visual."

"Put him on, Casco." Cross adjusted his tunic and ran a hand through his hair in the moments before the pickup activated. The bridge of the other ship was a flurry of activity behind the captain's chair. The commander nodded in his direction.

"Well fought, *Washington*. The rolling broadside was a useful tactic, one we will better defend against in the future, and one we will use against other less innovative Union ships." Cross cringed at his maneuver being used against his own side, but that back-and-forth exchange of technology, strategy, and tactics was a hallmark of the war between the divided children of Earth. "We require nothing from you at this time. Help has already arrived."

CHAPTER THREE

Captain Dima Petryaev arrived at the appointed time for his rendezvous with the *Gagarin*. The *Beijing* was one of the Alliance's biggest ships, and he had been in command of him for less than a year. The previous commander was now an admiral, and Dima imagined one day he might be forced to advance to that lofty posting. Then again, he wasn't very good at playing the political games required of the admiralty. At least at this level, he could take care of the crew under his command and watch with pride as they advanced through their own careers.

He took a sip of the strong, black gunpowder tea that was ever-present in the holder on his chair. The countdown clock on the screen clicked over to zero, and the ship transitioned out of the tunnel and back into real-space. Standard protocol required an immediate scan of the area, so his tactical officer should be—

"Multiple contacts, Captain. The *Gagarin* is here, but has taken damage. Computer identifies UAL *Washington, DC* also present. She is showing signs of minimal injury. Indications of weapons discharged from both ships."

"Sound General Quarters. Launch ready fighters in defensive

formation around us and the *Gagarin*. Maneuver the *Beijing* between those two." Dima's quiet commands were followed with calm efficiency. "Communication officer, please initiate visual contact with the *Gagarin*." He took another sip of tea. A long career had taught him to embrace the stillness between moments of action.

Once the connection was established, the main monitor screen split into thirds to display real-time view, battle schematic, and the damaged ship's commander. "Captain Petryaev, we were attacked without provocation by the Union. I ask that you destroy them. Slowly, if possible."

Dima laughed at the request. "Mikhail, we know each other well, do we not? So, tell me truly, *without* provocation?"

The commander of the *Gagarin* looked sheepish. "Nothing out of the ordinary, Captain."

"So, hotheaded boasting on both sides led to an exchange of more," he paused briefly, "pointed pleasantries?" Dima shook his head in mild frustration. "It's unfortunate that young rams need to butt heads using tools that endanger so many lives. Have you any casualties?"

"Negative, Captain. Only equipment damage. The *Gagarin's* design protected the crew from the actions of the *Washington*."

Dima shook his head again. It was difficult to compete with the mindset drilled into the Allied Asian Nations' soldiers and sailors during training. Everything from unexpected changes in weather to mistakes made from inexperience to legitimate transgressions were blamed upon the "evil" United Atlantic League. Actually, he thought to himself, that particular tradition started long before the two factions took their disagreements into space. The war on Earth that made all further planet-bound wars too dangerous to contemplate resulted from the same thinking. On both sides. Centuries later, millions of kilometers away from home, and they had gotten exactly nowhere.

"Continue damage control, Commander. We will speak in more detail once this crisis is behind us. At that time, you will transfer command to your executive officer and report to me on the *Beijing*. Petryaev out." He waved an arm and Mikhail disappeared from the screen. "Let's talk to the other hothead, shall we?"

The communication officer had served under Dima across multiple postings and had anticipated the command. After a moment of hushed conversation, a handsome young man with piercing green eyes appeared on the monitor. Dima sighed, remembering a time when his white hair was coal black, when his skin stretched over sharp bones in just that same way. *Youth.* A small smile curved his lips as he remembered at least he was smarter now, if not nearly so attractive.

"This is Lieutenant Commander Anderson Cross, in charge of the UAL *Washington, DC*. We have tracked your fighter launches, and note you have been in contact with the *Gagarin*. I urge you not to engage in any more hostile activity. I also formally request you leave this area of space, which is United Atlantic League territory." Dima admired the man's brash, unproductive confidence.

"I am Captain First Rank Dima Petryaev, in command of the *Beijing*. As you well know, Lieutenant Commander, we do not recognize your claim to this space. You have no bases here, no colonies, just words on paper that declare your ownership. I have little doubt that somewhere in my government, we have the same words on even fancier paper substantiating our own claim. Regardless, this giant rectangle of emptiness is not worth endangering the lives of your young men or mine. When he is ready for travel, I will escort the *Gagarin* from this sector into another, and you may go tell your higher-ups you defended this valuable source of radiation and vacuum."

He watched Cross process his words. It was a calculated insult, but not one that should trigger a violent response. Like the opening phase of a chess match, Dima was judging his counterpart's mental strength and command style. So far, he wasn't particularly impressed.

"That is acceptable, Captain Petryaev. I respectfully suggest that you send a more challenging opponent for future encounters. My crew can only improve by facing those of at least equal skill and intelligence. Anything else would again be only a waste of time and resources." Cross tipped an imaginary hat to him and finished speaking. "*Washington* out."

His screen reverted to the split display again—space and the battle schematic. He noted that his tactical officer had laid in several attack options to confront the Union ship. He gave the man a nod of appreciation, but implemented none of them.

"Lieutenant Zian, send a message to fleet, letting them know what happened here. Suggest a formal complaint against Lieutenant Commander Anderson Cross for an unprovoked attack on the *Gagarin* in a disputed sector of space." He paused, then continued in a more casual tone. "That ought to serve the arrogant young brat right. At the very least, it may make him think for an extra half-second before he engages next time." Two senior officers smiled in response to their captain's gambit.

"Captain," the tactical officer spoke, "we have indications that the *Gagarin* is increasing power to his drive."

Dima frowned at this information. "That's not a good idea. Communication, find out what he's doing. Wing officer, pull our fighters back to a safe distance in case something goes wrong. Tactical, images of the *Gagarin*, the *Washington*, and battle schematic please." The main screen rearranged itself into the requested view, and he saw the small triangles that represented his fighters moving away from the *Gagarin* in the most expedient direction available.

Lieutenant Loh Zian spoke, "He has refused our hails, Captain."

"What?" Dima barked incredulously and turned reflexively toward Zian. "No communication at all?"

"No, sir."

"What the devil—" Dima's voice trailed off as he realized there was only one likely explanation for Mikhail's actions. "Helm, keep us between the two ships. Communication, open a channel to the *Washington*. Tactical, strengthen defenses facing both. Weapons, compute firing solutions on both ships and standby."

Senior Lieutenant Svetlana Ivanova, content until now to assist the most junior officer on the bridge with her tasks, walked to Dima's side. "Both ships, Captain?"

"Aye, Exec. I believe Mikhail is about to do something incredibly stupid."

Anderson Cross appeared in a corner of the main screen. "Captain Petryaev, the *Gagarin* is coming under power. What are the two of you planning?"

Dima was formulating his response when Mikhail also appeared on the screen. By the way Cross reacted, Dima could tell that he was seeing the same communication.

"*Washington*, on behalf of my ship and my crew, I reject your claim to this space. Before I leave, I have a parting gift for you." The image cut off after a rude gesture from the *Gagarin's* commander.

"He's bringing his engines to full, Captain" reported the tactical officer. Before Dima could reply, the commander of the *Gagarin* delivered on his promise. Torpedoes erupted from all of his tubes, exploding together at a notable distance from the *Washington*, creating a momentary barrier to sight and sensors.

An officer on the *Washington* was the first to realize what was happening. Her shocked voice came through the connection between the ships. "He's going to tunnel with only one engine," she blurted out, the words running together in her haste to communicate them.

Both Cross and Dima snapped, "Evasive," at the same moment, and both vessels lurched into motion. Despite their immediate responses, there was not enough time to avoid the consequences of the *Gagarin's* decision.

The tunnel drive relied on a perfect balance of gravitational forces to create a stable connection between two points. In a ship, as large as the *Gagarin*, that balance required two engines working at peak efficiency. On the *Beijing*, it required four working in tandem. The engines on the *Gagarin* were wired in such a way that the tunnel drive should have been impossible to activate with less than two engines. Clearly the ship's crew had spent the time since Dima's arrival defeating those safety precautions.

The rip that the *Gagarin* tore in space wasn't stable. The gravitic forces displayed in wireframe on the battle schematic reminded Dima of a black hole. Several of his fighters were captured, their engines too weak to pull them free. They tumbled into the tear and imploded.

"Maximum speed, Helm," Dima commanded.

The ship lurched as he came up to full power. Dima wasn't concerned, he knew the *Beijing* had enough strength to avoid being pulled into the breach. "Wing commander, get our fighters back on board, right now."

With a single engine, the *Gagarin* couldn't resist the gravitational forces, and was dragged sideways into the tunnel. The comm connection with the *Washington* frayed, then dropped. Dima watched her in both schematic and real-time views as her engines struggled against the pull of the breach.

"Ideas, comrades. How can we assist?" The bridge crew was as lost as he was. This was an unprecedented event in their experience. His thoughts went on a tangent, and he realized it probably had happened before, during the development of the tunnel drive. But no one had survived to report it.

The words of Lieutenant Yegorovich at tactical jarred him back to the moment. "The *Washington* is going in."

Dima Petryaev clenched his fists in frustration as the tunnel consumed the *Washington* and then collapsed in upon itself.

CHAPTER FOUR

"But what would the gods have us do?"

Hierarch Kraada Tak's booming voice washed across his congregation, made up of the highest ranks in the highest castes. "The answer is present in those holy ones themselves. Creation and destruction, war and peace, pleasure and hard work. These things make up our lives, these are the things the gods demand of us. For the Xroeshyn, the gods have charted a course that requires us to soar between the currents, always aware of the forces seeking to pull us to the land."

Kraada gestured toward the ceiling, which depicted a perfect representation of a twilight sky—the single sun in descent balanced by the twin moons rising at the other end of the cathedral's crowning display. A careful watcher would see that elements within that sky were moving—a clever trick of technology and art that used a gravitational field to suspend autonomous representations of space objects. Seven statues, icons of the High Father and his six children —gods and goddesses—framed the display. The High Father looked down upon the altar, and three of his spawn flanked each side of the sanctuary. The eighth pedestal remained empty to remind celebrants of the final deity, Vasoi the destroyer. She was the guardian of souls as they passed between the portals of death and rebirth. The statues of her husband and children avoided looking in her direction for fear they would gain her notice and see their immortality proved false.

"That day will come, that day when the final paradise will open to us, as promised in the *Dhadas Ve Xroe*. But that day is not today. Today, we must adhere to the words the gods have given us in that most holy of books and set aside our petty differences in service of our greater calling." He warmed to his speech, facing down the center aisle of the sanctuary, his broad folded wings fluttering occasionally to emphasize his statements. His ceremonial black robes trailed on the floor behind him, the dark fabric setting off the shimmering colors of his skin. He pointed at a group of congregants clustered together in the front portion of the church. Their uniforms indicated membership in the warrior caste, and they were arranged as if in defense—lower ranks surrounding the highest ranks present.

"Our warriors have their mandate, and we must trust them to fulfill it." He pointed at another set of richly dressed congregants sitting across the aisle from the warriors. "Our leaders in matters political, bureaucratic, and spiritual have their mandate, and we must trust them to fulfill it." He turned and spread his arms and wings wide. "And you, the creators, the traders, the laborers, the backbone of our people. You have your mandate as well, to keep the Xroeshyn in ascent, ever-growing, ever-improving, until the day when we, together, achieve the victory that has been promised to us in the holy book."

His voice reached a crescendo as he addressed the lower castes. Then it fell into silence as he stalked back up the center aisle and took his position in front of the altar. He paused for a moment, looking up, as if in contemplation of the glory of Kidarr the High Father. In fact, he was seeing nothing, but organizing his next words. Kraada Tak believed he was the true voice of the gods. He never fully planned his sermons, relying on divine guidance to lead his congregation to the truth instead. He had yet to be disappointed, confirming his belief in his own quasi-divinity.

"But never forget that She is watching and waiting. If we falter, She will swoop down upon us without warning, bringing about the end of us, or our families, or our castes," he gestured now at the military grouping, "or our entire people. Leaving us awaiting our next turn on the wheel. Reducing all we have achieved in this life to vapor, swept away on a strong breeze." He felt that the proper notes had sounded and inspiration had left him, an unmistakable sign it was time to release his audience back into their lives.

"Go now, but do not forget what I have said. We may be of separate castes, we may have separate tasks, but if we fail to act as *one* people, we will be swept clean from the board to clear it for the next pieces."

AFTER THE SEEMINGLY ENDLESS one-on-one conversations with his departing parishioners, Kraada Tak reclined in his luxurious office chair. A gravity field allowed him to recline without crushing his wings. He preferred it to the garish, slit-back chairs that were more common. There were perks to being at the top of the religious structure, and he had earned them through decades of diligent and aggressive service to the gods. Had he not been born to the highest caste, made up of priests and politicians, he would have been a warrior. Maybe that's why he took a martial approach to spreading the truths of the gods.

He waved at his attendant, one of eight priests that saw to his needs on a rotating basis, spending one day each week in service to him rather than their own congregations. While Kraada was just a priest in charge of a single congregation, he'd been one of the eight to serve the last hierarch. He'd excelled in service to both and earned the right to take part in the ritual to select the new hierarch when the old one was called to the arms of Vasoi.

"Tisane for me, Bradii. Marshal Drovaa, the same or something stronger?"

"Tisane as well, thank you, Bradii. I have another long day of work ahead of me," Drovaa requested of the attendant.

Kraada's eyes widened in mock castigation at the soldier, and Drovaa Jat put up a hand to acknowledge it. "Yes, Hierarch, even on the holiest day of the eight, duty calls. I believe the gods will forgive me when we achieve the promised glories."

The delivery of a pot of hot tisane, accompanied by a light lunch of meat, fruits, and vegetables interrupted their conversation briefly. After fixing plates of snacks and steaming cups of the bitter herbal brew, Kraada got straight to the point, "I'm concerned. We're nearing the end of the cycle, and we've yet to discover the great enemy, much less destroy it."

Knowledge of the exact timing of the cycles was limited to the highest levels of the priesthood and the military, although they informed the emperor as a courtesy.

Drovaa nodded, frustration showing on his face. "Our exploration probes travel in as wide of a dispersion as is practical, but they've yet to encounter an appropriate opponent."

"And yet, we approach the close, which is only a fourth of an eight-year away." The Xroeshyn culture embraced sets of eight, in honor of the eight deities of their pantheon. It was acceptable to identify oneself with any of the eight, with deference given to the High Father by all. Kraada's chest bore a detailed tattoo of the symbol of Lelena, goddess of transitions and change. She had called to him from the time he was old enough to understand the differences among the deities.

"We do."

Kraada made a noise somewhere between a sigh and a growl. "Everything points to this cycle. Everything suggests that this is the moment that we will set our talons on the path that will end the cycle of rebirth and deliver us all to paradise when we cross over."

"It does."

Kraada gave the marshal a wry grin. "If I didn't know better, I'd think you were trying to calm me with your lack of engagement, Jat."

Drovaa laughed. "Perhaps, Tak. This isn't the first time we've had this conversation, and you do tend to get a little," he paused as if searching for the right word, "agitated when we discuss it. Not without reason, of course." The marshal leaned forward, holding his cup in both hands and meeting Kraada's eyes. "We're doing all we can. We must inform the emperor of the possibility that we've misread the cycles, that this won't be the one."

Kraada Tak's sound was clearly a sigh this time. "Yes. We do. You know he won't listen though."

"I do. And I know he'll pay the price for using this event as a popularity tool with the other castes if we're wrong. They will rend his flesh and send him to his next rotation in pieces."

Both men contemplated that image with some satisfaction. The current emperor had ascended to the title upon the death of his older, and much more qualified brother, and possessed none of the instincts essential to the position. Mistakes both large and small accumulated in his wake, but by virtue of his rank they went officially unrecognized. Unofficially, he had lost the respect and support of both the military and the priesthood. The bureaucrats and traders balanced the scales, finding him easily led to their viewpoints, thus securing their own positions and increasing the influence of their castes.

Kraada Tak rose gracefully from his chair, his wings spreading wide and then returning to their natural position on his back. "It so happens that I'm due at an appointment with our noble emperor in six eights, which is just enough time for us to brace ourselves and then arrive appropriately, but not completely disrespectfully, late. Would you care to join me?"

Drovaa Jat rose and stretched his own wings, then nodded.

"Bradii, small glasses of the iced brandy, please," Kraada requested as the door opened to admit his valet. The eight who served the hierarch were always listening, but would never speak of anything they heard, lest they betray their callings. It was a convenient arrangement that allowed them to better serve his needs and stay informed on important religious matters.

When they had their drinks, Drovaa raised his glass in a toast. "To our enemies, may they deliver us to paradise."

Kraada added his own request. "And may they do it soon."

JUST AFTER THE APPOINTED TIME, the two men entered the sumptuous reception quarters of Enjaaran Velt, Emperor of Xroesha and ruler of all creation. The party of underlings that had escorted them since they first set foot on the royal grounds departed, leaving only Enjaaran, his seneschal, a brace of guards in ritual armor and weapons, four servants, and the emperor's three favorite concubines. Kraada and Drovaa avoided making eye contact with one another, as they always did in this place, in fear that their condescension would spill over.

They also avoided eye contact with the emperor, for such things were officially forbidden in public spaces.

"Ah, welcome, protectors of my children's lives and souls." The emperor was always on stage when in public spaces, whether his audience was physically present or not. Kraada often wondered if recording devices preserved each of the emperor's words for the great benefit of his children for all eternity. He avoided snorting at the thought, but just barely. An involuntary flicker of amusement ruffled his wings. The two leaders mouthed appropriate courtesies. Drovaa made a small gesture, communicating using a silent code known only to the highest members of each caste, causing the emperor's seneschal to whisper to his master.

A frown creased the gregarious face of the emperor before he gave his seneschal a small nod. The seneschal locked eyes with each of the leaders, then turned and escorted the emperor toward a hidden door that swung open at his approach. After the four men passed through, the door closed with a soft hiss behind them. They were in the emperor's working office, a hermetically-sealed safe room that was only marginally less luxurious than his reception chamber. The emperor's demeanor changed the moment they crossed the threshold.

"What news, gentlemen?" He waved at a low table surrounded by several couches and reclined upon the most well-appointed with a theatrical groan. "I trust that this will not make me unhappy."

With no discernible instructions, a cluster of servants descended, placing each man's preferred wine and a tray of elegant small bites in front of them. Kraada and Drovaa both took delaying sips before speaking.

"As you know," Kraada began, "we have long believed this was the cycle in which the promise would be fulfilled, in which our divine enemy would be revealed. All the portents, all of our interpretations of the holy word, even the alignments of the stars themselves pointed to this conclusion. And yet—"

The emperor interrupted. "And yet, you are here to tell me that *somehow* the two of you are responsible for the most enormous mistake in the history of Xroesha, and that I must now inform my children that their infallible emperor is not nearly as infallible as we all hoped?" He rose with an incoherent shout, hurling his wineglass against an antique vase, causing both to shatter. "Unacceptable," he yelled. "Absolutely unacceptable."

The servants moving in to clean up shards of glass and porcelain caught his eye, and he growled, "Get out."

The emperor turned and pointed at Kraada. "You *promised* me that the divine day was at hand." His finger tracked like a laser to target Drovaa's face. "You *promised* me that we would find and destroy our foreordained enemy before the current cycle ends. Are you both completely incompetent?"

His agitation was apparent as he paced, before finally regaining his composure and taking a deep breath. "Gentlemen, your actions bring us to a dangerous point. We must consider the responses of the mob," he gestured as if to indicate the entire known universe, "to this dramatic reversal of the promises we have made for the past six years. What are your suggestions?"

Drovaa looked at Kraada and then cleared his throat. "Your highness, I'm sure we could make the claim that an undiscovered part of the *Dhadas* has been found, or some such excuse, to clarify that we acted on our best information. We can amplify this perception by making a show of sending probes and ships on a new vector suggested by this 'discovery'."

Kraada nodded in agreement. The emperor's face ran through a kaleidoscope of expressions as he considered the plan.

"That just might work," he began, but was interrupted by his seneschal entering the room. The man bowed to the emperor, then faced Drovaa Jat. "Marshal, your presence is requested in the Defense Center. Two ships are invading our reliquary."

Both Kraada and Drovaa stood in reflex. The emperor nodded toward the door.

"Do your duty, gentlemen. We'll continue this discussion at a less pressing time. But we *will* continue it."

THE DEFENSE CENTER protected first the palace, then the city, then the planet itself. It was dominated by a mammoth three-dimensional holograph, currently showing the holy site at the distant fringe of the solar system. Arranged around the central display were stations similar to those found aboard capital ships, overseen by specialists in offense, defense, sensors, and communication.

"Report," snapped Drovaa as he entered the room. Junior officers at each of the stations stood and saluted, holding their positions as the duty officer brought the two leaders up to speed.

"Two ships appeared inside one of the reliquaries within the asteroid belt. A sensor scan suggests they have been involved in combat recently and that one is heavily damaged. They have done nothing aggressive since appearing in the area. Our passive defenses are functional."

Drovaa took only a moment to think. "Regardless of what they're doing there, they are *not* welcome. We must protect the remains of our holy ones."

Kraada nodded.

"The ships appear to be a touch smaller than our cruisers according to the display. Tactical, does this match your assessment?"

The officer dropped his salute, moving to a parade rest with his hands clasped behind his back. "Affirmative, Marshal. Our estimates put them at six-eighths of our size. Initial analysis concludes that their weapons are likely less powerful than ours, although this is based purely on visual inspection and cannot be entirely relied upon."

The marshal's lips quirked at his subordinate's attention to detail. "Thank you, Lieutenant. Defense, dispatch the four closest ships."

Kraada caught Drovaa's gaze with a questioning look. Drovaa's smile widened. "Better too many, then not enough, Hierarch."

Kraada nodded in acceptance. Overwhelming force was not his personal strategic choice, preferring the hidden dagger to the obvious sword. He listened as the marshal repositioned support ships to act as a second line of defense.

Kraada placed a hand on Drovaa Jat's shoulder. "Your thoroughness is a testament to the rightness of your command, Marshal. I'm confident that you'll quickly sort out this trespass threatening the bones of our sainted ancestors."

Drovaa bowed his head as if receiving a benediction, which wasn't far from the truth, given their respective positions. Kraada had chosen his sermon voice so that every person in the room would hear his show of support over the distractions of their duties.

Drovaa stepped closer to the huge hologram that filled the center of the space. "Shift all defense reports to alternate displays," he commanded. "I want to see an area that includes only the Reliquary, the enemy, and our incoming ships." Turning to Kraada, he asked in a low tone, "What do you make of this?"

Kraada's expression was thoughtful. "I hesitate to ascribe more importance to it than random happenstance, Marshal. Then again, perhaps time will show us that it is the fulfillment of a promise."

At that moment, it was impossible to keep the hope out of his voice. Drovaa's eyes, bright and focused, showed that he shared that hope.

The duty officer spoke up again. "The *Jade Breeze* is entering the field."

CHAPTER FIVE

The lift glided to a smooth stop, and the door to the bridge slid open. Kate Flynn stepped out into chaos barely hidden beneath a thin veneer of ritual and order. Cross turned his head as she entered. Long experience with one another allowed her to see the suppressed fear he would never acknowledge.

He spoke in a casual tone that was almost, but not completely, inappropriate to the moment. "Welcome back, XO. We have ourselves a bit of a situation here. If you could take the sensor station and figure out where the hell we are, and how the hell we got here, that would free up Lieutenant Martin to focus on keeping the *Gagarin* at bay."

"Happy to oblige," Kate replied with matching false casualness. The bridge crew, accustomed to their wordplay, relaxed a little.

She sat, restraints deploying to lock her into place. As her hands danced without thought across the panel, activating systems and loading her operational preferences, she listened to Cross issue commands. "Tactical, protect us from whatever stupid thing that *Gagarin* will do next, but don't forget that we are surrounded by unknowns. Helm, maximum weapons range from the *Gagarin*.

Anyone," he trailed off, and offered a small laugh, "what the hell is going on out there?"

The tactical officer gave a situation report. "Location unknown, computers are still plotting the system. The *Gagarin's* engines are off-line. Our engines are functional at 50% capacity, but our tunnel drive is off-line. Weapons on both ships are powered and ready to go. The *Gagarin* seems to have taken minimal damage to several compartments during transition, and he is leaking gases in several places. We also took damage, with sections Alpha-three through Alpha-six venting atmosphere."

Cross directed a wry look at Kate before returning his gaze to the tactical officer. "It appears that the gods of tunnel space have something against our Marines, given that the only thing destroyed was their living quarters."

Most sailors harbored a fundamental dislike for the ground pounders of the Marine division. Kate was not among them. The Marines, like her, did their jobs they were assigned in the best way they knew how.

"Lucky that we're not carrying any this trip, sir."

"Lucky indeed, Martin."

Conversation paused as the *Washington* repositioned, the bridge crew keeping a close eye on the *Gagarin*. Kate, too, was captivated by the slowly receding image of the giant ship drifting through space. After a minute of silence, the communication officer's voice broke the moment, "Incoming communication from the *Gagarin*, sir."

"On screen," Cross snapped. Kate saw the tension in his face, heard it lurking behind his words. Her attention split as reports finally flooded into her system. She sent a quick message to engineering, informing Jannik of the processing delay.

The commander of the *Gagarin* filled the right half of the main screen. He looked unruffled, considering the damage to his ship and the unexpected relocation to an unknown sector of the universe. "What have you done, *Washington*? What new trick is this?"

Several bridge officers found his outrage amusing, quietly laughing and shaking their heads at the question.

Cross maintained his composure while facing his opponent. "It was your devious play that created the vortex that brought us here. Neither I nor my crew had anything to do with that, we just got to come along for the ride. I imagine your friend who joined us at the end of that little episode is commenting upon your stupidity right now."

The *Gagarin's* commander gave a small nod as if Cross had confirmed something for him. "Stupidity, is it? Perhaps, *Washington*, perhaps. Perhaps too, it was instead a noble effort to defend Alliance territory from the continuing and constant encroachment of the Union."

Kate tore herself away from the conversation and triggered several analyses of the images coming from the *Gagarin*. She linked them over to Cross's display. He glanced down, then look up with a predatory grin as the man on the screen finished speaking with a cheerfully vulgar suggestion.

"We've just analyzed the emissions from your ship, Commander. Very interesting reading. You're venting plasma gases vital to your cannons. That leaves you rather under-armed compared to my vessel. I suggest you stand down, acknowledge today's defeat, and return to your own space. Forthwith."

Kate saw him hit the small stud on his command chair that over-rode the comm and cut off the transmissions. He turned to her and said, "Okay, Kate. That should hold them for a while. Tell me what we've gotten ourselves into."

She had been waiting for the opportunity. "We're in a strange place. It's a significant distance beyond our explored territory. Given our transition time, we shouldn't have traveled this far. It's a very interesting discovery, because if we could figure out *why*, and harness that for our own exploration, ships—"

Cross cut her off, "Kate, do the science with Jannik later."

Kate snapped back to the moment. "Right, sorry. It's relevant in a military sense, though, because we want to make sure we don't get our tunnel drive shot out from underneath us or we'll be a very long time getting home."

Cross interrupted her with an almost gleeful expression. "Are you telling me that the *Gagarin* is stuck here?"

Kate gave him an exasperated look. "Appears to be the case. And *here* is a very interesting place. To start with, we are on the outer fringe of an eight-planet system. The planets are orbiting a star of similar size and mass to Earth's. They appear to be in stable elliptical orbits. Surrounding the entire orbital path is this..." With the tap of a few keys, Kate took over most of the main display, showing a diagram of the planets, the star they circled, and an oblong cylinder of asteroids that ringed the entire thing, curving to meet at each end, capping the shape.

Cross leaned forward as far as his restraints would allow. "That is the strangest shaped asteroid field I've ever seen. Do we know what's causing it?"

Kate shook her head. "There are some entirely strange gravitics going on in this system. The readings are so different from ours that the computer can't figure out what it's seeing. It's unlike anything in our exploration records. What's most interesting about it is this..." Kate zoomed the display to a tighter view. The closeup showed that individual sections of the asteroid field were themselves in motion, some seeming to move predictably while others moved randomly. "Again, we've never seen an arrangement like this."

"So, where are we in this mess," asked Cross.

"Right here," Kate replied, highlighting a section and zooming in. The two ships were near the middle of a cascade of rocks orbiting an obvious central point.

"What are they rotating around?"

Kate zoomed the screen again in response. "There appears to be an incredibly dense piece of rock in the middle. From our perspective, it is behind and above the *Gagarin*. I don't think we want to get any nearer to it, if it is exerting enough force to keep these rocks moving the way they are."

"That sounds like fantastic advice," Cross replied. "Recommendations?"

Kate thought about it for a second, opened her mouth to reply, then paused, shutting it again. What she wanted to say was that they should inspect those eight planets before tunneling out of the system. The scientific portions of her brain were excited at the opportunity to learn more about what kind of star could create such a strange phenomenon. Unfortunately, the executive officer carried a larger burden of responsibility. "We need to get out of here right away. We should also prep a beacon before we attempt it, in case something goes wrong. Finally, we may want to tunnel back to where we were to provide a report about the *Gagarin* being stranded to the Alliance ship."

Cross nodded. "I agree. That's what we'll do." He turned to the comm officer and said, "Send a message to the *Gagarin* informing them of our plan to depart and our promise to inform their fleet that they are in need of rescue."

Kate sighed. Even when Cross was being nice, he had to twist the knife. It was a trait she disliked in him. In time with her exhalation, the lift door slid open.

Before she could turn her head to look, she heard the sharp voice cut across the bridge. "Bloody hell and damnation, Cross. What are you doing to my ship?"

CHAPTER SIX

Cross flinched at his captain's words. He hit the button to release his restraints and vacated the center chair immediately. Given that they were in a battle situation, he dispensed with the usual officer-on-the-deck rigmarole, instead offering a quick summary to his commanding officer.

"We engaged an Alliance ship that misunderstood their right to encroach on one of our patrol sectors. We outmaneuvered them, then reinforcements showed up. The commander of the *Gagarin* launched a sneak attack and attempted to flee by triggering his tunnel drive on only one engine. The *Gagarin* and the *DC* were both pulled into a vortex, which we are still trying to understand, and we arrived here." Cross gestured to the display screen, which Kate had returned to normal operation as the captain entered the bridge. "His tunnel drive and engines are damaged. He's leaking atmosphere and plasma, and my XO and I agree that we should depart for home as expeditiously as possible."

Captain James Okoye ran a hand over his bald head as he sat down in the vacated hair. His height and dark skin would make him stand out on the bridges of most UAL ships, and his clipped British accent with undertones of continental Africa made him stand out everywhere. He spoke again. "And so, I am up to the moment. I have the deck."

Cross replied formally, "You have the deck, sir." He moved to stand behind and to the right of the captain's position, leaving the XO chair vacant for the tall officer that was just exiting the lift. Once there, Cross fumed in silence. It was fine for the captain to take command of the ship anytime he wanted. Cross had no problem with that. But he certainly could have been less condescending about it.

With one ear tuned to catch any requests from Okoye, Cross reviewed his actions since the moment the *Gagarin* had appeared on their plot. He saw no particular criticism that could be leveled at him for the way he handled the encounter. Every commander knew that showing weakness to the enemy was a fatal mistake, and he had upheld the honor of his service. The only thing he would change was to have gained more distance from the enemy after their initial exchange, so that his ship would have been less vulnerable to the surprise attack.

Voices pulled him back to the moment as Kate and the tactical officer announced almost simultaneously, "Energy signatures changing on the *Gagarin*."

Cross looked over at the personal display built into the XO's chair as Olivas adjusted it to zoom in on the enemy ship. The XO triggered an overlay of real time data that scrolled down the side of his screen. The enemy commander was up to something, but Cross couldn't figure out what it was.

Okoye had apparently seen this before, and his clipped voice sounded almost conversational. "He's rigged his engines to feed into the plasma cannon. That is why the engine numbers are small but steady. He's charging a capacitor with them. When it reaches an appropriate level, he will have a single, very powerful shot from that weapon." Okoye's discipline before entering command was engineering, and he had spent considerable time as an assistant chief engineer on one of the UAL's largest carriers.

Cross was sure that his assessment was correct. "We tried that once in simulation. The shot was even more effective than we expected and destroyed the enemy ship. It also exploded, killing the simulated gun crew right away and an additional fourth of the crew over the next day from plasma exposure."

"Recommend more distance, Captain," Commander Felix Olivas said, and Okoye nodded.

"Helm, increase distance."

Claire Martin's calm report followed. "Launches. He has fired all of his tubes."

The captain wore a look of regret as he looked over his shoulder and met Cross's eyes. He felt the judgment in that gaze and was forced to consider that perhaps there was something he could have done better to defuse the situation. As he opened his mouth to suggest that they continue with their plan to evacuate the sector, his words were overridden by the captain's stern voice.

"Sound brace for impact, Communication. Helm, set a course that brings our port broadside to bear. Campbell, fire energy weapons when we are in range. Launch all torpedoes when we reach 50,000." The distance readout on the main monitor showed 60,000, providing barely enough time to plot a firing solution and get the tubes open.

"Captain. Don't fire." Kate's alarmed voice rang out on the bridge. Without asking permission, she took over much of the main screen, showing the track of the enemy missiles. "Something is very wrong here, sir. The incoming torpedoes are not acting normally." Kate overlaid the entire path of the missiles, and Cross saw what she meant. The strange gravitics of the area were warping the torpedoes' tracks, pulling and pushing them in seemingly random directions. Only about a tenth of the launches would reach the *Washington* before their engines burned out.

"Thank you, Lieutenant Commander Flynn. Weapons, hold all torpedoes until we are in broadside position."

Cross saw Kate breathe out the stress of the moment and focus again on her instruments.

Martin spoke again, "Point defense cannons engaging." The dense rain of projectiles detonated each of the incoming torpedoes at a safe distance.

Cross thought it as the captain said it, "Our turn."

Where Cross's style of fighting the ship was precise and direct, Captain Okoye's style was notably different. As they approached optimal range, the captain sketched a spiraling path into his display, and linked it to the helm and tactical officers. The ship changed heading to follow the path, her weapons and shields compensating for the adjustment. Just as it became predictable, the heading would change again.

Cross felt that the captain's strategies were always too complicated, but it was impossible to argue with success. Captain James Okoye had never lost an engagement with Alliance forces and had come out of several with no damage at all. It was one reason he'd been excited to receive his current posting. The reality had proven somewhat different, as Okoye was a spiky mentor, and in Cross's opinion, overly critical. As was the XO, now that he thought about it.

In fact...

The time for musing ended as the ships engaged at broadside range.

Brilliant beams of energy lanced between the vessels seeking to overload the other ship's shields. A salvo of torpedoes followed on the same task. Both ships absorbed the first exchange with no damage, and traded shots from aft armaments as they positioned for another pass.

"This is the side we damaged before, Captain," Cross said, pointing to it on the battle display. The captain gave a nod of acknowledgment, but stayed focused on the schematic on the main display.

The clipped voice issued instructions. "Let's see how bright he is.

Weapons, as we come in for the broadside, launch torpedoes from our other side to loop around to his opposite side." The captain drew on his display and shared it to the weapons station. "Instead of holding our broadside missiles for a traditional launch, send them ahead on this path." He sent another diagram, this time charting missile strikes that would hit the top and bottom of the enemy ship. "Use our forward cannons to strike at the remaining side, and then we will dump everything we have into that side as we pass. Time the torpedoes to all strike simultaneously."

Against an unwounded ship, this tactic would have little effect. An unharmed ship would divert all of its available power into the shields, weathering the storm and countering with its own barrage. However, the *Gagarin* was far from pristine. His lost engine and rerouted power would decrease the efficiency of the energy transfer into his defenses. The tactical officer on the other ship would have to play the shields like a finely tuned instrument—performing an unfamiliar melody—to deal with it. Cross approved and filed the idea away in his mental toolkit.

The ships reached optimal range. "Fire," commanded Captain Okoye.

Cross felt the tremors of the launches where his feet touched the deck, and he imagined he heard the sound as they rocketed from their tubes. On the main display, the trails formed beautiful arcs as they traveled toward their destinations.

"Apparently, he's smarter than his conversational ability suggests, Captain" said Cross. On the display, the *Gagarin* had abandoned its broadside pass to climb upward, veering toward one set of incoming missiles. The position would allow his tactical officer to deal with the missile salvos separately.

"Not bad at all," Okoye said. He sketched a new course for the helm officer, and it was received with a crisp, "Changing course now, sir," from Lieutenant Smythe.

The *Washington* swung on to the new course, and side thrusters skewed her around the central point, reorienting the front of the ship even as momentum carried them in their original direction. The display updated with newly plotted trajectories for both ships, showing them intersecting near the gravitational anomaly at the center of the sector.

"Suggestions?" Okoye's baritone carried to include the entire bridge crew.

Lieutenant Stewart Campbell responded first, "How about we try to overload him? We approach using that spiraling path again, and once her momentum is strong enough, cut the engines and skew the ship, firing off both broadsides in sequence, right down his throat."

"I like it, good idea, Campbell. Felix, any observations on this plan?"

Commander Olivas looked thoughtful. "Aside from adding in cannon fire wherever appropriate, Captain, the only other suggestion I have is to deploy a couple noisemakers beforehand to screen the launch of the missiles."

Okoye nodded again. "Good call. Weapons, Helm, make it happen. Engage in fifteen seconds from my mark." The captain paused, tracking the two ships as they closed in on the display. "Mark."

Cross considered relocating to an empty bridge station, but instead secured his hold on a nearby support in preparation for the impending action.

A small timer clicked down in the corner of the main display. Each of the members of the bridge crew were busy at their tasks, but Cross saw each one of them sneak a glance at the countdown, except Kate, who stayed head-down over her sensors. Cross was sure she had mirrored the clock into her own display. Maximum efficiency was the hallmark of Kate Flynn.

As the timer reached zero, several things happened all at once. The *Washington* accelerated to her top speed and began an evasive course that still allowed her cannons to track the *Gagarin*. When those fired, bursts of energy crossed the void to slam into the *Gagarin's* forward shields. The noisemakers were launched from the ship's defensive tubes—four rockets each arcing out from openings on all six surfaces of the ship. These devices were designed to momentarily distract an enemy. They did their job well, coming together to create an explosion of light, sound, and radiation that blinded the *Gagarin*. Behind the screen of noise, the *Washington* cut her engines and pivoted, launching her first broadside at the enemy ship.

She continued to turn around her center point, thrusters redlined for maximum spin. Claire Martin worked hard to keep the shields aligned against possible fire from the *Gagarin*. While the noisemakers blinded the opposing ship, it left the crew of the *Washington* blind as well, prohibiting them from seeing the actions of the Alliance ship. The weapons officer launched each tube as soon as it was possible to make the shot, given the close distance between the two ships and the desire for a direct path.

"Evasive pattern beta" Okoye commanded as the final tube emptied. The ship strained as her main engines were re-engaged and driven to full output, creating enough pressure to push him back despite the ship's ability to control for inertial changes. As the noisemakers cleared, the display revealed that the enemy commander had again reacted unpredictably. In the thirty seconds they were obscured from one another, the *Gagarin* had also rotated, blasting hard for the gravitational disturbance to evade the *Washington's* weapons.

"He must be more damaged than we thought if he's running," Cross said just loud enough for Okoye to hear. The captain answered with a grunt, never shifting his eyes from the display.

Cross, Okoye, and the bridge crew watched the *Gagarin* curve strangely, his path taking him around the far side of the disturbance and reemerging beyond it at a full hundred-degree change of direction. Pieces of the ship scattered, torn from the superstructure by the force of the gravitational pull exerted by the anomaly.

They all watched as their torpedoes reacquired the *Gagarin*.

Cross, Olivas, and Okoye all yelled, "Abort," as the weapons drove into the mysterious phenomenon and exploded, reducing it to debris and dust.

CHAPTER SEVEN

Moments later, the arrival of an unknown ship set off a chorus of warnings on the bridge of the *Washington*. Several crew members pointed at the display while others called out the results of their sensor readings and computer analyses. Cross knew they were in trouble when not one report gave anything useful. The new vessel was like nothing they'd ever seen.

"Multiple launches from the unknown ship. Projectiles tracking for both us and the *Gagarin*." Claire Martin adjusted their defenses even as she reported the situation.

One thing that Cross had always admired about the captain was his unflappable discipline in the face of danger, and Okoye showed that now. "Helm, evasive pattern Delta, modified to take us away from the new arrival as quickly as possible. Weapons, do *not* escalate, hold fire. Tactical, strongest defenses toward the incoming missiles."

Commander Olivas issued commands to the communication officer, who sent out hails translated into every language the computer possessed.

"Its tonnage appears slightly greater than ours, Captain," Kate said into the quiet after Okoye finished. "Our computers cannot iden-tify the composition of its hull, nor any of the weapons it carries."

"Although, clearly, he has rockets to play with," Cross said.

The moment of inappropriate levity brought exhalations from the bridge crew and even put a tiny smile on the captain's face. "Rockets indeed, Lieutenant Commander Cross," Okoye said.

Tension mounted as the projectiles closed in on them. One half of the main display screen was devoted to a schematic showing the position of all three ships and the track of all things moving within the space. The computer had assigned the unknown ship a new color, outlining it in green. It joined the red of the Alliance ship and the blue of the *Washington*. Seconds before emerald tracks trailing the missiles connected the enemy ship and the *Gagarin*, a small dot representing his tunnel beacon separated and rocketed from the display.

The *Gagarin* flew apart as the enemy missiles struck. His weak-ened shields were no match for the apparent power of the weapons, seeming to provide defense against only the first of the eight that reached him. The others stabbed deeply inside the structure before exploding. On the camera, it looked as if the ship simply lost cohe-sion, jettisoning pieces to float freely in every direction. Noises of shock rebounded across the bridge, and Cross saw the captain exchange looks with his executive officer.

Cross spoke up, playing the assigned-doubter role of subordinate command officers. "We need more information about this enemy before we tunnel out of here, Captain. This may be our only chance to get it."

Both Okoye and Olivas glared at him, and he realized he'd over-stepped. That didn't make him wrong. Fortunately, they were smart enough to realize that.

The captain drew a curving path that would keep them at a distance from the enemy while providing a greater opportunity to analyze him. "Time to impact?"

A countdown timer appeared on the main display, starting at

forty-one seconds and descending. The alien ship wasn't moving, most likely awaiting the results of its initial launches before committing to any additional actions.

"Lieutenant Commander Flynn, are you getting anything else from this thing?"

Kate frowned. "His energy signature suggests that he's got defenses up, but they don't read the same way that ours do. It's as if they're hovering right at the edge of our instruments' ability to identify them. The computer has completed its analysis of the enemy and has identified twenty-four ports that could be missile tubes and eight projections that could house weapons. On one of our ships I would call them plasma cannons or lasers. On that ship," she shrugged, "who knows?"

Cross again felt the thrum of projectiles leaving his ship, and Lieutenant Martin reported that DC's countermeasures had taken out the incoming missiles. Everyone was riveted to the display. They all saw the enemy move toward them. Okoye spoke, "Tactical, based on what we know, what's the likelihood we can defeat that thing?"

Martin was silent for a moment, hands flying as she interacted with her display. "Battle computer suggests a 27% chance of outright victory, and a 14% chance of mutual destruction. The remaining 59% of the time, they survive and we don't."

"Huh. Those are some pretty bad odds. Flynn, assuming loss of our tunnel drive, how long would it take to get home from here?"

Kate had generated the answer to this question while attempting to identify their location. "This is uncharted space, Captain, so there's no way to be sure. The computer projects we would need at least two years and seven months to travel to our explored territory, and another eleven months to reach our point of departure. That's best case. The other cases are much worse."

The captain was nodding before she finished, his features tightening. Cross shared his frustration. Okoye's knuckles were white on the arm of his chair as he gazed upon the ship that had attempted to destroy them. Cross took in the two countdown clocks, one showed time to impact of incoming weaponry, the other showed time left until their tunnel drive was ready. Both read zero, although every member of the *Washington's* bridge crew knew another attack was imminent, and the impact countdown would soon begin again.

Cross thought, for a moment, that they would fight the other ship, and his pulse jumped at the foolhardy glory of it.

Then ever-dependable Lieutenant Claire Martin delivered bad news again. "Launches, Captain. Twice as many as before. All of them aimed at us." The countdown on the left side of the screen marked time until impact, beginning at seventy-six seconds.

Okoye depressed a small stud on his chair and spoke calmly. "Chief Jannik?"

The chief engineer's voice played out of the chair's speakers. "Yes, Captain?"

"An unknown enemy has appeared and we need to get out of here. I want everything extra that your engines can give me."

"Affirmative. Ramping up in fifteen seconds. Jannik out."

Captain Okoye turned and took a breath before implementing his escape plan. "Helm, all available speed to the nearest point we can transition the hell out of here. Tactical, if we can't outrun those missiles, I expect you to keep them off of us however you can."

Martin nodded, then cut her eyes quickly to Cross. He read the request in her look and joined her at the tactical station. "Communication, thirty seconds before impact, launch our beacon back to fleet. Flynn, download as much data on the newcomer and this area of space to it as possible." Olivas rose from his seat to take a handhold next to Lieutenant Casco, in case assistance was needed with the beacon.

There was nothing more to do. Torpedo tracks closed in on them as both ships increased speed. Crew members inserted new information into the display, showing the point at which the *Washington* would create its escape tunnel and the threshold where the other ship would enter cannon range even if they outran the missiles. After several seconds, it became clear they would escape just seconds before impact.

The captain tapped a finger on his chin. "We are cutting it too close. Tactical, deploy every countermeasure we've got, right now. Let's see if we can buy ourselves some time."

The *Washington* launched her full array of defensive tricks, attempting to distract the incoming projectiles with electromagnetic jammers and decoys that would appeal to sensors focused on sound, light, or heat. Antimissile rockets also shot forth, claiming several of the torpedoes in impressive blooms of fire. The countermeasures forced the remaining missiles to evade before reorienting on the ship, buying them an additional ten seconds until impact. A low whine trilled at their perception's edge as the point defense cannons spun up to do their protective duty.

Ricardo Casco shattered the silence. "Incoming communication, Captain. Sound and image."

Okoye's eyebrows rose as he swiveled toward the comm station. "Really? Now he wants to talk?" The captain swiveled back, released his restraints, and stood to face the main display, hands clasped behind his back. "On screen."

The bridge crew got their first image of an alien being a moment later. His skin shifted colors while they watched—different gem shades over a base gray that looked rougher than human skin. His impressive ivory wings were unfurled, making him resemble some strange mix of demon and angel, in Cross's opinion. The alien spoke, shaking his fist at them. The feathers at the crown of his skull stood up straight, giving him a menacing look. His tones were at times guttural, at times sibilant, and completely unintelligible to the humans. His face was a pleasant mixture of human and avian, the latter more than a hint but not dominant. Two gesturing arms and the tops of what Cross assumed were two legs completed the humanoid form. His uniform seemed to include selected pieces of armor at strategic locations, glinting in emerald green. Cross automatically categorized the being as male, even though there was no way to know for sure.

Cross caught Kate's eye, raising his eyebrows. Kate shook her head, her linguistic proficiencies inadequate to an understanding of the creature. The tirade wound down, and the being stopped speaking. He seemed to wait expectantly.

"I am Captain James Okoye, in command of the United Atlantic League starship, *Washington, DC*. We did not intend to enter your territory, but were brought here by equipment malfunction on the ship you destroyed. We seek only to leave in peace. Perhaps, at another time, when there are not torpedoes streaking toward us, we can find some common ground between our two people."

He paused, awaiting a response from the other side. The alien closed the connection, and the display returned to a view of its ship. Okoye sat again, and said to Olivas, who also returned to his chair, "I don't think he likes us very much."

He generated a couple of stifled laughs with his joke, which was all he could hope for at the moment, Cross thought. On screen, the *Washington* reached that point in the system that was in balance, the attractive forces of the planets, asteroids, and unknowns countering each other enough to provide stability for a tunnel.

Okoye wasted no time at all. "Helm, get us out of here."

Their countdown clocks were based upon technology that they understood. This was logical, but unfortunate as the enemy missiles didn't follow their rules. As the tunnel opened, the projectiles deployed a gravitic beam to latch on to the ship. With fifteen seconds to spare, the tunnel the *Washington* transitioned into closed, but not before the ship dragged several torpedoes into it with her.

CHAPTER EIGHT

With no other clear path to follow, Dima and the *Beijing* stayed in the sector to see if the ships that had been sucked into the errant tunnel would reappear. After nineteen hours, the beacon from the *Gagarin* tumbled into normal space from a tiny rip in reality and downloaded its data. Dima's executive officer woke him from a sound sleep to brief him. They met in the ship's galley, where the exec prepared a pot of bitter tea and doled out cold sesame noodles as a midnight snack. Dima raised an eyebrow at her, but accepted the food gratefully and ate while she brought him up to date.

When Senior Lieutenant Svetlana Ivanova finished her tale, and Dima finished his noodles, he leaned back in his chair and said, "I knew Mikhail for more than seven years. He was my executive officer several ships ago. He was a gentle man, for being so giant, but he was very easily provoked. It appears our Union friends found a pressure point and pushed on it until he felt the need to respond." Dima shook his head. "It is all so stupid, Svetlana. We fight each other over things that don't matter because that's all we know. We've lost sight of the reasons... if there ever were any to start with. Now it's just routine. If we could learn to work together, fewer young people would end up dead or damaged."

He levered himself up out of the chair with a sigh. "The situation seems to be moving from bad to worse, based upon what the *Gagarin* sent in his beacon. We should return to fleet and inform them about this new discovery. They will want to make sure they get impressive words on fancy paper claiming the aliens' space in the name of the AAN right away, no doubt." He straightened to his full height, and shifted his shoulders backward, mentally donning the mantle of command. He raised the communicator on his wrist and hit the button to open communication to the bridge.

"Lieutenant Zian, sound general quarters. Prepare the ship for action. Have the helm chart our fastest course back to the fleet." He turned to his executive officer and said, "What if the thing that killed the *Gagarin* knows where he came from?"

Ivanova froze, considering the implications.

"I think we had better get to the bridge."

"Indeed. I think we better."

Both officers had settled into their customary stations when the sensors officer spoke. "Radiation increase consistent with an imminent tunnel."

"Wide view on the screen, please, tactical." Dima looked at his executive officer. "Another beacon?"

"We can hope."

"It's not particularly likely, though."

"No, it's not."

"Well, then."

"What if it's the ship that destroyed the *Gagarin*, Captain?"

"We run, Exec. We run really, really fast."

CHAPTER NINE

The *Washington* transitioned from tunnel space unaware of the trailing missiles. They announced their presence by striking the unreinforced aft portion of the ship's starboard side. The shields held out against the first torpedo, but the second and third drilled deeply inside and exploded. A fourth followed them in but failed to detonate, preserving the *Washington* from destruction.

The torpedoes created a chain reaction of explosions that marched through the ship. The *Washington* bucked with each detonation. Cross was flung into the air, a victim of a weakened strap at the engineering station and his own reluctance to engage the manual restraints. Felix Olivas also suffered a failure in his safety equipment as the XO chair partially broke free from its mooring, severing both the manual and automatic restraining belts. Cross was lucky and snagged a support column to wrap himself around at the cost of only a cracked rib and heavy bruising. The executive officer did not share his luck and tumbled about, smashing his skull sharply into a bulkhead.

"Medical team to the bridge," Captain Okoye's clipped accent announced, cutting through the noise and confusion. "Damage report."

Martin coordinated the flow of information from throughout the ship. "Sections one through five on decks alpha, bravo, and indigo are vented to space. The crews who survived the initial blast were suited and have minimal additional injuries. Medical teams are responding."

"What hit us?"

The tactical officer responded, "Unknown. But the only contact on our screens is the *Beijing*."

At a nod from the Captain, the communication officer left his station to administer first aid to the XO. Cross climbed up from the floor, using the column as a support. Once he had stabilized himself, he said in a low tone, "The *Beijing* doesn't know how badly we're hurt, sir. A surprise attack would take him unaware. It may be our only chance, given the damage." The battle display told the tale, showing a schematic of the ship with shields missing and sections that were venting atmosphere outlined in orange. There was a lot of orange.

The captain looked thoughtful. By the time that Okoye finally answered, Cross would have already fired off his first salvos. "You spoke to the captain of the *Beijing* before, did you not?

"I did."

"Did he seem to you like the sort of person to fire upon another ship without provocation? He did not do so last time."

Cross's face betrayed his discomfort, as he answered his captain with a touch of a scowl. "Not a single thing has happened how I thought it would, Captain. I'm not sure I can judge the intentions of the Alliance commander."

Okoye acknowledged this with a nod. "Fair enough. Take the XO station, please."

As Cross limped to the chair, the captain issued a stream of orders. "Helm, chart a tunnel out of here toward the nearest base. Start moving us slowly in that direction, in as nonthreatening a way as you can. Weapons, all arms at ready status, but do not fire unless fired upon. Tactical, keep our defenses attuned. Sensors, anything?"

Kate answered when her position was called, "No signs that the *Beijing* has fired at us, Captain. But, of course," she glanced at Cross, "it's possible he did and we're just not picking up the evidence."

The medical and damage control teams arrived on the same lift and dispersed to attend to their tasks. As the communication officer returned to his position, the captain called for a channel to the *Beijing*. Moments later, the image of Dima Petryaev appeared on half of the main display.

"Captain Petryaev. I am Captain James Okoye, in command of the *Washington, DC*. I believe you have spoken with my executive officer, Lieutenant Commander Cross. I am assured that both sides were to blame for the foolishness that ensued between my ship and the *Gagarin*. After we were in the tunnel, I assumed command, and your man attacked after we exited. Although we fired at him, it was an alien vessel that destroyed the *Gagarin*. There were no signs of survivors, not that we could have stopped to help them had there been. You have my condolences on the loss of your ship."

Dima nodded in response to this diplomatic gesture. "Mikhail was a big man, big in all ways. His sense of personal honor got him into trouble more than once, and it appears to have been his undoing. If I may briefly address the Lieutenant Commander?" Dima's eyes focused on a different spot, "There may be a lesson in Mikhail's fate for you." Dima focused back on Captain Okoye. "You have suffered damage, Captain. Do you require assistance?"

There was a limit to the amount of diplomacy Okoye was willing to engage in, and he appeared to have reached it. "No thank you, Captain Petryaev, although I appreciate your generous offer. Our damage control teams have the situation well in hand, and we will tunnel to our nearest base as soon as our drive is ready."

Dima nodded. "Then I guess there is not much left for us to say to each other, Captain. The circumstances are unfortunate, but it is always heartening to meet people on your side who are willing to converse before launching into combat."

Captain Okoye nodded in reply. "I was just thinking the same about you, Captain Petryaev. Safe travels. *Washington* out."

Okoye pointed at his tactical officer after the connection dropped. "You keep a close eye on that ship, Martin. The moment he does anything unexpected, max our shields, fire countermeasures, go evasive, and get us to the tunnel."

Cross saw him look over at the medical team attending to the XO. The ship's doctor had come himself, and he stood, peeled off his gloves, and shook his head. "Bloody hell," the captain swore.

Softly, so that his voice wouldn't carry beyond its target, Okoye had only one command to give. "Lieutenant Commander, you are dismissed. We will talk later. For now, get off my bridge."

Cross departed with as much dignity he could manage. After the door closed with a hydraulic hiss and the lift glided into motion, he bloodied his knuckles on a wall, stifling the scream that wanted to erupt from his chest. He headed to engineering to kill time before the captain summoned him for the inevitable *conversation*. Okoye could flay the skin from a statue with the sharpness of his tongue. He was not looking forward to enduring it yet again.

CHAPTER TEN

The doors of the lift closed and Kate cringed in sympathy. Okoye had always held Cross at arm's length, not out of any malicious intent that she could see, but just because their personalities didn't match particularly well. A captain wanted an executive team that thought differently than he did, but perhaps not as differently as Cross. It had caused friction before, and she figured he was in for another intense verbal expression of that friction in short order.

She manipulated the sensor array, gathering as much data as she could on the *Beijing* while they were in proximity to him. She also shared Lieutenant Martin's coordination of damage repair teams, taking the lower half of the ship as her responsibility. It was an engrossing task, and she lost track of time while submerged in it. Erin Smythe jolted her out of her efforts with the announcement, "The tunnel drive should be ready to go."

The captain responded by contacting engineering and found that Jannik agreed with Smythe's assessment.

Okoye addressed Martin. "Are we stable enough to last through transition in and transition out?" Kate linked the status of her damage control teams to the tactical officer's display.

"Yes, Captain, we should have no problem making it to the base with the repairs we've already completed. Some of the structural damage will require a starbase to fix, but we are stabilized."

"Excellent, thank you, Lieutenant. Helm, take us home with all speed."

"Aye, sir. Engaging tunnel drive."

Transition was a sight she never tired of, the way the blackness of space split into an array of colors, some of which seemed to exist only in the moment of transport from known reality into the unreality of tunnel space. Once in the tunnel, there was not much to see other than a smear of speed that was incredibly hard on the eyes. Rare were the people who wanted to experience that more than once, as it very much emphasized they had left their own universe far, far behind.

The captain spoke again, quiet reverence in his tone. "Lieutenant Casco, please record the death of Commander Felix Olivas on this date. He died in the line of duty, and should receive full military honors when we return to base. Please update the ship's log and list Lieutenant Commander Anderson Cross as the *DC*'s executive officer. Lieutenant Commander Kate Flynn is now third in command."

Her heart pounded at the announcement. He gave her a confident look and a nod. She hadn't imagined the sound of those words would be so pleasant on her ears, and found a sense of pride in her accomplishment, even though she wished that the cost of it had not been so high.

"Tunnel time expected to be twenty-eight hours to the UAL forward base," Smythe announced.

"Thank you, Lieutenant."

Kate wrapped up her oversight of the damage control parties and sent the final information to the tactical officer. "Permission to leave the bridge to confer with Jannik, Captain?"

He looked at her questioningly.

She hastened to explain, "The computer is having a difficult time translating the recording we received. We want to put our heads together and see if we can speed up the process. It would be useful to understand what that alien was saying. I'm not sure about you, but I've got a bad feeling about it."

Okoye gave a short laugh. "There's not much right now worth having a good feeling about, Lieutenant Commander Flynn. But your idea is excellent, and you should absolutely confer with Chief Jannik about it. Your initiative is appreciated. I will update the duty rotations and copy them to you. When you're done with Jannik, go off-shift and get some sleep. As long as nothing unexpected happens, we're safe in the tunnel. And, frankly, if something does happen, we probably won't even have a chance to notice it."

Kate nodded. Problems that occurred in tunnel space tended to be fatal to ship and crew alike. "Thank you, Captain. I hope we can make some progress before we get home." She grabbed her computer pad and headed for the lift.

WHEN SHE ARRIVED IN ENGINEERING, the ensign monitoring the engine readouts gestured toward Jannik's office. The door was open, allowing the chief engineer to listen to the engines. He claimed he could hear a problem coming before the instruments would show it, and long experience had given her no reason to doubt him. She was rather surprised to see Cross in the room. The short glasses of dusky liquid in front of each man were less of a surprise.

As she sat, Jannik poured a glass for her and slid it across the table and into her grip with expert precision. The two men raised their drinks in a toast and Kate followed suit.

Cross spoke, "To Commander Felix Olivas, who served with honor, and has reached the final port of call."

Kate and Jannik finished the ritual in unison, his deep baritone a melodic counterpoint to her own higher tones. "May he find home, hearth, and happiness there; here, he will be remembered and honored."

Cross tossed his drink back, then stood and stretched, stopping the movement halfway with a wince. "If I know you Kate, and I like to think that I do, you're here to work. I have no interest in working right now. I'm going to stop by medical and then go to my quarters and crash for a while. I need to build up my strength before the *conversation*."

Jannik grimaced, while Kate barely kept her own face neutral. For a moment, she considered mentioning his appointment as XO, but realized that the captain probably had a plan and that she was best kept out of it. She rose and gave Cross a careful hug. He sank into it for a second, allowing her to comfort him. Then, with a crooked smile, he took his leave.

Jannik shook his head at Cross's retreating back. "Not the best of days for that boy, is it?"

"Definitely not. Although, I'm not positive he did anything that could strictly be called *wrong*."

"Sometimes things just go sideways, and there's not a damn thing you can do except hold on for the ride. I'm sure the captain knows this. After all, he was an engineer before he was the captain."

Kate laughed. "Everyone knows that engineers are on top of the heap."

Jannik toasted her in reply, finishing off his drink. "Okay, down to business..."

AN HOUR LATER, they were deep into rewriting computer code to better attack the problem of the alien's foreign speech. They had been compelled to listen to the mostly familiar sounds arranged in seemingly random ways until both were exhausted from the aural assault.

Jannik, who had been cursing steadily but with no force behind it, finally said, "There's only so much we can do here, my girl. I think we've optimized it as well as we can, and we've devoted as much computer power to it as is available on the ship."

"I still think wiring the entertainment computers into the server farm was a bit excessive."

"Every processor counts, Kate, you know that. Still, it will probably take days and days to get through it at this rate, if it's even possible with our limited resources. What we really need to do is to set up a call that goes out when we leave the tunnel. We can request all the linguistics databases from all the Union ships and installations in the area. That additional data ought to speed up the process some."

Having resigned herself to leaving the translation issue for the time being, she looked up at Jannik. She recognized the look on his face, and Kate tilted her head. "You've got a secret, don't you? Spill."

Jannik's scraggly face split into a wide grin. "You know me too well, Kate. It just so happens, that I know the Union maintains a duplicate copy of its entire linguistics database at every starbase. If there is anything like this in all of human history and experience, it'll be in there." He leaned back with a self-satisfied smirk.

"You make everything you do appear to be magic, when really it's just that you know a guy who knows a guy who knows a thing that he shared with you over drinks in some seedy base bar."

"Pretty much."

"Well played, Chief."

"Thank you, Kate."

She looked at the clock and decided she had time for a quick stop before bed. "I'm off to sleep, magic man. Try not to let the ship explode, okay?"

Kate walked out, leaving Jannik grumbling amiably about the lack of stamina among the new officers, who needed to sleep all the time, while he poured another finger of amber into his glass.

CROSS'S CABIN was not exactly on the way to her quarters, and yet somehow, she found herself there. During the short trip from engineering to the third deck where the officers' cabins were located,

Kate had debated whether talking to him was a good idea or not. On the one hand, he needed to internalize the events of the day at his own pace. She could see that he'd been cut, and she shared phantom pain from his wounds. On the other hand, she knew this could trigger a cascade of self-doubt and recrimination inappropriate to what had happened.

The decision was taken out of her hands as she stood outside his door. With a quiet hiss, it slid open, revealing a shirtless and bandaged Cross standing in the doorway.

"I knew you'd come."

"You did *not*," she said indignantly.

"I did. Even when we're at our most distant, we are always friends. So of course, you would come."

"Okay. You did know. Now move and let me in."

Cross stepped back, and Kate entered his spartan quarters. Officers on rotation learned not to grow too attached to a certain cabin or even a certain ship. Even though his role as third—now second—commander on the *DC* was a longer-term posting, Cross had rid himself of most creature comforts along the way and seemed disinclined to add any back. An ornate wooden case held mementos of the successes he'd had, of the honors he'd won. Aside from that artful display, the room was bare, except for a photo frame showing a succession of people and places.

Kate sat in his desk chair and rotated it to face the bed, motioning Cross to sit down. He lay down instead, grabbing the pillow and putting it at the foot so his head would be closer to her. "Talk, Cross."

"There's nothing to say."

"There's plenty to say. You need to vent some pressure before the captain calls you to a conversation or your brain will explode, making a mess of his lovely sitting room."

Cross exhaled a long breath. "I've gone over it and over it, Kate. I'm not sure what I should've done differently. There are places where I might've made different choices, but all paths seem to lead to the same place. It's our absolute mandate to hold the Alliance at bay.

That ship was trespassing in our space. I did what any commander would do in that situation."

Kate offered noises of agreement, refraining from pointing out that he had shied away from using the Alliance ship's name. A depersonalizing signifier of a guilty conscience. "Say more."

Cross clenched his hands into fists as he sought his next words, then forced himself to relax. "I gave him every chance to back down, every chance to end the conflict with no damage to either side."

Kate was sure he had caught the look on her face when he corrected himself and said, "Okay, minimal damage to both sides."

"Let's be honest, Cross. You provoked him. You did it on purpose. It was a good psychological play, and it worked too well. There was no way for you to know that his particular personality would become irrational in response. You're right, it's what any of our commanders might do." Kate was troubled, and she knew that he could hear it in her voice. "That's what makes this whole situation so stupid. We provoke each other, we use gigantic ships to spar over useless prizes, as if they were only boxing gloves in a practice ring. And then we act surprised when something goes wrong and a catastrophe occurs."

Cross set up to face her. "You know that's not what I—."

Kate cut him off with a wave of her hand. "I know, Cross. I know that you're not a warmonger, not someone who delights in the sadistic joy of inflicting damage for its own sake. However, I know at the same time that you love the game, that seeing an Alliance commander crawl away with his tail between his legs is a win for you. And I think that's probably true for most of the captains on most of our ships."

She stood, and walked toward the door, stopping and leaning against the wall beside it. "But that doesn't make it right, Cross. We have to do better. I don't know what better is, but I have faith that when we find it, you'll be one of the good ones who takes the chance to change."

Cross stood, walked to her, and put his hands on her arms. "And I have faith that you'll be one of the good ones who figures it out for us, Kate."

From another person that would sound patronizing. From him, with all that lay between them and behind them, she knew every single word was true for him. "Thanks, Cross. I hope you're right. I should go get some sleep."

He looked down at her, that familiar gleam in his eye. "Sleep's overrated. I have a better idea. Stay."

Kate grinned slowly, letting the stress of the day fall away in favor of embracing the moment at hand. "Only if you promise to make it worth my while."

Cross answered with a kiss that was quite promising indeed.

CHAPTER ELEVEN

Kraada Tak's knees ached where he knelt on the hard floor of the cathedral—where he had been kneeling for over a day. The implications of recent events were staggering. He replayed those critical events over in his mind.

HE AND DROVAA JAT were in the Defense Center when everything happened. They watched the battle play out in close to real-time courtesy of the *Jade Breeze*'s sensors. Even as the torpedoes chased the *Washington* into the tunnel, the two men were considering the implications of this transgression.

The marshal issued commands to bring the ship home, but only after conducting a thorough damage report on the reliquary. Kraada stared at him, then cut his eyes toward a secure area used for high-level discussions during times of conflict. Drovaa took the hint and announced they should only be disturbed with matters of great importance.

Once the door swished closed behind them, locking them into the room's safety, Kraada asked the obvious question, "Could *they* be the ones? The timing is notable if nothing else."

Drovaa nodded, but deferred, "This is your area, Hierarch. I'm just a dumb soldier."

Kraada snorted, and leaned forward in his seat, tapping his sharp nails on the table. "In the final analysis, it matters less whether they are truly the ones than whether the people will *believe* they are the ones. Even with that in mind, they fill many of the requirements spelled out in the *Dhadas Ve Xroe*. They are a species we haven't encountered yet, they've attacked us without provocation, and more-over, they've violated a holy site. They are within the designated cycle, though a little late, which will force us to ramp up against them quickly."

Drovaa agreed. "That won't be a problem. We've been ready for six years now, awaiting deliverance on the promise of the gods. We can launch the first wave in weeks, not months. The ships out exploring, or on other details, can serve as reinforcements or a second wave. At your word, we'll put out the call to bring them all back."

In that moment, Kraada felt the weight of his faith and of history upon him. Although, he'd been waiting for this *exact* development for all of his adult life, its arrival was a shock that resonated down into the marrow of his bones. He paused for a moment in quiet reflection and realized this decision was too momentous to make on the spur of the moment. "As much as it pains me to say it, my friend, we need to await further information and seek the counsel of the gods before launching ourselves at this enemy."

Drovaa nodded in acceptance of this plan, exactly like a member of the faithful should when the head of the church indicates a religious preference. "I will bring my forces to full readiness, just in case, Hierarch."

Kraada matched his formality. "Very good. I must meditate on this development."

Drovaa stood and left the room, returning with several men in uniform. "These men will serve as your honor guard, and escort you to wherever you wish to go, Hierarch. They are remanded to your service until such a time as you release them, so please use them as you desire."

"Thank you, Marshal." Kraada strode through the door, his ceremonial robes trailing behind him. His honor guard hurried to take positions around him and cleared his path all the way back to the cathedral.

Kraada noticed none of it, as he was lost in thought.

HALF A DAY LATER, he rose from his knees in the center of the vacant sanctuary. His meditative trance had shown him many possible futures spiraling out from this decision. It was not precognition, just a vivid imagination, but he wouldn't be shocked if there *was* a touch of the divine guiding his thoughts. He faced each of the icons in turn, gazing up at them and offering thanks for their guidance. Three received special attention, his patron Goddess Leleana, Kidarr the High Father, and the empty pedestal representing Vasoi. To this last, he offered his doubts and his fears about the cost this campaign would exact from his people. He prayed to all the gods that he was doing their will.

Then he straightened, unfurled his wings and flung his arms wide. He shouted, "Praise be to the gods of the Xroeshyn! Our destiny is finally at hand!" His guards and servants heard his muffled cry through the closed door of the sanctuary. Before they had time to ponder his words, the inner doors slammed outward as Kraada burst through them and began issuing orders.

He found time for a brief nap as his eight attendants mobilized. When they had assembled, he joined them for a formal meal—one of the many rituals set down in the *Dhadas*. Issues of import were never discussed while dining. Sharing a meal was a bonding experience, a way for the participants to focus their minds before embarking on pivotal discussions. It served this purpose well, creating a sense of transition before moving on to business. They shifted to a cozy den, all eight of them seated and watching Kraada expectantly.

"We are called, brothers and sisters. The time has come. The portents and signs we have been gifted with over the last six years have pointed to the discovery of a new species. A new species which launched an unprovoked attack upon the reliquary devoted to the All-Mother. There can be no doubt that this is the promised foe, especially given their transgression against the goddess of the beyond. When we defeat them, the gates of paradise will finally be open to our ancestors, who have dwelt in the in-between for too long, awaiting their final deliverance or their next turn on the wheel."

This declaration elicited gasps, prayers, and mild skepticism. One did not rise to the lofty heights that these men and women had achieved without being aware of the church's history. There had been three other moments identified as fulfillment of this promise of the gods. However, when the promised signs of success failed to materialize after the obliteration of those enemy races, the church was grudgingly forced to admit each time that its interpretation had been in error.

Kraada addressed the understandable skepticism. "This is not like the other times, brothers and sisters. The attack was on one of our holy sites. This is the final sign. However, past examples urge us to use caution in how we share this news with our congregations. Be hopeful, but make no promises. Exhort them to remain faithful and to thank the gods for the delivery of what may be the final enemy. Tell them that our forces will leave soon, within weeks, to determine whether these are the ones."

One of the eight, a priestess, stood to face him. "Let's cut the ceremony, Hierarch. How sure are you?"

Several fellow priests looked around uncomfortably at this frank opposition to their leader. The rest seemed as if they were in support of her question, as if she was speaking words they themselves would speak if they were bold enough to do so.

Kraada paused, looking her up and down, taking her measure.

Her skin reflected hues of orange and red, a combination that was quite pleasing, he noted. Her robes were less ostentatious than her peers, making her natural beauty all the more noticeable.

"Radith, thank you for your courage. This question will be on the minds of our people, and unless I miss my guess, is also on the minds of several of our brothers and sisters. There is no way to be completely positive until we engage them in formal battle." He paced, keeping his eyes on her, his gestures timed to emphasize the pivotal words in his speech. "However, I have meditated for over a day on this question, as prescribed in the rituals. I saw many possibilities. *If* they are not the ones, at the very least they will serve to bind our children together in common cause and reinforce their faith in the gods. If they are the ones, then our faith and our efforts will be rewarded as never before in our history."

His path led him to stand right in front of her, his head slightly declined so he could meet her gaze. "The rewards are well worth the risks, sister, don't you agree?"

She nodded, seeming to be convinced by his logic and his emotion, and sat again, cradling her drink and looking at him through half-lidded eyes.

"Thank you for giving voice to the doubts in your soul, sister. We will only succeed in our calling through honesty and partnership. Brothers and sisters, let us give a prayer of thanks to our gods and go forth to serve our people."

As Kraada escorted them from the cathedral, he touched Radith's arm in a silent invitation to remain. After the others left, the two religious leaders retired to the luxury of his bedroom to offer a vigorous demonstration of worship to Trensun, the god of love.

KRAADA WAS BACK at the Defense Center early the next morning, at the request of Drovaa Jat. The *Jade Breeze* had returned during the night, and its captain and religious officer were reporting in person to the marshal. Drovaa waited for him just inside the center's entrance. As soon as he caught sight of him, Drovaa took him aside for a word before they entered the secure room where the officers awaited them.

"Have you decided?" The hopefulness in his voice was apparent.

"I have. Regardless of what tidings the crew of the *Jade Breeze* brings us, we must pursue these aliens and exact revenge for their trespass. In doing so, we will discover if they are the ones."

He nodded at the look of ferocity that took over Drovaa's face and put his hand on the marshal's shoulder. "Yes, my friend, it is time to stop waiting and act."

"My people will speed up preparations immediately after this meeting. We've been on alert since that ship appeared, and much of the preliminary planning is already complete." He took Kraada by the arm and steered him toward the secure room. "Now let's find out what happened."

Captain Traan Aras and Religious Officer Reenat Srav awaited them, hot cups of tisane in front of each of them. They glared at one another across the table. Drovaa spoke first, as was appropriate in this location. Had they been in the cathedral, Kraada would have taken the lead. "Gentlemen, welcome back. You are to be congratulated on your handling of the situation in our reliquary. Captain Traan, please summarize what occurred during the battle."

As he obeyed, Kraada watched Reenat. The feathers on the man's wings were ruffled, showing his extreme displeasure, which only grew as the captain explained. When the man finished speaking, Kraada interjected before the marshal could ask any more questions.

"I take it you have a different view, Deacon Reenat? Please tell us your perspective."

He shot up from his chair and pointed at Traan. "*I* told him we must follow these trespassers, these offenders, these destroyers. But he was content to launch the torpedoes and return to the safety of the base. They needed to be punished," he yelled and pounded his hand on the table in time with his last word. His wings were fully extended, and his eyes were aflame with a zealot's frenzy. His next words were measured and directed at the captain. "He was derelict in his holy duty."

"Strong accusations, brother." Kraada's voice had the tone of ritual, an invocation. Kraada looked at Drovaa, who knew his part.

"Captain Traan, how do you respond to the accusation you have failed in your holy duty?"

The captain stood to attention and faced them, ignoring the religious officer. "I demand he retract his statement, or face me within the lines of eight." The two leaders nodded, and Kraada addressed his subordinate.

"Do you wish to retract your statement, Reenat?"

"I will not do so."

"Then it is decided," Drovaa intoned. "Tomorrow at dawn you shall meet within the lines. Go, and prepare yourselves."

AT SUNRISE THE NEXT MORNING, the two men reported to the combat ground outside the cathedral. The large octagon had a tall pole at each point, and plasma beams connected each at one-meter intervals when activated, sealing the combatants within. The cage would open only when one had joined his ancestors in the in-between.

Kraada and Drovaa stood as officiants to the ritual. As allowed, each combatant had brought a second, who would replace him should his courage fail. The second could serve as a champion, with the primary sharing the champion's fate, but this approach reeked of cowardice and was rarely invoked. On this morning, the seconds were present, clad in ritual armor, but all knew they would only bear witness.

The combatants arrived, Reenat Srav from the cathedral where he had passed the time in prayer, and Captain Traan Aras from his quarters, where he had spent the night which might be his last paying homage to the god of love, Trensun. Each wore armor befitting their caste, the captain's in shades of green and silver in honor of his current posting on the *Jade Breeze*. The religious officer's armor carried an icon of his patron, Ibrena, the goddess of peace and justice, and was primarily sapphire with golden trim—the traditional colors of that divinity.

The two men approached their leaders, and descended to one knee before them, their heads bowed. "Brothers," Kraada said, "will you set this argument aside? Blood need not be shed on this day."

The two men answered in unison, "I will not."

Drovaa spoke next. "Are you then determined to face one another in combat?"

Again, they answered together, "I am."

"Will you consent to having the matter decided with first blood, rather than death?"

The two men answered as one a final time, "I will not."

Kraada completed the formal words. "It has been asked, and you have answered. You will now enter the eight, where one or both of you will join your ancestors. May the gods give righteous strength to he who deserves it, and through that strength cast down he who has failed them. So may it be."

Drovaa echoed his final statement, "So may it be."

The two men faced one another. "So may it be."

In a ritual battle fought to first blood, this would be the moment where the combatants grasped hands and prayed together for the safety of their battle. In this case, they shared only a vicious glare.

An attendant motioned them into the arena, and the plasma barriers activated behind them. Kraada murmured to Drovaa, "It seems like this must be something that's been growing for some time, given their intransigence." Drovaa confirmed that these were his own thoughts as well with a nod.

The two leaders moved to their seats to oversee the combat, climbing high enough to have an unimpeded view down upon the proceedings. Small cameras hidden in each post fed an array of monitors at their feet, vital to judge first blood battles, but nothing more than additional perspective in a fight to the death. They would also record the battle so, that others might learn from it.

It was Drovaa's turn to speak, "Combatants, prepare."

The two men in the octagon moved to opposite sides. The captain drew his weapons first, a longsword in his left hand and matching short sword in his right. Although they were ancient blades, handed down through generations, it was clear from how they caught the light that the edges had been refurbished with modern technology to make them laser sharp. Each was curved, a testament to the martial technique that relied upon fluidity and speed. The captain enacted a formal warm-up, flowing through a set of motions with the swords and stances with his body. It culminated in a crouched, ready pose with the longsword raised over his head, the point forward, and the short sword positioned over his front knee, ready to defend.

The priest chose the standard weapon of the clergy, a heavy spiked mace. In his off hand, he held a large edged shield. The purpose of the mace was obvious, and it was weighted to compensate for the priest's lack of bulk. Kraada himself had won many a battle with a similar mace in his hands. The shield was atypical, a family heirloom modified over several generations. As a defensive tool, it was designed not only to block incoming strikes, but also to catch a blade on the many tiny projections in its uneven surface. Properly used, the shield could wear down the edge of an attacker's weapon over the course of a battle. The edges were sharp enough to cut flesh even if not enough to pierce armor. The priest closed his eyes for a moment, spread his wings, and looked up to the sky in prayer. When he finished, he banged his mace against his shield, indicating his readiness to begin

Kraada spoke, addressing the crowd that had gathered and the two combatants. "Today we ask the gods to watch over us, as we put a question of duty into their hands. Regardless of the outcome of this battle, by turning to the gods, we give them the honor that is their due, and we trust in their beneficence and their goodwill toward all the Xroeshyn."

He paused, waiting for his words to sink in, hearing scatterings of the closing phrase, "So may it be," from the onlookers that had gathered to witness the battle.

"Combatants, begin."

THE CAPTAIN of the *Jade Breeze* took a cautious approach, moving forward carefully, always on balance, ready to attack or defend. The priest was wrapped in a burning, holy anger that had been building from the moment that the captain refused to follow the alien ship into the wormhole. He vented it in a screaming charge, rushing forward and using the momentum to launch a spinning attack. His shield swung in first, clearing the defending swords out of the way. The mace followed, a quick strike intended to end the battle with one blow to his opponent's head.

The captain evaded with a spin that followed his deflected swords and dropped low under the swinging mace to aim a cut at the priest's legs. Armored boots stopped the blades, and the priest chopped down with the point on the bottom of his shield. It struck the captain's right hand and his short blade fell to the ground.

Sensing his advantage, the priest increased the rate of his attacks. The captain retreated, raising his sword in defense where necessary, but more often choosing to dodge.

Drovaa leaned over to Kraada and whispered, "Are all of your priests this aggressive?" He raised a hand to hide his grin, the dark humor inappropriate in this time and place.

He shook his head in reply. "Actually, Reenat is one of the most peace-loving of the brethren. Most of the rest of us claim at least twice-eight victories within the lines."

Their attention was recaptured by the combat below, where the priest had backed the captain into one post of the octagon. The shouts of the crowd easily displayed which combatant they supported. Those on the side of the priest cheered loudly, as the captain's supporters watched quietly. The latter group erupted into cheers as Traan counter-attacked. Blocking high with the hilt of his sword, the captain interrupted a downward blow from the mace at its apex. Kraada noted that on these grand strikes, the priest's shield arm swayed backward for balance, leaving his chest exposed It seemed that Traan had come to that same realization. Although a strike wouldn't get through that armor, the captain had other plans.

After knocking the priest slightly off-center with the block, Traan delivered a jumping kick to his chest, both heels slamming him backward. The captain recovered quickly, rolling and levering himself back to his feet.

The priest lost his footing and tripped backward to the ground. His skull made an audible crack as it hit the hard surface of the arena. When he rose, it was with a wobble, shaking his head as if to clear it.

"Uh-oh," Drovaa observed.

"Indeed," Kraada replied.

The priest did his best, but once damaged, he couldn't match the captain. His armor protected him from many slashes, but he failed to connect with the heavy mace, and the shield drooped lower and lower as the battle waged on. Eventually the captain found a seam in the priest's armor with the point of his blade, piercing the elbow joint of the priest's left arm, causing the shield to fall from nerveless fingers. At that point, the priest raised a hand, and Traan stopped his attack, moving out of range to wait.

The priest reverently set down his mace and knelt on the floor of the arena. He clasped his hands in front of him, bowed his head, and prayed to each of the gods and goddesses while his blood dripped to the ground, where it was absorbed and added to that of countless combatants reaching back through time. After several minutes, during which the captain stayed respectfully at attention, the priest met his eyes, nodded, and bowed his head again.

A sweeping move covered the space between them, and the captain's long curved sword removed the priest's head. As the sensors in the poles registered the end of a set of vital signs, the barrier dropped. The captain walked quietly out of the circle to the excited cheers of his supporters and the grudging respect of those who wished for a different result.

Kraada leaned over to be heard over the tumult below. "It appears that Captain Traan's decision to hold back has been recognized as the right one by the gods."

Drovaa dipped his head, "Or, on this day, he was simply the better warrior. In either case, the *Jade Breeze* has earned its place in the vanguard of our first wave."

"Send them as soon as you can. Time is precious."

"As you say, Hierarch."

The two men rose, gripped hands, and then separated to attend to the many moving parts required to begin the destruction of the trespassing alien race.

CHAPTER TWELVE

Cross awoke from turbulent dreams and reached for Kate. She wasn't there, of course. She never stayed the night aboard ship; that was a luxury reserved only for when they were truly off-duty during shore leave. He understood why she did it, but it didn't make the dull ache of her absence go away.

He shrugged it off and hit the shower. When he emerged from his cabin half an hour later, he was cleaned, pressed, and ready for action. He also had a destination. The captain had summoned him for the conversation.

Cross entered the captain's quarters, easily the most luxurious space on the ship. The admiralty consisted of former captains, and the design of the suite reflected their time as line officers. It had a working area, a sleeping nook, and a large reception area with couches, chairs, and low tables. It was there that the captain awaited him, offering a short glass of spiced whiskey as he approached and sat.

The two men drank without exchanging a word, and Okoye refilled the glasses. He then leaned his tall form back, resting his feet on the table.

Cross waited, and the silence stretched.

As the tension become unbearable, the captain spoke, "Cross, you are an excellent officer, and your accomplishments throughout command rotations have earned you the opportunity to be the second-watch commander aboard a starship. This experience is as much a rite of passage as anything. It is the place where your mettle is truly tested, where we discover if you possess that mysterious gene that will allow you to rise to great heights as a captain in the UAL Navy." Okoye levered himself up from the grip of the couch and walked around the room as he warmed to his speech, adding gestures at appropriate times.

"On the plus side, you exhibit several of the obvious skills of command. You are confident, you are consistent, and you treat the majority of your subordinates fairly and evenly."

Although the captain didn't mention the relationship between Cross and Kate, Cross knew he was aware and tolerated it only so long as it caused no trouble on his ship. Even though fraternization between officers of the same rank was permissible by naval regulations, the captain's word always trumped the letter of the law aboard his vessel.

"You have the intellectual capacity and the strength of will that are essential to success," the captain continued, pausing to look down on Cross.

"On the minus side are your aggressiveness and your focus on tactics at the expense of strategy." Cross had heard this from the captain before, and bristled, biting his tongue to keep from interrupting. "I reviewed the data from the beacon log generated during the encounter with the *Gagarin*. From the first moment, you pushed harder than you needed to. Where quiet diplomacy between equals might have worked, you sought the psychological edge. That is the correct opening move one time out of three or four. On the other occasions, it serves *only* to escalate the situation, which is exactly what happened here. That leads us to the second problem."

Okoye sat again and leaned forward to meet Cross's eyes. "You need to think bigger. It's not enough to win the battle by any means necessary, because the purest tactical victory can be the first step toward wholesale defeat. No position you've held thus far has demanded a strategic focus, so naturally it's somewhat foreign to you. That, after all, is the purpose of rites of passage, to take you beyond what you've mastered into the knowledge that follows it."

Cross thought the captain's expression couldn't get any more serious, but then it did. "I challenge you, Lieutenant Commander Cross. I challenge you to rise above your old ways of thinking. I challenge you to think broadly, to let strategy define your tactical choices. Use your aggressiveness where it is the right move, but expand your options for when it isn't. You are made of the optimal raw materials to build a successful career in command of any ship the admirals may assign you to. Rise above, and you'll find yourself in one of those glittering new vessels that are the shining prize for young captains."

Okoye leaned back again and took up his drink. "Fail to do so, and you'll protect colonization convoys with the oldest ships of the fleet for the rest of your career." He took another sip, using it as a transitional moment. "I'm confident you can accomplish tremendous things. Rise, Cross."

He nodded and opened his mouth to speak, to defend himself or at least lessen the negative judgment of the captain's words. He closed it again without uttering a syllable. As with all of his *conversations*, Okoye had narrowed the problem to a laser focus, and offered a solution for fixing it. To protest that truth would accomplish nothing. Instead, he only said "Thank you, Captain."

Okoye spoke once more as Cross rose to go, his voice softer, "Anderson, it's not your fault. Felix accepted the risks knowing, as we all do, that space is as unforgiving a place as has ever been imagined. It was the actions of the aliens that caused his death. Not yours. Not mine. We will remember him with appropriate honors when we reach the base. Between now and then, put him from your thoughts. Like any of us, he wouldn't want to cause distraction or pain to his fellow sailors."

Cross paused in his departure and turned toward the captain. "It's hard, sir."

"I know it is. But it's the captain's role to set it aside until an appropriate moment. Then, likely over a drink, we can allow the feelings to exist for a time. We must do the duty we're called to do, and that requires staying on target."

Cross nodded and took a deep breath. "Yes, sir. I—"

The intercom in the room interrupted Cross as the communication officer's voice radiated from hidden speakers. "Captain to the bridge, please. Tunnel exit is imminent."

Okoye spoke to the air, "Acknowledged." He stood and gestured at the door. "Lieutenant Commander Cross, it appears we need to get to work."

"After you, sir."

A SHORT LIFT RIDE LATER, the two officers strode onto the bridge, filled with first-watch officers. "Status," Okoye announced as he took his chair. Cross a moment behind him, slid into the XO seat and entered the codes to bring up his custom displays.

The helmsman spoke, "Tunnel jump took less time than projected, Captain. The currents must be with us today." The ongoing joke likened tunnel space to a river, invoking the days of sailing ships.

"True enough, Lieutenant Lee." Cross watched the countdown clock as it descended to zero and the ship reverted into chartable territory.

The communication officer spoke next, "Starbase 14 control requests course change to 37°, 15 high. We are assigned to berth twenty-seven."

"Oblige starbase control, Lee," Okoye said. His voice registered an almost imperceptible relief at being back in Union-controlled space. Apparently even experienced captains preferred the comfort of home—they just did a better job of hiding their discomfort when they were away.

The tactical officer reported on the other vessels present at the base and routed an image of each one to the main screen for the captain's review. The last was the gem of the fleet, the UAL's flagship *Rio*. It was the first example of the new dreadnought class, massing almost twice as much as the *Washington, DC*. She never traveled without her escorts, two cruisers from the generation after the *DC*'s— the *Toronto* and the *Montreal*. That trio had enough firepower and defensive capability to withstand any six Alliance foes at a time.

"She's beautiful," Lieutenant Allen Jacobs said.

"She's unproven," Okoye replied. "Give me a ship that's been put through her paces over a shiny new toy any day, tactical."

Fond laughs swept the bridge crew, as that was the only reaction someone on the *Washington* could offer and maintain loyalty to their own vessel. Secretly, though, there were many who would willingly transfer to enjoy the relative luxury of the larger vessel.

Kate spoke in the gap between reports from the engineering station, "Captain, the computer has finally decoded the message sent by the aliens."

Okoye sat forward in his chair, "Impressive work, Flynn. On-screen."

The screen divided again, showing their starbase approach on the left side and the alien frozen on the right side. Kate had served under Okoye long enough to know he would want a visual translation so he could still hear the tones used by the alien, and it was already set up. The image moved, and the entire bridge crew leaned forward as if increased proximity would grant greater understanding.

"Trespassers. Defilers. Mutilators." The alien's voice was harsh, but exuded a sense of control. "You have destroyed one of the most holy relics of the Xroeshyn."

Across the bridge, sharp indrawn breaths sounded in recognition of their plight. Though religion was no longer ascendant among Earth's children, officers didn't rise in the ranks without understanding the past of their home planet. The ways in which deity had been used as justification for actions both military and political were key parts of that history.

On screen, the power of the alien's delivery was increasing. "We offered you no offense to trigger this attack upon our gods." His wings spread as he pointed at them. "Demons. Heretics. Blasphemers." The second hand joined the first in the air, gesturing to the heavens. "You will be repaid for your trespass. As commander of the *Jade Breeze*, I swear it on my life." His voice reached a crescendo. "You have been marked, and there is no escape from our vengeance."

He dropped his arms and looked down for a moment before raising his head. His gaze traveled from left to right as he appeared to meet the eyes of each person on the bridge. "Despised, you are. Destroyed, you soon will be. Run, cowards, but know this. We are coming for you. And I will not cease hunting you, until you are delivered to the in-between. I am Captain Traan Aras, and this is my vow before the gods."

CHAPTER THIRTEEN

The captain left the bridge half an hour before, when starbase command revealed they would have to hold before docking. Cross sat in the captain's chair, bored, waiting for the moment they could dock and get off of the *Washington* for the first time in what felt like an age.

Cross could tell that the rest of the crew had seen the change in Okoye's attitude toward him and that the tense situation had been successfully resolved. They were meeting his eyes again, no longer associating him with the dismal failure of the *Gagarin*. *A positive sign*, he thought. Still, a good week on base would be just the thing to put this terrible event behind them.

Unless the aliens stayed true to their word. The likelihood of that seemed small, because the vortex that delivered them to the aliens' territory was random, and no known or imagined technology could determine the destination of another ship's tunnel.

Finally, they received permission to dock and Lieutenant Lee took them toward the berth at minimum thrust, staying alert for the traffic that zipped around despite the best efforts of control to route them. Cross used the opportunity to admire the gleaming starbase, the most recent version of the UAL's fourteen installations. While smaller in size, it exceeded the others in many other important ways. Defense, shields, amenities, these were greatly improved in the new construct.

A giant cylinder formed the core of the base, with rotating hubs at the top and bottom providing kinetic energy used to create gravity within the station. Once again, Cross was vague on the science, but glad it worked. The *Washington* matched rotation with the ventral hub, and then moved forward toward the dock. The motions in multiple dimensions made this a challenging maneuver, but with computer assist it was within the helm officer's skills. Of course, no starbase docking procedure was complete without a last-second unexplained hold from control, and the *Washington* received hers just before sliding into the berth.

Cross itched to be a face in the crowd, to avoid his crew, and to lose himself for a couple of days. Jannik was always good for that, the two of them spending copious amounts of time over drinks and across the gameboard from one another during shore leaves. He hoped to spend a substantial amount of time with Kate as well, although in their roles as second and third in command they would split shifts with the Captain aboard the *DC* in case of an emergency recall.

Cross's display screen lit up with a message from Okoye. It read, "Admiralty briefing. Tomorrow 0800." He acknowledged and clicked the display off. Putting his head in his hand, he felt a headache grow. A briefing of the admirals was without a doubt the thing he was least interested in doing in the entire universe. He'd rather have another "conversation" with the captain. He'd rather spend three watches in a row on the bridge. The list went on and on.

But at a minimum he would have some time to himself before the briefing. If they ever docked.

SEVERAL HOURS LATER, Cross reported as off-duty to the ship's computer, and walked across the gangway separating the ship from the starbase proper. Once there, he grabbed a lift to the center of the complex, which was set up much like a city block. Its circular design made it unfamiliar for most of the people who grew up on Earth, as did the artificial sun that was more a diffuse glow than an actual orb in the sky. In spite of these things, it hit the senses with a reassuring sense of "real." A breeze rustled through the trees and the grass gave off a fresh scent. The park in the middle was an actual living, growing thing. All the sailors visited it at least once to take off their shoes and feel something other than metal under their feet. Radiating out from the greenery in all directions were an assortment of restaurants, shops, and nice hotels for those with the means and the desire to avoid standard, military quarters while on base.

Cross had the desire. And drawing an officer's pay with nowhere to spend it left him with enough in his accounts to cover at least a couple of nights in reasonable comfort. He checked in to a simple room in one of the nicer hotels, then used his command access to pinpoint Jannik's location on his pad. He downloaded the information to his wrist comm and headed out.

If the base had a seedy district, Cross was confident that Jannik would find it, and the chief came through again. It wasn't that the physical surroundings were downtrodden in any way, because the entire facility shined. Rather, an aura hung in the bar, accented by smoke from a variety of vices and the surly edge that certain crowds got as their collective blood alcohol content went up.

Cross had experience with tough environments and navigated without offending to find Jannik seated with two other people who looked like engineers of a similar age. Cross took the empty seat in silence and punched in his request to the table's computer. In short order, he had whiskey neat, and the other three men had a new glass of whatever they had last ordered. Without a word, the four toasted one another with raised glasses and drank them dry. Cross leaned back and closed his eyes, letting the noise of the bar and the rhythm of his tablemates' discussion take his brain off-line for a while.

After a hazy eon, the other men left, leaving Jannik and Cross alone.

"Glad you survived the conversation, my boy."

"What's a few more scars to old warriors like us, eh, Jannik?"

The older man laughed at him. "You don't know scars, Cross."

"The damnable thing about his conversations," Cross said, "is that he's always right. Just once, I would like to see him not be right."

Jannik leaned forward, giving Cross a serious look that didn't look at home on his face. "No, my boy. You do *not* want to see the captain, any captain, be wrong. Generally, when a captain is wrong, somebody dies."

Cross winced. That one had hit a little too close to home. "I'm sure you've heard the whole story by now. I still can't figure out where I could've turned that failure into a win, can you?"

Jannik shook his head. "There's no way to predict what an enemy will do until you trade your first moves. There was no way to guess that this one would go crazy on us. Both sides been playing this game long enough, by now everyone should pretty much know the rules."

"Kate said something similar."

"She's a smart woman, that one. Don't know what she sees in you."

Cross laughed as they found themselves once again in familiar territory. "It's either my perfect physique, or my dreadnought-class good looks."

Jannik snorted and gave a forlorn stare at his empty glass. "For an arrogant lie like that, you get to buy the next round."

Cross countered, "Only if you'll indulge me in a game," and gestured at the chessboard inlaid into a table in the corner. Jannik's dive bar choices were rarely without a board. The old man loved pitting his mind against others' minds. He claimed a bit of competition told him more about a person than hours of conversation could. As a matter of routine, he played against, and instructed, every crew member who worked under him in engineering.

Jannik smiled. "Of course, Cross. I'm always willing to take your money."

KATE JOINED them a little over an hour later when they had traded victories, and Jannik was steadily encircling Cross's pieces on the board.

"The captain took the next shift, but mentioned that the two of you have a meeting tomorrow?" She hit buttons on a nearby table to order herself a drink.

"That's true," Cross said. "An admiralty briefing no less. I'm sure that will be entirely useful, and go very, very well." He saw one trap closing on him and made a bold move with his Queen to evade it. Jannik had set him up for just that response, three layers deep, and Cross lost a bishop in exchange for a pawn. He cursed creatively.

"Any clue what the admiralty wants to talk about?" Jannik asked.

"I'm guessing it's got something to do with our discovery of a new alien race," Cross quipped.

Kate nodded, and continued, "One that seems to want to destroy the *Washington*, at least, but probably would prefer to wipe us all out."

"Except for the beautiful women like Kate, of course," Cross said. "After all, it's a fundamental understanding of our culture that Mars needs women." Both Jannik and Kate laughed at this reference to early 20th century history.

"It is wise of them to want to keep the smarter gender," Kate replied.

"My guess is that they're going to eat all of you, tasty young people, but treat your elders with dignity and respect." Jannik's threat didn't impress Kate and Cross.

"They'll probably eat all of us," Kate said, "but it's true you, older types will be much more stringy and gamy." All three of them burst into laughter together, feeling the warmth of family despite the lack of blood connection.

The game ended with Cross losing after fighting a strong battle to the end. Another round of drinks was ordered and consumed, and they staggered slightly as they headed together toward the door. Cross invited Kate to stay with him, but she only laughed and said, "First, you're too drunk to be of any use. Second, you get to visit with the admirals in the morning, and you need to get your sleep."

She gave him a kiss on the cheek and said, "Rain check, Ace. Ask me again tomorrow." She linked arms with Jannik, and they wandered off together toward the base officer housing, merriment carrying back to Cross as he watched them depart.

The combination of bar games and Kate's use of his fighter call sign reminded him of their academy days and put a smile on his face that stayed with him through the walk back to his hotel. He was out when his head hit the pillow, but the smile had been banished by the sense of impending doom in the form of his morning meeting.

CHAPTER FOURTEEN

Cross met Okoye in the lobby of the hotel. The captain had also chosen the place as a residence during his leave. As they walked together toward the block of buildings that made up the military working space on the base, he saw the look—Okoye was going to give him a pep talk. They were only slightly less painful than his *conversations*.

The older man cleared his throat. "Just report the facts and do your best to strip emotion out of it. They will push, and will be inappropriate and disrespectful. They don't care about your past, about your skills, about the subtle nuances of the situation. The admirals have three jobs. First, and most importantly, they must keep our people safe from the many threats awaiting us as we explore further and further into uncharted territory. Second, they need to protect their positions and power bases. They do this through their third job, which is to fully and completely cover their asses at all times and in all respects."

Cross caught the laugh as it tried to escape. Only his dread of the upcoming meeting allowed him to contain it. "That's telling it like it is, Captain."

"Truth, Lieutenant Commander." Okoye laughed. "The admirals don't know you well enough to like you yet, Cross. They are very well acquainted with me, and like me hardly at all. Consider this a *conversation* with both of us on the receiving end." Cross raised an eyebrow. "Yes, I know the crew calls them conversations. The knowledge that there will be one when something unpleasant occurs reassures everyone that I'm on top of things. When you get your own command, you'll understand. A good captain knows everything that happens on his ship and uses every bit of it to the advantage of his crew."

Cross shook his head as he held the door open for his senior officer to precede him into the building. Both men presented their identification at the security gate and offered fingerprint and retinal verification. In even more secure facilities, a small drop of blood would be extracted and tested for genetic match to the records on file. A dour ensign wearing the perfectly, crisp white that signified starbase crew led them to the lifts. Both he and Okoye were in dress blacks signifying their postings aboard active duty vessels. Each had a newsteel badge engraved with the letters *DC* pinned at the top of each sleeve. They each also wore appropriate rank insignia on their shoulders. The captain's sleeves showed multiple combat recognition tokens as well.

The lift opened upon a spacious room that overlooked the park many stories below. A large semicircular table filled the space, with a seat for each of the admirals. Behind the chairs was a giant picture window showing the upper level of the other half of the base across the way. Cross and Okoye had a nice view as they sat at a two-person desk inside the arc of the circle to await their superior officers.

They didn't have to wait long.

Doors at one side broke open with a crash, and the admirals flowed in, awash in a myriad of colors and insignias. They were all older than the officers from the *DC*, at least in their fifties. Each had risen to their positions through exemplary work in their chosen fields, combined with extensive networking and politicking. Cross couldn't imagine ever leaving the bridge of his starship for a planet- or base-bound office, no matter the perks that might come with those gold stars.

Admiral Chloe Durand was the most senior member of the Admirals' Council. Cross had heard through the grapevine that she had avoided several attempts by subordinates to supplant her from the position and send her out to an "honorable retirement." She wasn't having any of that nonsense and maintained a firm grip on the rest.

She began the proceedings, "This council will come to order. The matter before us today is the recent encounter by the *Washington, DC* with an alien race in an unknown territory."

Each admiral looked stern and a few appeared slightly curious. "Gentlemen, it's my understanding that Captain Okoye was not on the bridge at the start of this event?"

Okoye replied, "That's correct, Admiral."

"Then we'll will let Lieutenant Commander Cross begin the tale, and Captain Okoye can continue it from the moment that he joined the action, so to speak."

Cross nodded and began to talk.

AN HOUR LATER, the officers had shared the entire story with the admiralty and answered the first round of incredulous questions. After a short break, the group reconvened to grill the two men more.

"Would you say you provoked the alien species?" Admiral Hugo Silva was the head of the UAL Engineering division and sported a long dark mustache that Cross desperately wanted him to stop stroking.

Cross remained silent, following his captain's directions. "I would most emphatically respond that we offered no provocation, Admiral," Okoye responded. "However, we were informed afterward that our exchange of weapons with the *Gagarin* destroyed an item holy to the aliens. I emphasize that this was not our intent, but it was a byproduct of the battle with the Alliance ship."

The admirals grumbled, each apparently judging they would've done better. Cross could read the attitude on their faces, and it caused his blood pressure to rise. It was always easy to criticize those at the front from a comfortable seat in the back.

The next admiral, Thomas Bryon, was in charge of the UAL Medical Corps. "What can you tell us about the aliens, Lieutenant Commander?"

Cross thought this was a particularly stupid question because the admirals had already seen the video of the alien species. He suppressed his temper and responded in as level a tone as he could muster. "They appear to have the characteristics that we associate with avian life, including wings, a few remaining feathers, and an overall body type that tends toward tall and thin. Their skin appears to have overlapping scales and has strange color effects associated with it."

The admiral pressed the issue. "Didn't you notice anything else?"

Cross gritted his teeth. "With all due respect, Admiral Bryon, we were a little too busy running for our lives to form a more detailed impression."

Okoye gave him a warning look, and he backpedaled. "I believe the crew did all that they could in this area, sir."

A third council member spoke up. "I'd like to start by saying that the *Washington* acquitted herself well against the, *Gagarin*, was it? Yes, the *Gagarin*." He looked down at his notes a lot. "It's not our fault that the idiots engaged a malfunctioning tunnel drive, and the chaos that ensued isn't of our making. It's my opinion that Captain Okoye handled the situation in an acceptable manner."

Cross blinked. He wondered if he had missed the question. It seemed he wasn't the only one, as a fourth admiral asked the third, "Do you have a question? Or is this just a political statement for the record?" There was clearly little love lost between the admirals in charge of Colonization and Forward Fleet.

"In fact, I do have a question, Admiral Campos. Gentlemen, what is your assessment of the enemy's offensive capacity? We all recognize that this is only a single engagement, and we have reviewed the battle recordings ourselves several times. But you were there, in the thick of it. What is your judgment of their military might?"

With a look, Cross again deferred to Okoye. The captain spread his hands out on the table, palms up. "My instincts tell me that their weapons are more powerful than ours and do not operate on the same principles. This makes them virtually unknowable. The aliens appear to use both projectile and energy weapons. I am at a loss to explain how their torpedoes crossed the threshold into the tunnel with us. I also fail to comprehend why our torpedoes were affected by the gravity in that area while theirs weren't. We have far more mysteries than we have answers where the enemy's capabilities are concerned. On a personal level, I find them extremely threatening, because we don't know how they think, we don't know what they can do, and we have no way of knowing how they'll respond to anything we might do."

Several of the admirals nodded in agreement, others scowled, and at least half wore poker faces that would make a professional gambler envious. The senior admiral waved at them. "Gentlemen, we must discuss this matter amongst ourselves. Refreshments are available next door, where we ask you to remain in case more information is needed."

The two officers stood, saluted, and exited the room.

THE VICTUALS WERE NOT as bracing as either officer would have liked after the grilling they'd undergone, but snacks prepared for the admirals were certainly more sumptuous than they were used to aboard ship. Both men piled their plates high and moved to a small table. Every member of the military knew that when there was a chance to eat, it was taken, since there was no way to know what might prevent the next meal. Cross snorted, thinking that a few members of the council had taken this mandate a touch too far.

Okoye leaned back after his first several bites. "Best case is that the admirals accept that the aliens are a dire threat and ask us to take part in the defense of this sector. I imagine that the *DC* will be among the front-line ships if the aliens appear. The council will want to test the opponent's strategy and ability before committing their full firepower."

Cross nodded in agreement. "It's what I would do. Not exactly cannon fodder, but certainly more a pawn than a knight. The crew wouldn't appreciate that analogy though."

A smile crossed Okoye's face. "Lieutenants Campbell and Walsh, among others, would be quite offended. We must make sure they know just enough to keep them sharp, but not enough to demoralize them." Cross frowned at him. "I know what you're thinking, Lieutenant Commander. You would prefer to be honest with the crew, and believe they could handle any knowledge we might give them. Am I correct?"

Cross sighed and paused before taking a bite. "As always, sir."

Okoye laughed. "It's not magic, Cross. Just a lot of years working with a lot of different personalities. You'll learn how to read them as the same thing happens to you. In any case, captains have a higher calling than the truth. We're responsible for the safety of our people, and sometimes that requires that they not know every detail to keep their own psychology from sabotaging them."

Cross mulled this over for a time, then decided that he agreed. *As always.*

The two men spent the next hour detailing several possible approaches to use when the enemy came calling. The most creative ones included the coordinated activities of up to sixteen ships. They were more conceptual exercises than actual plans, but both men enjoyed the process. Along the way, Cross learned a little more about large-scale strategy, and Okoye filed away some interesting tactical options. Both felt guardedly optimistic when summoned back into the presence of the council.

ADMIRAL DURAND ADDRESSED THEM, "Gentlemen, thank you again for the information that you have provided on this day. As you are no doubt aware, the admiralty operates on a principle of two-thirds majority for all decisions where unanimity cannot be achieved. Today's decision was not unanimous, but it meets the requisite threshold. I will ask Admiral Wesley Matthias to share our statement with you."

The head of Logistics for the UAL rose and faced the two men, who also stood, following the long tradition of respect accorded to the highest officers of the fleet. "Captain James Okoye and Lieutenant Commander Anderson Cross, you are each awarded the combat star in recognition of your actions against the Allied Asian Nations ship *Gagarin*. Well done." He paused, and Cross saw him trying to ignore the glares that were now coming from a few of the other admirals. "It is the decision of the majority that this alien race, the Xroeshyn, does *not* pose an imminent threat to the United Atlantic League. There is no practical way for them to have tracked you through the tunnel, and if we were in normal-space proximity to them, our expansion probes would already have discovered them. We will not overreact to this encounter, but will establish a higher state of defensive readiness for a time, and increase the number of patrols in the forward sectors."

Cross and Okoye both attempted to keep neutral looks on their faces. Okoye was better at it, Cross saw out of the corner of his eye. He was sure that the heat in his blood showed in his own expression.

The admiral continued, "When repairs to your ship are complete you are ordered to resume forward patrol. Until then, the *Washington* is on repair and re-provisioning duty. You may cycle your crew to shore leave as you see fit. Please coordinate with the starbase chief engineer. Gentlemen, you have our thanks for your efforts. You are dismissed."

There was no opportunity to respond, which was probably a good thing for Cross's career. The same pristine ensign led them from the room, and then from the building. He inhaled to speak, and Okoye held up a hand. "Now is not the time, this is not the place. I'll return to the *Washington* and coordinate repair activities for the next twenty-four hours. After that it's you, after you it's Flynn. Make good use of your shore leave, Lieutenant Commander."

Cross watched him walk away, then stomped back toward his hotel to scald the residue of being in the admirals' presence from his skin with as much hot water as he could get. He felt in his gut that the aliens were already on their way, or soon would be. He just hoped to find a way around the admiralty's poor planning before the Xroeshyn arrived. He groaned. His luck was never that good.

CHAPTER FIFTEEN

Kraada had spent the last few days preparing his underlings for the first attack wave. That included assigning one of his eight to be the new religious officer on the *Jade Breeze*, the flagship for the attack force. Kraada was confident she would serve effectively in that role, and would communicate back any pertinent information that the official communications might not include. They had discussed the posting in settings both public and private, and were bound by a singular shared purpose—to discover whether this opponent could be the one that was foretold. He had ample reason to believe she had the passion necessary to accomplish this task. Passion to spare.

But Kraada was a man of immense strategy. He never depended on any single individual. Those who reached lofty heights without building a network of weather gauges to warn of incoming storms didn't stay in those lofty heights for long.

Exactly at the appointed moment, there was a knock on his office door, and his attendant for the day ushered in a tall woman in a naval commander's uniform.

He stood and crossed the room to embrace her. "Niece, it's good to see you. It's been too long."

Returning his hug, she said, "It's wonderful to see you too, Uncle." Indraat Vray was his sister's daughter, and he shared a good relationship with his niece, much more so than with his own sister. "Thank you for the invitation."

"Unfortunately, it's not just a social request that brings us together today."

"I assumed as much. I've heard rumors. Does this relate to them?"

"It does."

"How can I and the *Ruby Rain* be of service to the church, Hierarch?"

Kraada smiled. "There is no need for titles among family, Commander." He turned the last word into a gentle tease, before he grew serious. "We're at a turning point, one way or the other, and before we continue, I must know where your loyalties lie." He could've explained more, but he was certain her sharp mind would jump to the right conclusions.

"My first loyalty is to family, Uncle. Then to my service, then to the gods. In most situations, I find these three are served equally well by the same actions."

"And if they were not?"

"It is as I have said."

"Very good," Kraada said, clapping his hands. He moved to a nearby cupboard and retrieved a bottle of wine and two glasses. As he poured for each of them, he said, "You're as honest as ever. There's an emerging situation that will almost certainly stress one or more of those loyalties before it is resolved."

Indraat's wings fluttered as she moved toward the low couch at Kraada's gesture. Her skin inhabited the red side of the spectrum, reflecting hues of scarlet, orange, and purple. The contrast with her ship's uniform, a lush black with accents of red throughout, made her stunning. The sheaths on her outer thighs lacked the vicious duo of daggers she routinely carried, and he noted that the shoulder holster underneath her jacket was also empty. "I'm sorry that my attendant took your weapons. You should've been permitted to keep them."

She shrugged. "It has been some time since we've seen each other, Uncle. It was a sensible precaution for your staff to take. As long as I get them back undamaged, I'm comfortable being weaponless in your presence."

Kraada gave her a knowing look. "As if you're ever weaponless, Vray." She gave a small nod, conceding the point. She might be weaponless, but she was in no way defenseless. He was one of the few people aware of her advanced hand-to-hand training with the ground troops. Her experience with them wouldn't be appreciated by the majority of her service comrades. "In any case, I have a strategy meeting today with Marshal Drovaa, and I'd like you to join us."

They finished their wine and spoke of family matters until it was time to visit fleet headquarters.

THEY WERE USHERED into Drovaa's office as soon as they arrived. While Kraada knew the other two had encountered one another before, he felt it necessary to introduce them again, anyway.

"Marshal Drovaa, this is Indraat Vray, Commander of the *Ruby Rain*, and daughter of my sister." Drovaa returned her salute, then shook her hand. "It's a pleasure to meet you again, Commander. I believe I was there when you graduated from the Academy." She nodded, clearly pleased to be remembered.

Kraada gestured for her to take a seat, taking the one closest to the desk for himself. "We have several matters to discuss, Marshal."

"I presume you mean other than outfitting, provisioning, crewing, and launching an invasion fleet on an unexplored trajectory, correct?"

Kraada laughed. "Exactly. It's good you have the simple parts well under control." Indraat and Drovaa both smiled at his lightheartedness.

"Indeed, Hierarch."

The moment of levity fell away against the seriousness of the situation. "What's the status of our force, Marshal?"

Drovaa stood and paced. "Six ships are ready to depart, including the *Jade Breeze*. Seven, if we include the *Ruby Rain*." He looked at Indraat, and she nodded. "Seven, then. The eighth should be on station the day after tomorrow, but getting the ship re-provisioned will take at least a day."

Kraada was shaking his head before Drovaa finished speaking. "This cannot wait, Marshal. It is imperative we strike while passions are high to maximize public support for this move. Doing so protects the emperor and ourselves."

"It will *not*, however, protect my ships and crews if we send them in as less than a full eight."

"And yet, it must be done," Kraada replied.

Drovaa turned angrily toward him, but was stopped by Indraat's voice. "The *Ruby Rain* can tow a re-provisioning module. It'll slow us down, but not more than a few hours. The other ship can join us at a staging point instead of stopping here first. We can transfer the cargo upon arrival."

Both men looked at her, considering. "Your ship is at full operating specifications?" Drovaa asked.

"Of course," Indraat replied.

Kraada took over. "That situation is resolved, then. The next issue is our destination. Have our analysts figured out where they went?"

Drovaa shook his head, waited a beat, and gave a wicked grin. "We have something better than the analysts. The *Jade Breeze* tagged the ship with a marker. One of our probes has detected a trace of its signal, and all the other probes in that area have been retargeted to follow and triangulate its position when it comes to a stop."

Kraada let out a deep breath, jettisoning a long-held worry. "It's fitting that we'll be able to track the ship that trespassed on our reliquary and make it the first casualty of this action."

Indraat nodded. "And fitting that the *Jade Breeze* will lead the charge."

Drovaa squinted at her. "You're angling to be second in command, aren't you?"

"If it serves the needs of the fleet, sir, yes," she replied.

Kraada gave the marshal a shrug. "She's got the experience." Left unsaid but understood by all was that Indraat would be Kraada's representative among the initial force.

Drovaa shrugged. "Sounds fine. All seven ships have commanders with about the same time in command, so it shouldn't be an issue to place you at the head of the line."

With this matter decided, Kraada dismissed Indraat to prepare her ship for departure and arrange the re-provisioning module for towing. After she left, he brought up a touchier subject. "Have you had discussions with the emperor on this subject?"

"I have."

Drovaa's face told Kraada all he needed to know about those conversations.

"I imagine that we're on our own in this endeavor, unless and until it succeeds, at which time the emperor will take full credit for it?"

"You have an astute understanding of politics, my friend."

Kraada snorted, the feathers on the top of his head spiking up. "I have an astute understanding of our emperor, at least." The two men had agreed on many occasions that Enjaaran was not an ideal leader. They both also understood the system of family rule was not one to be challenged lightly. The last attempt—a military coup centuries before—had ended in a purge of both soldiers and civilians that discouraged further attempts.

Kraada stood and wandered the room, his wings stretching, feeling something at the tip of his mind. "What are we forgetting, Drovaa?"

Drovaa shook his head. "Nothing, Hierarch. It's only that this is a much less predictable scenario than any we've faced during the many years of our friendship." He moved over to Kraada and extended a hand. "Together, though, we *will* succeed regardless of the obstacles that appear in our path."

Kraada met his eyes and shook his hand. "So may it be."

THAT NIGHT, Kraada hosted Indraat to a private dinner in his quarters, served by two of his attendants. The eight, minus the one now assigned to the *Jade Breeze*, were all in attendance at the cathedral, and would remain so until the current crisis was resolved. Underpriests watched over their congregations as they watched over their leader. An eighth was already en route to replace Radith.

Kraada didn't wait until the conclusion of dinner to talk about matters of import, placing the need for action ahead of civility. "I'm not positive what Drovaa will give you as a mission as you embark into alien space, but I hope you remember the church's stake in this at all times. I'm counting on you to be more than just a military commander."

Indraat nodded acceptance, setting down her utensils and focusing all her attention on him. "I understand. I will do this."

Kraada had predicted her answer, but the reassurance was welcome, for the next thing he had to ask was far more difficult a task.

"I also need you to be my eyes and ears on the front lines, and to report anything you judge important directly back to me."

Indraat took a delaying sip of her wine, then set it down and met his gaze. "To clarify, Uncle, you're asking me to evade the normal chain of command and feed you information in secret?" He nodded. "Done," she said with a shrug, then picked up her utensils to resume eating.

Kraada smiled. "Just like that?"

Indraat returned the smile. "Just like that. Family, then duty, then the gods. This serves two of the three, so it must be a worthy task."

Kraada nodded, taking her words as seriously as he would any declaration of faith. "You risk a great deal in doing so. If you're discovered, the rules of battle say—"

"—that I will be shot as a traitor and my body launched into space, trapping my soul in this world rather than allowing it to depart for the in-between." She nodded. "I understand the risk, Uncle. I also understand that some things are too important to leave solely in the hands of the military. That is why there is a religious officer on each ship after all."

Kraada leaned back, appreciating her logic. "But in some circumstances, that officer cannot accomplish everything the church needs, because they're not in command."

"You need not convince me any further. I'll do what needs doing."

Kraada changed topics without warning. "What is the consensus about Marshal Drovaa?"

Indraat registered surprise, her expression quickly changing to one of thoughtfulness. "It's not as if we talk about him much, in his own person, but he is discussed as a representative of the military high command. He's reasonably popular, but some commanders question whether he's aggressive enough to lead us over the enemy once we find them. Because it has been more than a decade since our last efforts at conquest, many officers only know him as a theoretical war leader, rather than an actual one."

"Would you say there's a belief that he may be out of touch with the current reality?"

"I would say among a small but significant portion of the commanders I encounter, that would be a true statement."

"How do they feel about the emperor?"

"All the Navy's commanders revere and honor our glorious emperor." It had the sound of something delivered by rote, and the twitch of her lips reinforced that perspective.

"And when they're talking amongst themselves, instead of to a higher-ranking individual?"

Indraat looked around as if fearing to be overheard even in this place. "In private, the opinions of our emperor rate him somewhere on a continuum between a hedonist who doesn't care about his people on one end, and a brainless neophyte who doesn't understand his people on the other."

Kraada coughed into his wineglass, having chosen an inappropriate moment to take a sip. When he recovered, his laughter rang out, echoing around the room. "That," he choked out, "is not something you should say beyond this haven, as you well know. Of course, it also happens to be hopelessly accurate."

She laughed along with him. "I know to never breathe a word of that beyond these walls. I do value my life."

"Niece, my instincts and meditations are telling me the same thing. We are on the verge of a great change for our people. I cannot see what form it will take, whether it be delivery to paradise through the destruction of this enemy as we all hope, or something unexpected. I ask you to keep your loyalties as you have stated them, and act as my sharp talon, invisible to the eyes of everyone but the gods."

Indraat nodded and sank to her knees beside him. He swiveled in his chair to face her. "Uncle...Hierarch, I vow to do this thing, to be your hidden weapon, and to cleave to my promise: family, service, and the gods."

He placed a hand on her head in benediction. "May those gods bless you and keep you ever in their sight, and protect you as you go forth to battle our enemy."

"So may it be, Hierarch."

Later that night, as he climbed into bed after another eternally long day, Kraada said a small prayer for the safety and success of his niece and her force who were set to depart in the morning. He prayed that she would deliver victory to them, and paradise to all Xroeshyn. "So may it be," he whispered as sleep took him.

CHAPTER SIXTEEN

With the *Washington* in a repair dock, there was little for Kate to do during her hours in command. A skeleton crew occupied the bridge, with only two others sharing the watch with her. While they acquainted themselves with positions they didn't normally operate, Kate used the sensor station and its priority computer access to learn as much as possible about their new foe. Cross had shared the admirals' perspective with her, and Kate didn't believe it any more than Cross and Okoye did. She'd witnessed the righteous fury blazing in the eyes of the alien commander and knew in her soul that his vow was true. He would not stop looking until the *Washington* and her crew were dead in space.

Cross's guilt had to be tremendous, and she hurt for him. Immersion in work kept those feelings at bay.

She cleared the low hanging fruit, performing a quick search that revealed no encounters with sentient life of any kind since humans had reached the stars. Even the reports from the most forward colonies and starbases mentioned no sightings of unusual or unknown ships or beings. Ever. So, she'd have to start from scratch.

She reviewed the recording one still image after the next, examining everything in the foreground and background. The computer offered a high probability that the species descended from avian genes. This would have implications for how they thought, how they reacted, how they lived.

The obvious telltales of feathers and wings were clear. Less so was the computer's calculation of their mass, which suggested bones of lesser density than her own, and possibly a continued ability to fly, at least in gravity less than Earth's normal. For a moment, Kate wondered what their planet might be like—imagining cities in the clouds and swooping aliens. It was an appealing picture, or would be if the aliens in question weren't trying to end her existence.

She asked the computer to analyze the shimmering skin tones of the alien. The exact composition was beyond the computer's ability to pinpoint, but a magnified image revealed it was made up of small overlapping scales. The way colors seemed to move of their own volition across them had no clear match in Earth's experience. Possibly the chameleon was the closest analogue, if one assumed that the hues changed intentionally or in response to some instinctual imperative, rather than at random.

She shook her head as she considered just how much they didn't know. As she entered the next request for information on the alien, she decided it was time to quit calling them aliens. Xroeshyn is what he had called himself, so henceforth she'd use that name. The computer overlaid measurements on the image, making Kate realize that the furniture and equipment was slightly larger than human equipment and furniture. The speaker was quite tall, probably over two meters. His face and head depicted a blend of recognizable features and avian influences. Everything about him was sharp, from his mouth that inspired comparisons to a beak to the slanted eyes, set above a curving ridge of bone that started at the nose and ended at the cheekbones.

The background revealed parts of two more aliens. The computer suggested they were of similar height, but their exposed skin showed different colorations for each. In some places, the brilliant shades strained her vision, as if they straddled or exceeded the boundaries of human optical capacity.

The alien's speech had been translated through brute-force processing. It was unlike any known language, except for having a basic noun/verb structure that placed adjectives after the subject. But even these conclusions were suspect, because it was impossible to know how much of the result was generated by the computational equivalent of guesswork. Either way, Kate mused as she leaned back and stretched, the words seemed to match the body language and tone of the message pretty effectively.

Kate shifted her analysis to the ship itself, particularly how it moved through space. She imagined that was tied to the reason its weapons functioned during their encounter when the *Washington's* didn't. Playing back the battle sequence, she charted each influence she could see. After staring at it for at least an hour, ceaselessly demanding that it tell her its secrets, Kate sighed and took a break. She walked to the galley and made herself a comforting cup of hot cocoa through a careful application of steamed milk to real chocolate purchased on the starbase.

Her mind wandered while she sipped, savoring the blissful quiet. It was rare to be on board and not hear the thrum of the engines, which were off-line at the moment. With the ship tethered to station power while she underwent deep maintenance and repair, the engines weren't needed to make her operational. As Kate stood, her tired hand dropped the cup, and it fell toward the deck. She got a foot under it, saving it from breaking, and stored it in the cleaning rack. She exhaled and pushed her hair out of her face with both hands.

On the way back to the bridge, she decided she probably needed to take a break and summoned another officer to stand watch in her stead. She went to the captain's ready room and lay across three chairs, which combined to make a reasonable approximation of a cot. She fell asleep to dreams of cascading colors warping madly through an asteroid field.

WHEN SHE WOKE UP, she knew. It had been right on the tip of her mind, and the few hours of sleep she'd snagged had set it free. With navy coffee in hand, created by following the age-old recipe with maximum caffeine and bitterness, she sat at the sensor station and brought up the battle schematic playback again. She watched it through to verify that her thoughts were least plausible and was rewarded with a positive result. She wrote a quick program to map the gravitic currents in the Xroeshyn sector during their time there. After processing for a half-hour while Kate sipped her stimulant and discharged some of the paperwork associated with her command, the computer reported as ready.

Kate toggled the playback to the main display and walked in front to watch. Just as she had thought, there were unpredictable gravitic happenings throughout the sector. First, the artifact that their torpedoes had destroyed exerted a strong attractive wave. She had seen the effects of that pull, in how the *Gagarin* curved as it sped past, the force of the gravity altering the ship's course and causing the missiles to retarget too close to the artifact, which pulled them in as they approached. The asteroid belt itself was home to several strange currents of attraction and repulsion that couldn't be explained by the available information, but appeared systemic, as if the whole solar system was the center of some unexplainable gravitic power.

Kate was surprised to see that the alien ship also seemed to exert a repulsive gravity wave. The computer illustrated a weak pulse emanating from it. Finally, the projectiles that followed the *Washington* through the tunnel exerted their own gravitic waves. *That's one mystery solved*, Kate thought.

At the conclusion of her shift, all three commanders met during the crossover. Kate reported her findings to the others, and both were impressed and alarmed in equal measure. Cross grumbled something about the admirals, but Okoye cut him off. "The two of you take one last day of shore leave. We embark tomorrow morning, and I need to be aboard to make sure everything's prepared. There's no need for you to be here as well. Go."

Kate and Cross went.

KATE HAD FIGURED she'd be aboard for the rest of their time at the starbase, so she had transferred her belongings back to the ship. She led Cross to her quarters, slipped into the shower, and came out dressed for a casual night on the town. Throwing a few things into a bag that she tossed over her shoulder, she left the *Washington* arm-in-arm with Cross.

Two hours later, they relaxed over a fine meal at Cross's hotel restaurant. He shared the full tale of his adventure with the admiralty, and she told him the deeper details of her research into the Xroeshyn. They reminisced about the fun times they'd had at other starbases and teased each other about their prowess at various games of chance. She could tell something was bothering him, and she had an idea of the topic.

Over coffee and dessert, he finally broke his silence. "Kate, look, with the new duty rotation—" he began.

Kate stopped him with a raised hand. "Allow me to finish for you." She dropped her voice lower to imitate Cross and put a clueless expression on her face. "With the new duty rotation, we'll have less time to spend together. I know this means you'll spend all of your off-hours lying in your quarters, hand to your forehead, moaning, 'Woe is me. Oh, woe.' Because of this, I feel guilty, but because I'm a particularly stupid specimen of my gender, I have only a tiny ability to actually express my emotions. So, uh, I just don't want to feel bad, so if you could proactively let me off the hook, that would be awesome." Kate looked across the table at Cross, then reached over and pushed up on his chin to shut his mouth.

"Did I get it about right, Ace?"

Cross nodded, looking like he still felt guilty. Kate wasn't sure whether to pity him or laugh at him.

"Okay, Cross, I'll only say this once so listen up. We're two separate people. You don't complete me, I don't complete you. We're each committed to things beyond one another. At times, these things will create physical distance or other complications. During those times, we're each free to follow our hearts wherever they lead. During the times we can be together, we will renegotiate where we stand based upon these other factors in our lives. I know for a fact you never saw us settling down on a colony with the stereotypical white picket fence. You need to realize that I never saw that either."

Kate leaned across and gestured him forward, so that their mouths almost touched. "I won't deny that I love you, Cross. You're a great friend, a pretty good occasional boyfriend, a lot of fun to socialize with, and a tiger in the sack. But that doesn't mean that right now I want to be your one and only, or that I expect you to feel that way about me. So, let your masculine, patriarchal nonsense go, and take me back to your hotel room. We still have ten hours before we have to report to the *Washington*, and I'd like to sleep for at least three of them."

Kate stood, pulling the speechless Cross to his feet. She hooked her arm in his, and he walked her to the door on auto-pilot. She looked up at him and smiled. "You know, honestly, you're kind of sexier when you don't speak. Perhaps that should be a thing for you."

Once they reached the room, he conveyed how he felt about her using no words at all, which suited Kate just fine.

CHAPTER SEVENTEEN

Dima Petryaev and the *Beijing* were on patrol at the front edge of Allied Asian Nations' territory. He had communicated the fate of the *Gagarin* back to headquarters by using one of his own tunnel beacons, but had opted to stay in the field. He could admit to himself, if not to anyone else, that he was unsettled by the idea of an alien race. Further, he was concerned because the path from wherever the aliens were to where they might somehow know the humans had gone came right through the forward sectors of each faction.

It had required some small bending of the letter of the law of his orders, but he had locked himself into a patrol pattern that would take him back near the sector where the *Washington* and the *Gagarin* had met. Dima had a feeling if problems were to occur, they would start there, and he wasn't mistaken.

The invasion began quietly, with the simultaneous encroachment of seven ships onto the forward edge of his sensors. The bridge of the *Beijing* erupted in announcements. Dima kept his ears open as he issued his own orders, taking in information from sensors, tactical, and helm officers. "All stop. Shields to maximum facing the unknown ships. Ready weapons, but do not target." He hoped these were Union forces. His gut told him they were not.

"Captain Petryaev," said the tactical officer, "ship configurations are similar to the one that destroyed the *Gagarin*. They are tagged as alpha-one through alpha-seven." The battle display on the main monitor updated to show the tags. "Standard shield frequencies not detected." Dima raised an eyebrow at his tactical officer, who stammered as he resumed speaking. "Of course, we must assume that the ships have defenses we're just not sensing." Dima nodded. He never missed a teaching moment.

"Thank you for the information, Lieutenant Yegerovich. Communication officer, are you picking up any transmissions from that sector?"

The rapid reply showed Junior Lieutenant Loh Zian had been working on that question even before he asked, "No sir."

"Hmmm." Dima mused for a second, then thought out loud. "So, we have one of two situations. Either they already have their plans set, and don't need to communicate, or we cannot detect their transmissions." Nods of agreement appeared and Dima continued speaking. "If it is option one, what does that mean?"

The crew knew that he never asked rhetorical questions. Junior Lieutenant Evelina Germanova spoke up from the sensor station, "It means they may be waiting on an external trigger, such as reaching a certain time, to begin whatever it is they are here to do."

Yegerovich picked up the thread, "Perhaps they're making final checks after arrival before moving on."

The helm officer pointed at the main screen, which showed a heavily magnified view in which the alien ships looked surprisingly like ants. "I think they may be waiting for that." Every head turned to face the display.

A tidal wave of energy in shimmering hues of blue, red, orange, and yellow flew through the sector. It left behind an eighth ship, automatically tagged as beta-one by the battle computer. The artistic way the aliens traveled through space made their own tunnel drives look like something a child would create. Zian swore quietly in Chinese while Dima's executive officer echoed the sentiment in her aristocratic Russian.

"Keep an eye on our friends, Exec. Call me if anything happens. You have the deck."

"Aye, sir, I have the deck," Senior Lieutenant Svetlana Ivanova replied.

Dima strode from the bridge, heading at a fast walk to his quarters.

SEVERAL MINUTES LATER, he requested that the ship's last remaining tunnel beacon be used for something other than its primary purpose. When the communication officer signaled it was recording, Dima spoke into the camera of his computer pad, "Admirals. This is Captain First Rank Dima Petryaev, commanding the AAN *Beijing*, sending to you from our forward exploration sector."

He leaned forward, hoping to portray an intensity that would convey the gravity of the situation. "In the sector where the *Gagarin* departed for unexplored space, there are now eight alien ships. We are unable to identify their defensive capabilities and have so far been unable to detect any communication among them. It is my initial assessment that this is an attack force, with the best-case scenario being that they are targeting either the UAL ship *Washington, DC* or the UAL as a whole. The worst case, gentlemen and ladies, is that the attack force is either one of opportunity or one that specifically wishes to eradicate us as a species."

He took a deep breath before he continued, making certain to temper his words. "To guard against the possibility it is an attack force of opportunity, I recommend evacuating our ships from the projected path of the squadron, which I will append before launching this beacon. To guard against the possibility it is a force determined to eradicate humanity, I recommend and request that you forward this information on to the admiralty of the United Atlantic League."

Pausing to consider his words, he steepled his fingers beneath his chin. "I know this may seem counterintuitive, and it flies in the face of the old adage that the enemy of my enemy is my friend. However, consider for a moment the potential ramifications if this is the first wave of a conquest force. If we don't at least equip the UAL to blunt that attack to the best of their ability, we put ourselves in a less advantageous position than if those two sides inflict significant damage upon one another. Eliminating the aliens' element of surprise will allow us to gather far more information about their capabilities than allowing them to attack the Union forces unhindered."

His body pressed forward to convey the sense of urgency he felt. "If I'm wrong, and these aliens are here only for the UAL, we have only to watch. Should the Union prevail, it will doubtless be weakened, leaving it ripe for our own conquest afterward. In the absolute worst case, providing a warning to the Union admirals is the first step in creating a partnership that may help us to avoid our own destruction by this unknown alien threat."

He leaned back and spread his hands. "I beseech you to act immediately upon receipt of this message, and send word to the *Washington, DC* and to the Union admiralty. In my opinion, it's the best play that we have at this time, even though it requires us to sacrifice a possible short-term masterstroke for a more likely long-term strategic victory."

Drawing upon every skill he had to convince them to act as he advised, he made his last pitch, "I also recognize that I am but the leader of a single ship, speaking to the leaders of our entire military. Nonetheless, I believe this is a pivotal moment, when actions taken or withheld will have effects that resonate into the future. Please consider my request. With deepest respect, Admirals. Captain First Rank Dima Petryaev of the AAN *Beijing*, signing off."

Dima watched a replay and grunted at the forced formality of the message. What he really wanted to say wouldn't sit well with the admirals' egos. He hoped that he had been persuasive enough to convince, but not pushy enough to offend.

THREE HOURS LATER, Dima was on the bridge when the alien ships moved. "Tactical, project the path of those ships. Once you have it, upload it to the tunnel beacon. Communication officer, when the beacon has the information, launch it."

He sat down in the command chair and waited for his crew to complete his orders. When he felt the thrum of the departing communication, he addressed the helm officer. "Follow, but maintain distance. Maximum range to keep them in our sensors." He turned to his executive officer. "Crew rotations at four-hour intervals, Exec. We need our people fresh since we cannot anticipate the aliens' actions."

He thought for a second before deciding this was important enough to break a few rules.

"Communication officer, should we get within hailing range of any Union ship, please establish a connection and inform me." He knew two UAL officers by name after all. He gave a short laugh, thinking that they would be very surprised to hear from him, if random chance awarded him that possibility.

CHAPTER EIGHTEEN

The three commanders of the *Washington* were separated, Captain Okoye in a briefing with the admirals, Kate on board, and Cross wrapping up his hotel stay when his communication alarm went off. Cross frowned, wondering who needed to reach him as he stepped out of the lobby and triggered playback of the recording.

Unexpectedly, it was audio only, and the sender data was blank. He recognized the Russian accent when he heard it, from their brief encounter after the *Washington* exited the wormhole.

"Captain, Lieutenant Commander, I hope this message finds you well and your ship rebuilt. The next time we meet, I can guarantee you that the outcome will be different."

Cross frowned. This was a very strange thing to say, given the positive nature of their last meeting. Captain Dima Petryaev's voice continued after a short pause.

"I send this to warn you that another lesson for the Lieutenant Commander is imminent. As he requested, the opposing player will pose a much greater challenge than did the *Gagarin*. Until I see the *Washington* in my targeting sights again, good luck to you both."

It took Cross several seconds to parse the words, and realize that

Petryaev was trying to preserve his own deniability while sending a message about something else entirely. Something very scary, he realized as a cold shiver traveled through him. He broke into a run and hit the buttons to connect to Captain Okoye. The Captain's comm was unavailable, a typical precaution to avoid distraction during meetings with the admiralty. Cross barked an obscenity, startling a pair of cadets as he dashed past them. He contacted Kate instead.

"What can I do for—"

Cross interrupted her. "Kate, sound emergency recall on my authority as executive officer. Get everyone to the *Washington* as quickly as possible. We will depart as soon as I arrive. My ETA is," he checked the map on his comm display "twelve minutes. Preflight the ship and secure approval for undocking with any excuse you can think of."

"Affirmative. Emergency recall, preflight, undocking approval. See you in twelve."

Thirteen minutes later, Cross was aboard the *Washington*, entering on her lowest deck. He opened a communication channel to Kate again. "Status?"

"We're ready to go. Seventy-three percent of the crew is on board, enough to operate all vital systems. If we can wait another seven minutes, we will get above eighty percent."

Cross growled at the lack of specificity in Dima's message and said, "Okay, seven minutes then. Captain Okoye?"

"We had an ensign break into the meeting. He's not pleased with you, neither are the admirals. He should be on board in six minutes, but specifies that he is continuing his briefing by remote and will not be immediately available when he arrives."

Cross cursed again. The captain must not have had time to review his messages, or he would head straight to the bridge. Given the vagueness of the timing, it wouldn't be a problem. Probably. "Acknowledged. When everyone's on board, pull out. I will grab a uniform and be on the bridge shortly. If we're clear before I arrive, put us on a vector between here and where we reverted from tunnel space after the *Gagarin*. Shields to full, weapons ready."

"Affirmative. Want to tell me what this is about?"

"You have to hear the message for yourself, Kate. I'll fill you in when I get there."

CROSS STEPPED onto the bridge and into a cacophony of voices blaring from the speakers. He glanced at the communication officer, and Lieutenant Ana Fitzgerald brought him up to speed.

"Enemy vessels detected, similar or identical to the ones that destroyed the *Gagarin*. Starbase defenses mobilizing, all ships cleared to launch on designated vectors."

Cross threw himself into the captain's chair and looked at Kate. She nodded, answering his unspoken question about her promise that the captain and eighty percent of the crew should be aboard by now. He could see on the main screen that the *Washington* was in motion, backing out of her berth. He reached down and tapped a spot on his display.

"Helm, take us to the position I've marked and hold. Maximum safe speed. Remember that it will be chaos with all of these ships clearing the area. Comm, inform the starbase, the *Rio*, and her escorts of our plan. Tactical, sound battle stations and prepare to engage the enemy if they come within weapons' range."

All Cross could do was wait. His crew would scramble to their duties, and the captain was probably conferring on an entirely different topic now that the enemy had been sighted. He allowed himself a small smile at this proof of the admirals' shortsightedness, then adopted a neutral expression appropriate to the commander of a starship.

The copy of Dima's message reached Kate, and he watched her eyes widen as she listened. She nodded in affirmation of his choices.

Cross returned the gesture, always willing to accept a little positive reinforcement.

"Tactical, set up battle display with enemy forces in green. Project area of influence from the starbase's weapons and overlay." Cross watched as the data materialized and decided his initial positioning was optimistic. "Helm, revise destination. Same vector, but keep us within the weapons range of the starbase. Make it so we can strike the enemy," he paused and did some quick calculations, "with half of our maximum range outside the starbase's sphere."

Okoye's irritated voice was a surprise when it came through his earpiece. "Cross, I'm helping to coordinate the larger battle from the auxiliary bridge. Keep us out of trouble and follow the plan from the *Rio*."

"Affirmative," Cross growled in return. He knew the crew from his original command shift that had made it back to the ship would take the duty stations on the aux bridge to support the captain, and he couldn't think of any other way to assist. He returned to the task at hand.

The bridge crew was glued to the battle display, watching as the enemy ships crept forward and the defenders interposed themselves between the starbase and the incoming threat. Fitzpatrick added the *Washington* into the starbase's command network, which included the commanders of all the military ships and starbase defense control. The captain of the *Rio* was the senior ship commander present and was coordinating the tactics of the ships in the sector. Cross listened in as Captain Javier Montoya supplied orders to the *Rio's* escorts and the newly arrived *Mexico City*. A signal ordered the *Washington* to adjust position to fit better into the overlapping defense spheres, and Cross echoed those instructions to his helm officer.

He noted that the entire bridge crew was primary rotation officers, Okoye's team. He sent a quick message to Kate asking about the status of his own people. She responded that all were on board and at their positions on the auxiliary bridge. The speed of her response meant she'd expected the request, and he shook his head at her intellect.

And then they could do nothing but wait as the enemy crept closer and closer.

THE BATTLE BEGAN WITHOUT CONVERSATION. Hails had been repeating since the aliens appeared on the sensors, but they were apparently uninterested in talking. The incoming force split into four pairs, and each launched a complement of torpedoes before arcing in different directions toward the starbase, one high, one low, one port, one starboard. All the missiles sped along a direct line ending at the *Washington*.

Cross grimaced. "Well, I guess they remember us."

At this distance, they had almost forty-eight seconds before the missiles would reach them, and twenty before they could launch in defense. The *Rio* was not as limited by range as her smaller allies and she launched two counter-torpedoes for each incoming weapon. She also disgorged a fighter screen that split in half and raced to intercept the high and low targets.

The *Washington* and *Mexico City* were assigned the port target, and the *Rio's* escorts moved toward the pair of enemy ships on the starboard side. The *Rio* herself stayed in the center, coasting backward toward the base, waiting for the full array of weapons she carried to be in range.

Eyes on the display, Cross thought time must have jumped forward, placing the opponents instantly within range of one another. All the ships started firing at once. The *Rio* rotated ninety degrees, bringing her port and starboard broadsides to bear on the enemies going high and low. The fighter screen scattered with computer-controlled precision, opening a lane to each pair, and the *Rio* fired both of her broadsides at once.

As with all the ships of the dreadnought class, the *Rio* boasted an impressive number of weapons of every kind known to the UAL. Her torpedoes fired faster, were stronger, and could fly for longer. Her lasers were half again as powerful as those on the *Washington*, and her plasma cannons were double the intensity. Plus, given how big she was, there was a lot of room for them. A single broadside included six lasers, six plasma cannons, and twenty-four emplacements, some housing torpedoes and the rest magnetically accelerating orbs of newsteel a meter in diameter at incredible speed toward an enemy. Her disciplined crew managed their tasks well, coordinating the various shooting speeds to maximize the damage of each broadside. A single blast would be enough to significantly wound any ship that the AAN could field.

They proved less effective against the defenses of the Xroeshyn ships. The strange shields that had generated such an odd gravitic pattern when analyzed, bent the incoming energy of the plasma cannons and lasers, curving it away from the ship and leaving the gunners aghast. Some of the torpedoes fared better, impacting the enemy shields, but in most cases, failing to get through and cause any damage.

The newsteel rounds, a recent innovation that had yet to see action against the Alliance forces, struck the enemy ships with most of their force intact. Gravitic defenses pulled them off of the direct-line path from their guns, but weren't powerful enough to stop them. Ablative hull pieces fragmented and fell away from the alien vessels, yet they continued undeterred toward the starbase.

Clearly daunted by the lack of effectiveness of the first salvo, the commander of the *Rio* projected a new vector onto the ships' battle displays. Cross saw he was directing them all to converge on and overwhelm the topmost vessel. He issued the appropriate commands, and the *Washington* changed course.

Then he noticed an opportunity. One of the enemies that had gone low was faltering, falling away from its escort as the other seven continued driving toward the starbase. His conversation with the captain about thinking strategically evaporated from his brain as if it had never occurred. He used the controls on the arm of his chair to designate that ship as the *Washington's* primary target.

"Helm, come to 213, 60 low." The ship altered direction again, and Cross felt the uncertainty of his crew. He had no time for doubt, his own or others', and focused on his prey.

"Tactical, keep us safe from random shots, but reinforce bow shields as much as possible. Weapons, try sequential impacts instead of all at once. Space them at one second apart, plasma first, then laser, then torpedoes. Fire once we are inside maximum range and keep firing." Cross leaned forward in his chair, ignoring the discordant chaos of the command net in his earpiece. It took forever, but finally they were close enough to engage.

Both ships engaged at almost the same moment. Incoming energy blasts hammered the *Washington's* front shields, but they held. The enemy ship skewed, continuing on the same heading but presenting her starboard broadside, which fired as it gained its target. It continued through a full spin, discharging its port broadside as well.

The *Washington's* shields held against the enemy's energy blasts, but were substantially depleted.

"Countermeasures." Cross's voice was calm and deliberate, a sign that he was in the zone. "Tactical, pick a point." The shorthand told the tactical officer to mark the enemy ship with the *Washington's* targeting lasers, mounted on the top and bottom of the ship right at the midpoint. Once locked on a target, they would maintain that spot regardless of the ship's movements. "Lock all weapons on the point. Helm, evasive pattern gamma."

The *Washington* careened onto a new vector, incrementally increasing the enemy torpedoes' travel time to them. Cross saw his mistake as he reviewed the battle display. His racing brain processed the fact that two other ships had peeled off and were closing on the *Washington*, which had left friendly cover behind. He bared his teeth and gave a head tilt of respect to the enemy commander. Fortunately, there was still time to alter the trajectory that was taking him into the teeth of the ambushing vessels.

"Helm, new course." He traced the tightest arc that would direct his ship back into the starbase defenses while avoiding the enemy's trap onto his display. "Tactical, full power to shields all around, watch for incoming from starboard." He judged the distances and was confident he had reacted just in time. The commander of the *Rio* gave him an earful for deviating from the plan and provided new orders. The *Washington* was now tasked to intercept any escapees from the imminent converged attack.

Icons came together as seven Union ships attacked the enemy pair. One of them turned, taking the attack head-on and charting a collision course with the *Rio*. The other enemy ship dove sharply, evading the engagement and orienting itself on the starbase. An array of sparkling items ejected from the front of the enemy ship, and they fired tiny engines to accelerate toward the starbase. Point defense cannons activated, but only defeated one in ten as they were too small for the targeting radar to lock on to. The remaining three ships came in undeterred by the base's defenses and the harassing fighters and launched their own tiny projectiles, followed by traditional attacks that were absorbed by the starbase's shields.

The tiny flickering items adhered to the starbase, then appeared to fall dormant. An astute observer would've noted that they'd landed in particular patterns, a spiral on the upper part of the base, and a spiral on the lower part of the base. That same observer might wonder why that pattern, and why that location, since there was nothing in the science of humanity to explain it. This perplexed observer would soon discover what those tiny destructive devices were for.

CHAPTER NINETEEN

Captain Okoye strode onto the bridge, projecting calm confidence all around. Cross, who'd turned at the sound of the lift door, vacated the captain's chair and strapped himself in to the XO position. After almost falling for the enemy trap, he was more than willing to relinquish command to the captain.

"Status," Okoye said in his clipped accent.

"No damage, our objective is highlighted on the battle display, our target is the one running from the *Rio* and the ships with her." Cross tapped instructions into the arms of his chair while he spoke, bringing up his personal displays. He hadn't fully set up the XO station, an oversight that, if he was honest with himself, probably had a lot to do with the way the previous executive officer vacated the position.

"Very good, Lieutenant Commander. I have the deck."

"Yes, sir. You have the deck."

"Tactical, any success against their defenses?"

"No, sir, nothing in particular. A staggered attack may work, but we had to break off before we could try it fully." Okay nodded in response to Lieutenant Allen Jacobs's words.

"Also, Captain," Cross said, "Several of the enemy ships launched small projectiles toward the starbase, which seem to have struck and adhered. Their purpose is unknown."

He looked over as if to say "really?". Cross shrugged. They were all operating in new territory now.

The captain turned back to the main screen in time to see the result of the battle at the highest point of the enemy attack. The smaller UAL ships pummeled the target, while the *Rio* made only one pass then reoriented herself toward the next enemy in line. That single salvo was adequate to reduce the enemy vessel to floating wreckage, the *Rio's* broadside barrage overwhelming the enemy's already stressed defenses. The battle display didn't show it, but Cross imagined the bodies of aliens cartwheeling through space away from the ship. It offered him no satisfaction.

All the ships ceased firing as they repositioned for the next round. The Union tended toward a direct linear strategy, moving on sharp vectors. The enemy followed a more organic approach, using arcing paths to approach their targets. Based upon Cross's assessments so far, the enemy vessels were nimbler than the UAL ships, and carried about the same amount of firepower and better defenses than the destroyers and cruisers. Their single dreadnought appeared to be more than a match for any enemy ship currently in the field, at least over a protracted timeline.

The remaining seven enemy vessels organized themselves into two pairs and a trio, the latter curving toward the *Washington*. The captain frowned at the screen. "Did you do something to irritate them, Cross?" The moment of levity in the heart of the battle allowed the crew to release the breaths they had been unconsciously holding. Cross noted this, and remembered what the captain had said about using every tactic that presented itself to benefit the crew.

"Nothing in particular, Captain. Apparently, I just have that effect on people. Even alien people. Present company excepted, of course."

Okoye smirked. "Of course." He turned back to the main screen.

"Helm, I don't think we want to tangle with these three on our own. Please set a path that curves us behind the *Rio* and her consorts. Tactical, choose one and mark it, then when we're eclipsed from the enemies' view, launch all tubes targeted on that mark." Cross checked to verify that the battle display was showing proper transponder readings, so that the torpedoes wouldn't hit friendly ships.

Okoye paused for a moment, then flicked the switch on his chair that allowed him to speak into the battle net. "This is Captain James Okoye, commanding the *Washington, DC*. We will circle behind the *Rio* and fire all tubes at a single ship. It is marked on display as echo-one. Request a second flight of torpedoes to launch five seconds after ours, and another five seconds after that."

Cross heard the responses in his own earpiece as the commander aboard the *Rio* designated the ships to assist. The *Rio* and her consorts adjusted their trajectory to intercept one pair of the enemy ships, and the remaining Union forces oriented on the other pair. The three on the *Washington's* tail were ignored.

Moments later, the foes were within battering range again. The starbase proved ineffective in engaging the enemy ships, which danced and darted around lasers, plasma, torpedoes, and point defense cannons. It served as a distraction at least, causing multiple enemies to be out of position and unable to support the other ship in their pairs. Working together, the *Rio*, *Toronto*, and *Mexico City* made short work of one of those orphaned ships, the smaller vessels again overwhelming the enemy's defenses and allowing the dreadnought's weapons to punch through.

The rest of the Union forces didn't fare so well in their individual matchups. The staggered torpedo attacks that the *Washington* had started were ineffective, because the torpedoes seemed to lose their lock on the target and shot off in every direction as they got closer. Okoye sighed and offered, "Anyone that can figure out what kind of defenses the enemy ships are putting up gets The Admiral's Reward the next time we have shore leave." The highest informal recognition that a ship captain could provide, the Admiral's Reward was three nights at the location's nicest hotel, complete with all the food and drink that a sailor might want. The expense came out of the captain's own pocket.

Like a school of fish that had scattered, the enemy ships formed up in a graceful combination of movements, and launched another salvo of torpedoes, evenly split between the *Toronto* and the *Mexico City*. Countermeasures bloomed as the aliens again peeled off onto separate vectors, firing their energy weapons at the two ships.

As the missiles closed in, the other ships in the Union's defense force attempted to intervene, but they were too distant. The destroyers attempted every evasive tactic they could manage in the short window between launch and impact, but failed to shake the majority of the torpedoes. Cross's eyes were locked in horror on the real-space view as he awaited their destruction.

The *Rio* saved them, coming up from below and interposing herself in front of the smaller vessels. The dreadnought's shields glowed with energy discharge as they absorbed the enemy's blasts, and then the ship itself was engulfed in explosions as the torpedoes impacted the barrier. When the surrounding space had cleared, the *Rio* was still flying, albeit with a large trail of debris that had been blown off her hull. In several sections Cross saw atmosphere venting and supplemental explosions, but she had survived.

All six of the remaining enemy ships broke off the attack and made one more pass at the starbase, moving at higher speeds than the Union forces had yet to see from them. A glittering storm of the small projectiles rained out again, adhering to the installation's skin and continuing the patterns of both spirals. The *Washington* and the other UAL forces raced in pursuit, but couldn't close the distance.

A communication came from one of the departing vessels, and the computer provided an almost real-time translation of it. The crew of the *Washington* recognized the alien who'd addressed them before.

"I am Captain Traan Aras of the *Jade Breeze*, and I am in command of this honor squadron representing the Xroeshyn people."

He paused, his hands clasped behind his back, his wings folded gracefully, and much more in control than the last time they'd seen him. "It seems only fitting that as you've taken something of import from us, we've taken something from you. Before we leave, and until we meet again, we'd like to send a special message to those that trespassed upon our holy place. You are marked. Your defeat is certain. You will spend eternity in the in-between, serving our ancestors."

Torpedoes exploded from all the enemy ships, bearing down toward the *Washington*. In the next moment, a wave of shimmering color swept through the sector, and the enemy ships were no longer there. The torpedoes remained and were closing fast.

Okoye snapped orders to his crew. "Helm, evasive pattern theta. Keep our aft to those missiles. Tactical, full power to aft shields, minimal everywhere else. Launch all countermeasures." The *Washington* flipped over and hung in space as she fought off the inertia of her original path before pulling away from the torpedoes. Devices intended to block heat seekers, radar heads, and visual locks spread out behind them, failing to distract even a single missile.

"What the hell," Cross spoke without thinking, then caught himself and fell silent. The countdown clock in one corner of the screen showed the time until impact of the missiles, currently at twenty-three seconds.

Okoye was paying attention to the battle net and nodded in acknowledgment of something he heard. "Helm, come to 290, 40 high. The *Rio* will take out some of those torpedoes." As the *Washington* reoriented itself, the *Rio's* lasers and countermeasures picked off several of the missiles, and she interposed herself in the path of others. After her efforts, only twenty torpedoes remained locked onto the *Washington*. Cross was sure their defenses wouldn't handle that many.

Okoye's deep experience saved the ship. Cross wouldn't have thought of it, and none of the other bridge crew had mentioned it as an option. As soon as he heard the command, the helm officer automatically hit the button, as he'd been trained to do in drill after drill, until the memory was built into his muscles and required no thought at all.

"Tunnel jump. Now." The *Washington* took a shortcut from one end of the sector to the other, reappearing almost instantly on the opposite side of the starbase. As she reverted to normal space, she was in the path of another ship that went evasive to avoid her. Standard protocol was that a ship emerging from tunnel space stayed on course and those around her dodged—another procedure burned into the muscle memory of every helm officer.

The torpedoes reacquired the *Washington* and turned to follow, but the distance was far enough that the starbase point defense cannons, along with those of her sister ships, were able to destroy the incoming projectiles before they could reach her.

"Tunnel jump. Brilliant, Captain." Cross's admiration was clear in his voice, and he was sure he was speaking on behalf of the entire crew of the *Washington*.

Okoye shrugged. "Sometimes the oldest tricks are the best tricks, XO."

The sense of relief that the crew felt was punctured by an announcement that overrode all communication systems. "This is Starbase 14. Full evacuation protocol initiated. Repeat, full evacuation protocol initiated."

The communication officer switched to another starbase channel. A recorded message said, "We have been attacked by enemy forces that have left devices embedded in the base. Analysis has revealed an increasing gravitic force emanating from each. Initial analyses show that these are arranged in a deliberate pattern to reinforce one another and tear apart the base. We estimate only eighteen minutes before they reach full power and the base cracks." The time remaining, reduced with each replay of the message.

Okoye paused for a moment, allowing the message to sink in. "Helm, take us back to our original berth. Communication, send a recall to all of our personnel still aboard the base to report to that berth." He paused, listening to messages over the command net. "It appears we are picking up some Marines assigned to a ship that can't make it back. Make it happen, people, as quickly as possible."

He turned and looked at Cross. "Get down there and coordinate getting them aboard. Take Flynn with you, she can compensate for your frequent lack of people skills. Especially where Marines are concerned." Cross winced, but there was no denying that his history with Marines was less positive than it should have been. It wasn't fantastic that the captain brought it up in front of the entire bridge crew though.

Cross unbuckled and dashed for the lift, stepping in just after Kate. The door swished closed behind them, and the lift dropped them down toward the boarding deck.

"Perhaps you should let me do all the talking," Kate teased. Cross just shook his head.

"You can't talk to Marines. They don't have the brainpower to understand actual language. Only grunting."

She stifled a laugh. "No wonder the captain sent me along. You seem to have a bias."

"Me? Never."

Then the lift opened on the boarding deck, and the time for humor was over.

CHAPTER TWENTY

Kate and Cross stepped out into a strangely ordered chaos of bodies. Some crew members were changing shifts at battle stations while others were clearing the way for a rapid influx of people and things from the starbase.

"There's no way to tell which side of the ship they'll come from. Let's cover both," Cross said. Kate nodded and pointed to the airlock on the left. Cross advanced in the opposite direction.

She weaved with a fighter's grace through the throng—dodging and ducking, always aware of her target. Finally, she reached it, only to find Jannik had gotten there before her.

"This is a fun one, isn't it?"

"Fun is not quite the word I'd use for it," Kate replied, calling up external views of the *Washington* sliding into her docking berth.

The helm officer's voice came across the intercom, "We're not going to latch on. I'll hold her in position here. Start boarding."

Kate and Jannik both hit buttons, and a section of the *Washington's* hull pushed out and slid sideways, revealing a hatch in the starbase fifteen meters away. A gangway emerged from the deck to extend across the gap separating them from the space station. A long flexible tube extended with it, curving above and below the gangway, and would eventually contain atmosphere for those crossing from one airlock to the other.

As she waited for the connection to be established, Kate called up Cross's view on another display, seeing a mirror of their own procedure on the other side of the ship.

After several seconds, the tube showed a clean seal and filled with breathable air. Kate hit the button to release the airlock on her side, and someone aboard the station did the same. Both doors slid open almost simultaneously, and the waiting crew started across the gangway at a run. Kate nodded to Jannik, who had his hands on the controls in case something went wrong, and moved to the doorway.

"Go, go, go. Faster, faster, faster," she called to every person within range of her voice, and they responded by offering just a little extra speed as they cannonballed into the *Washington*. A quick look at the monitor showed that Cross's side was boarding people too, and Kate's fear they would have to leave their crew behind diminished with each passing second.

Finally, the crew was aboard and the Marines began their transit. They came in pairs, dragging equipment crates between them. The boots of their power armor thudded on the gangway as they drew closer to the ship. Kate escorted the first pair arriving to a side area of the boarding deck, yelling, "Make way, make way," to the members of the *Washington's* crew who were still catching their breaths, in some cases pushing them physically along toward the left in order to create room for the incoming personnel.

"Jannik," she continued yelling, "release the maintenance ladders." He nodded and hit the buttons that opened the between-deck hatches throughout the boarding level. She pushed sailors toward the ladders, and the congestion cleared out a little more quickly as people climbed rather than waiting for their turn on the lifts.

She ran back to the airlock door, sparing a precious second to check how Cross's side was faring when Captain Okoye's voice delivered more bad news. "Cross, Flynn, you have ninety seconds to wrap-up boarding before we undock."

Kate cursed under her breath and yelled across the gangway, "Sixty seconds. Go, go, go."

There was a jolt as the starbase shuddered from the pressure being exerted by the gravitic mines. "I don't think we're going to get all of those seconds," she muttered to herself, as she tended to do during times of emergency, and quickly assessed the number of Marines remaining. The numbers didn't add up. Some of them would be left behind when the ship pulled away.

She beat her hand against the hull once in frustration, then came up with a new plan. She ran across to one of the Marines standing in the side area, speaking when his helmet swiveled toward her. "We're going to have to improvise, there's not enough time. Tell your people to attach to the lines when they come out."

He nodded, and Kate raced to the controls again, cycling the inner door of the *Washington's* airlock closed and retracting the atmosphere tube. She knew the power armor would have internal air sufficient to keep the Marines breathing until they could get on board —assuming her idea worked.

She crossed to Jannik's position and edged him out of the way. There was just no time to explain. The *Washington* carried magnetic grapnels, used to pull ships together so their airlocks could connect. There were six of them surrounding the airlock—two on each side and one above and below. She fired the grapnels, which locked onto the starbase. Next, she hit the button to retract the gangway. From there, she dug into the programming. She found enough time for a brief look at the Marine, who gave her a thumbs up.

The helmsman's voice sounded over the intercom. "Disengaging now." Kate accessed the subroutine she was looking for and defeated the automatic retraction that came with the release of the magnetic seal. Just as the ship started to move, she released the magnets on the grapnels, and the *Washington* pulled gently away from the dock, trailing six lines of Marines who were climbing hand over hand through the weightlessness to get to the *Washington's* airlock.

"Good job, my girl," Jannik whispered in her ear as he guided her away from the controls. "Maybe you should sit down, though."

Kate realized that she was shaking from the adrenaline coursing through her, and followed Jannik's advice, finding a seat on a nearby crate and pushing sweat-dampened hair out of her face.

"Nice work, Lieutenant Commander," said a mechanical voice next to her, and she looked up to see the Marine that she had interacted with earlier looking down at her through the lenses of his power armor. "All of our people are on board or on the lines."

She noted the use of "our," and thought Cross would be perturbed to find she had apparently adopted a contingent of Marines.

CHAPTER TWENTY-ONE

As the lift door slid open, Cross and Kate emerged to hear the sector command net playing over the bridge speakers. Each officer on the bridge was intently working at his or her console, dealing with the massive flow of incoming information to give Captain Okoye the largest number of options. Kate moved to the sensor station, and Cross strapped in to the XO chair.

Okoye acknowledged their entrance with a loud, "Good work, Lieutenant Commanders." Cross felt the glow of confidence that came with the recognition, and knew the captain had done it on purpose. Psychological manipulation in the service of good. Okoye continued speaking after a brief pause. "You're in time to see the finish."

Cross looked up at the screen where a third countdown had joined the two that were always present. The new one marked the life left to the starbase, and it was already under one minute. The battle schematic showed that all the ships were at a good distance and were accelerating away on the most efficient vectors available to them. He shifted his eyes back to the real-time display at just the right moment.

Each of the mines was aglow, displaying the spiral pattern of their arrangement even against the similar color of the starbase's exterior. The stresses that each exerted on the structure of the base had already resulted in small cracks radiating out from each mine. As the cracks from separate mines touched, the integrity of the starbase vanished. It was as if a pair of giant hands had grabbed it above and below the midpoint and twisted each half in opposite directions.

Debris exploded outward as giant fissures appeared, spiraling through the starbase from its center point. Built to withstand the direct pressures that human science understood the need to defend against, it had minimal resistance to the twisting attack of the gravitic mines. Within seconds, the two halves separated from the sheer power of the opposing torques, and floated freely in space. Also floating freely was jetsam of all kinds, which sadly included the bodies of those not able to escape the base in time.

A small percentage of those jettisoned had deployed emergency beacons, and over the command net, each ship was tasked with the retrieval of the ones nearest to them. Rescue operations were automatic, requiring nothing more than a gesture from Okoye to get the ship underway. The crew worked in a haze of disbelief, none of them ever having seen anything as large as a starbase fall victim to violence. Even the dreadnought *Rio* was tiny in comparison.

Okoye shook his head, and Cross wondered what he was thinking. That secret was not revealed in the dry delivery of the captain's next words, "Continue rescue operations. The captains are going to confer with the admiralty, and I'd like to do it somewhere that I don't have to look at that." He shook his head again. "Lieutenant Commander Cross, you have the—"

Cross lurched in his seat in response to the huge fireball on the screen. Unlike the death of the starbase, the explosion of the *Toronto* was unheralded, a sudden new star aglow in the sector. Shocked outbursts erupted, followed by a stunned silence.

Okoye snapped "Report. What happened to her?"

Every member of the bridge crew dove into their instruments, including Cross. Kate was the first to respond. "From the playback, there are many small glowing objects that appear across the ship, increasing in intensity until the moment that the ship's engines explode."

The tactical officer confirmed, "That's what I see too. No evidence of external weapons other than the glowing objects. No way to tell what activated them—"

"Or how many more of them there are," finished Cross.

The heavy silence returned as everyone considered that more explosions might be imminent. When they didn't materialize, the tension reduced, but only a little.

Okoye said, "All right. We can only control what we can control, so let's do our jobs. Helm, our destination has been linked to you. Set up to engage tunnel drive to get there with all speed once we complete rescue operations."

"Captain, respectfully," Cross said, "the admiralty may be wrong on this one. There is information about the enemy we can only gather here and only gather now." Okoye gave him a sideways look that communicated nothing. Cross forged ahead. "We need to stay and discover as much as possible. They have already attacked us here, it's not likely they'll be back soon."

"You're making a big assumption, Lieutenant Commander Cross." His tone was less collegial, more professorial. "Why, exactly, do you think the enemy won't return? Leaving the sector could be a feint, prior to returning for a second round of attacks."

Cross didn't back down. "Captain, it is my opinion that the aliens were testing our defenses here. The goal was to assess our capabilities, not to achieve our destruction. The aliens must have more than eight ships in their fleet, given how fast they were able to respond when we were in their part of the universe." He shrugged. "If they had wanted to destroy us, they would have brought more ships. Clearly their technological level is such that they could coordinate such a thing. Hell, Captain, it's not like we forced them to leave. The eight they sent probably could have finished us all off. We would've inflicted some damage, but there's no way we would've defeated them."

He paused, searching for a further argument, and realized he didn't have one. "It just felt like they were testing, sir, and left when their experiment was complete."

Okoye sighed and drummed his fingers on the edge of his chair. "Not that it's a democracy, but let's see what the third in our command triumvirate thinks." Cross and Okoye both turned to Kate.

She cleared her throat, buying a moment to think that fooled nobody. "I'm with Cross on this one, Captain. They sent a small sortie, they tested out the efficacy of their various weapons against us and against our starbase, and then returned to analyze the results. For all we know, they left behind sensors or something to continue gathering data on our response." Her voice grew darker as she contemplated that possibility. "Whatever we do, we don't want to leave this sector directly for our destination. They figured out where we were somehow. Maybe they can identify tunnel destinations from the source?"

"Impossible, according to all the science we have." Okoye raised a hand to cut off Kate's objection. "I know, we don't know what science they have. Still, it does us no good to imagine that they are omnipotent or omniscient." His fingers, drumming, finished in a decisive tap on the chair. "My instincts are telling me the same thing as yours. They could've done much worse to us, so they must've had a reason not to. Let's hedge our bets."

Cross followed Okoye's gaze as he turned forward again and saw that most of the ships in the sector were moving toward a departure vector that would put them in position to tunnel directly to the rendezvous point. The *Washington* was following in that same direction, albeit much more slowly than her sister ships. Cross gave an appreciative nod to the back of the helm officer's head. Without a direct order to do so, Lieutenant Zachary Lee had slowed the ship, staying within the parameters of their orders while also giving the command crew time to deliberate. It was the sort of thing a confident captain encouraged in his crew, and a less confident one chastised them for. Cross was sure that Okoye had noticed and declined to comment.

"XO, you have the deck. I will politely suggest to the admirals that we take a two-step progression to our destination, rather than a single jump, even though this will cost us some time. In case I fail, keep moving as slowly as possible toward our departure point while you all," he waved his arms to indicate the entire bridge crew, "find as much information as you can before we leave this sector. Staying for more than a few hours would invite trouble, I think."

Cross stood up from his chair. "I have the deck, Captain. We'll be ready to depart in three hours barring orders to the contrary." Okoye nodded and left the bridge. Without sitting down, Cross addressed his crew, "You are all experts in what you do. Spend the next hour running every analysis you can think of. At the end of that time, we'll share information and decide how to progress.

He walked over to Kate and asked, "Anything I can do to assist you?" She was already face down in her instruments, hands moving across the console.

"Yes. Go away."

"If I had a dollar for every time a woman told me that, I'd be able to build my own starbase."

Kate-and several others-laughed. Cross gave a small smile, then moved to the next station and asked the same question.

An hour and fifteen minutes later, the officers shared their discoveries. Only two offered avenues for further investigation, one from the tactical officer, and one from the communication officer. The former reported that the gravitic mines that destroyed the starbase and the *Toronto* were the same, and a replay of the battle showed when they had been attached to the side of the ship.

"It was a clever move," Jacobs observed, "sending in enough primary weapons to distract, and launching the mines from a passing torpedo that appeared to miss its target. The computer reduced it to a lower priority when it was no longer a threat and didn't track the incoming, tiny projectiles."

Cross folded his arms in front of him, his lips pursed. "Impressive. Difficult to guard against. Let's work up something for the computer to keep a better eye on torpedoes that have missed their targets." He turned to the communication officer. "What did you find?"

The communication officer's face was crinkled, her eyebrows drawn together into a small frown. "I would've said this was random, except that analyzing it for just over an hour has shown that it occurs in a sixty-four-minute cycle. It's in a section of the electromagnetic spectrum where we usually encounter space noise. Radiation. That sort of thing. This, however," Ana Fitzpatrick continued, pointing at her own display screen, "is communicating something, but I have no idea what."

Cross's face mimicked Fitzpatrick's look of confusion. "Is that all we know?"

"No sir," she said slowly. "We also know where it's coming from." She paused, and shook her head, crinkling her face up even more. "It's coming from us."

CHAPTER TWENTY-TWO

In the deepest level of the cathedral, underneath the areas accessible by the public, underneath even the areas permissible to most clergy and staff, was a cavernous training space. Along the walls were weapons of every sort—modern and archaic. There were stations appropriate to each weapon where the select could come to practice. Primarily, this was a place for the guards that served the priesthood, who dedicated part of each day to maintaining and improving their skills.

This morning, there were eight guards present, befitting the status of the august individual who spun and slashed inside the lines of eight etched into the rock floor. Kraada Tak held a huge broadsword, both hands wrapped around its elongated hilt, weaving it through a variety of forms for attack and defense. Four guards were in the arena with him, attacking whenever the opportunity presented itself. Kraada rebuffed the majority of the attacks, his form almost flawless. When one slipped through and struck him on the light armor he wore covering his torso, he nodded at the guard and returned to a ready stance. The clash of weapons allowed him to retreat into a state where his thoughts didn't task him. He wasn't sure if it was holy, but it was a useful form of meditation—one he couldn't allow himself often enough.

Eventually, there would be a challenge. What sort of hierarch would he be if he allowed a second to serve him as champion, rather than entering the arena himself? His thoughts changed direction as he saw an opening for an attack, and he wove gracefully past an opponent, using the occlusion provided to tap a second on the helmet with the tip of his sword. A look of surprise was crisply replaced by a frown as the guard waited to be chastised.

Kraada instead put the broadsword back into the scabbard running down his spine, between his wings, and clasped hands with each of the guards, thanking them for their time. This was one of the few activities that released the weight of the mantle he wore, and he planned to keep it that way. He was toweling off when an attendant broke into the room.

"I know I am not supposed to interrupt you, Hierarch, but the message you've been waiting for has arrived."

Kraada dropped his towel on the floor and clapped the messenger on the shoulder. "Good work." He pointed at the four guards he hadn't been battling and ordered, "Escort me." They fell into line around him as he hurried toward his apartments.

He reached his suite just as the cathedral's communication staff signaled that the message had been decoded and was ready for playback. Kraada dismissed his guards and sat in the chair behind his ornate desk. He pulled out an earpiece and put it in, an extra nod to security that was most likely unneeded, but still reassuring. Indraat's voice came through clearly, the robotic alteration of her tones a result of the encoding-decoding process. The Xroeshyn message system used some of the same technology that their wave travel system did to send messages that arrived considerably before the ships that sent them. Decreased fidelity was a fair trade for the increase in speed.

"Hierarch," it began, "our first foray against the enemy was a complete success, though not without the loss of two of our own ships. The *Jade Breeze* survived unscathed. Included with this message are data files showing the details of the battle. Our weapons are effective against their smaller ships although we will have to combine efforts to take down their largest vessels. Our mines were highly effective against both their station and an individual ship." The voice paused, and Kraada was annoyed at the crackling that filled the empty space.

"I see no evidence to suggest that they are not the promised enemy. Their technology fits the description, their morphology fits the description, and the reference to division among the enemy seems to apply as well. It is perhaps not as precise as you may have wished, Uncle, but as you well know, the gods have a tendency to be less than transparent." The implied levity in her final sentence disappeared as she concluded, "We will engage the wave drive after sending this message, and should arrive within a day of it. I will submit myself to you upon my return to address any questions. Indraat, out."

Kraada dropped the earpiece on his desk and leaned back in his chair, eyes closed, thinking.

———

HE WAS STILL RECLINED two hours later when there was a soft knock. He shifted forward again, stretching. "Enter." The door swung open, and both an attendant and his valet entered the room. The priest was one of Kraada's least favorite, a sycophant whose rise to his current position had more to do with the politicians he knew than with his efforts to serve his congregation, his church, or the gods.

Even his voice was slimy as he announced, "Marshal Drovaa is here to speak with you, Hierarch. It is a matter of some urgency." Unspoken was the opinion that the military leader ranked higher in the attendant's estimation than did Kraada. Kraada gave him a grin that showed his teeth.

"Thank you, Skraan. Please ask the marshal to give me a short while. Provide him with refreshments while he waits, and you may deliver dinner to both of us while we meet." He turned to his valet, who was already laying out appropriate robes for the meeting, and motioned for him to follow him into the dressing room.

Once properly attired, he received the marshal. "It's good to see you again. We must stop allowing our only meetings to be those inspired by moments of crisis."

"I couldn't agree more, Hierarch," Drovaa said, sitting down across from him at the short dining table. "I've had a report from the *Jade Breeze*."

"Indeed? How did our attack fare? What have we learned?" Kraada's excitement was not entirely feigned. Even though he knew some of the answers to those questions, he was interested to know what Drovaa's sources had reported to him. Once he'd heard the other man's information, if appropriate, he would share some of Indraat's.

"I am sorry to break this news to you, my friend, but the commander of the *Jade Breeze* tells me it's impossible that these aliens are our promised enemy."

Kraada froze for a beat with his fork on the way to his mouth, then recovered and chewed slowly before responding. "Indeed," he said again. "On what does the good captain base his opinion?"

"It's his estimation that neither their technology nor their strategies make them a significant threat to our forces. As the holy book declares we'll find the true limits of our strength and faith in fighting the promised enemy, this opponent doesn't appear to rise to that standard."

Kraada took a deep drink of his wine, swirling it in his mouth before swallowing and offering an appreciative sigh. "And your opinion on this matter, Marshal?"

"I wouldn't have shared my subordinate's observations, if I didn't believe them correct, Hierarch. This may be a case where we're hoping so intensely for a certain result that we see that outcome where it doesn't exist."

"Indeed," replied Kraada a third time. "In any case, it hurts us not at all to consider how we may deal with them as a thought experiment over dinner, while we await the ability to question the captain of the *Jade Breeze* on this matter, don't you agree?"

Kraada saw the scowl the other man smothered before it had a chance to do more than quirk at his lips. "Of course, Hierarch. In exchange for such a fine meal, I'd be happy to engage in such a flight of imagination."

After his guest's departure, Kraada vented his annoyance on the dishware and wine glasses, hurling them skillfully one by one into the room's fireplace. Drovaa, that damned fool, was playing games. Apparently, it had been too long between campaigns for him, and he was entertaining himself by placing pieces in Kraada's part of the board. He punctuated that thought by lofting the wine bottle through the air to crash into the flames as well. The noise brought guards and servants, who burst into the room and then stood back looking uncomfortable.

"Clean it," he ordered, "and do not disturb me until Indraat Vray arrives, save at the word of the emperor." He stormed out and entered the set of rooms he used as a sleeping chamber, closing the sound-proof door behind him. His nightly habits calmed him, and by the time he was ready for his last task before sleep, his mind was centered. He walked to a corner of the room and sat cross-legged before the avatar of his patron goddess. Bowing his head, he spoke ritual words of supplication, adding requests for patience and strength, and promising death to the enemies of the Xroeshyn that the gods had delivered to them.

His last thought as he slipped off to sleep, wrapped in heavy blankets that surrounded him like the arms of the goddess herself, was that the gods keep their promises, and these aliens must therefore be the ordained ones. With a sleepy snarl, he added the addendum that if Drovaa Jat played him false, he would discover that Kraada played a much better, much deeper game than did he.

A LONG NIGHT'S sleep put him in a much better frame of mind to meet the next day's challenges. He shared breakfast with Indraat, the finest breads, proteins, and fruits that his staff could provide.

"The captain of the *Jade Breeze* is convinced these aliens are not the enemy we've long awaited."

Indraat Vray snorted in response. "The captain of the *Jade Breeze's* idiocy is only interrupted by the occasional thought with some tenuous connection to reality, which he then rejects out of hand."

Kraada laughed at this blunt critique of her fellow officer. "You seem to have a very complete view of the good Traan Aras."

"This is true, Uncle. He has, on several occasions, attempted to engage me socially." Her wings fluttered theatrically in what a human would have called a shudder. "Trying to make small talk with him requires one to carry entirely too much of the burden. I cannot imagine it is any better for his crew."

"Perhaps this explains dearly departed Reenat Srav's frustration with him?"

"Reenat also exists... existed, that is... in a world of his own making, where reality had little purchase."

"My, Niece, this is a side of you I haven't seen before."

She looked up at him through lowered eyelashes. "Before, I wouldn't have deemed it appropriate to share these thoughts with the Hierarch of the Xroeshyn." Switching from demure back to her normal tone, she continued, "But with my uncle, who knows many of the players, and who needs to know all of them as well as possible to arrange the board most effectively, I feel confident that truth will be welcomed as a positive."

"Between us, always. I pledge it. If I am foresworn, let the gods deliver me to the in-between and leave me there for all eternity."

"So may it be."

"So may it be."

"May I then end the life of the useless being in command of the *Jade Breeze*?" She took out the dagger sheathed at her hip in a smooth move, twirling it in her fingers before sliding it back into its home. "It is past time that someone did."

Kraada gave an approving nod to her attitude, but not to her idea. "His existence must continue for a while longer, Vray. First, we need to see what information he can provide when I question him. More importantly, though, he may be useful as a distraction in the middle part of the game."

Indraat Vray sighed. "I understand, Uncle."

"However, when he's no longer useful, you may do the removing."

Indraat smiled. "I will hold you to your vow."

Kraada's face fell into the lines of worry that had been present far too often as of late. "How sure are you that these aliens are the promised ones?"

"Seven of eight, Uncle."

"Seven is good, Niece. Seven is very good indeed."

INDRAAT RETURNED to her ship after the meal, and Kraada headed to the Defense Center. He planned his arrival to interrupt Drovaa's interview with the captain of the *Jade Breeze*. When he arrived, he discovered that no such meeting was taking place, and was instead ushered into the marshal's presence.

"Hierarch, good to see you again so soon."

"Marshal," Kraada replied. "Have you finished already with Captain Traan?"

"I have. There wasn't much new information to be had, other than data that we've supplied to our tactical and defense personnel."

"Do you continue to believe they aren't the promised enemy?"

"They call themselves humans."

Kraada hoped he kept his irritation from showing. "And are these *humans* our promised enemy?"

"They are not."

Kraada stood and paced. "It hasn't happened often before, Marshal, but I find myself disagreeing with you in this case." He waved an arm to forestall any reply. "However, at this point, we need not commit publicly one way or the other, so let's not worry about doing so." He turned back and sat across the desk from Drovaa again. "Whether they are sent by the gods or not, they have destroyed a holy relic, and in so doing have damaged our honor. The only way to regain it, is to destroy the offenders, don't you agree?"

Drovaa spread his arms wide. "I agree, Hierarch, and nothing would please me more. I will ready two squadrons for departure in the next eight-day."

Kraada toasted him with his wineglass in reply. *It's a start, Marshal. It's a start.*

CHAPTER TWENTY-THREE

With the ship safely in tunnel space, Cross and Kate could take some essential downtime and have a drink with Jannik.

"So how did you manage it?" Cross asked.

"Secret engineering techniques," Jannik replied, taking a sip of his whiskey.

Kate laughed, discharging a little more of the tension they all felt. "But seriously, how did you?"

"Well," Jannik leaned back and scratched at the center of his chest, "once Fitz discovered that the signal was coming from the *DC*, there were limited options. Inside the ship, or outside it. I figured that the likelihood of them getting a bug into our computers was smaller than them sticking one of those tiny things on our hull since we've seen how good they are at that. We deployed spiders on the ship's hull, and sure enough, they found one."

Cross remembered from his rotation in engineering how useful the tiny spider-like robots were, constantly crawling the insides of the ship looking for problems. "Clever idea, to use them outside. I didn't know they were vacuum-rated."

Jannik recoiled in mock offense. "Of course, they are, my boy.

Everything that the engineering division does is first-rate, with tolerances far higher than needed. For instance, they also have built-in magnetics in their tiny legs that allowed them to stay attached."

Kate interjected, cutting him off, "So after you found it, the spiders just yanked it off the hull?"

Jannik turned back to her, sitting forward in his chair. "Not at all," he said, sweeping his arms on the surface of the table. "The little ones were too small for that task. We had to get out the mongoose."

Cross snorted into his drink, thankful that he wasn't taking a sip right at that moment. "Does everything down here have an animal name?"

"Yes. You're referred to as the sad puppy."

Kate laughed some more and then said, "Let me guess. And I'm the happy kitten?"

Jannik smiled. "Crafty owl."

While she sat back with a pleased expression, Cross protested, "I'm not a sad—"

"Anyway," Jannik said loudly enough to override him, "the mongoose is an articulated robot, kind of like a caterpillar, but with all of its legs on the inside of a flexible membrane made of ballistic cloth and the thinnest newsteel we've ever been able to produce. It costs about the same as a laser cannon." Cross whistled, and even Kate looked impressed. "Being the types that we are in the engineering division, we always have two, a primary and backup."

Kate nodded. "You'd have a backup set of drives if you could."

"We do, actually" said Jannik.

"What?" Kate and Cross expressed their surprise at the same moment.

"The *Washington* has a backup drive."

"Jannik," Cross said, "have you been brewing moonshine with the fusion engines again? The ship's not big enough to have two drives."

Jannik shook his head in apparent mourning for the complete lack of knowledge possessed by everyone younger than him. "My boy, the wormhole drive doesn't take up much space." At the mention of it, Cross remembered reading about it at the Academy, but it hadn't entered his mind since. He could see from the look on her face that Kate had also forgotten.

"Okay, but let's get back to the point at hand, brilliant engineering man," Kate said. "What did you do with the mongoose?"

"Well," Jannik said, "the spiders weren't strong enough to detach it from the hull, nor are they intelligent enough to do much more than crawl around where we tell them to and report. We tried using them before we deployed the mongoose, but to no avail. We sent him—"

Kate interrupted, "What's his name?"

Cross read the expression on Jannik's face and put his forehead down on the table. "You did, didn't you? The mongoose has a name too."

Jannik's voice conveyed reluctance to share the information. "Jo."

Cross looked up, his face wrinkled as he attempted to figure out the moniker. Kate's lips formed a perfect O. "You did not," she said.

"We might have," Jannik replied. "You can't argue that it's inappropriate."

"You named—" Kate began, then stopped. "You named the mongoose—" and then she stopped again, as if saying it out loud would somehow be breaking a rule. "You named the mongoose after the captain?"

Cross laughed, and then couldn't stop for quite some time. Kate joined him after a few seconds, and Jannik a few seconds later. When they finished, Cross leaned back, wiped tears from his eyes, and took a much larger sip of his drink that he had before. "Okay, naming issues notwithstanding, how did it fare?"

Jannik sighed. "Sometimes what's best for the ship isn't quite as good for its crew, especially crew as disposable as the mongoose. We sent it out over the hull, and it reached the device with no problem. It was able to encircle it and get a few of its useful tools into cracks and crevices around it. We burned out three motors prying it off, but that's the beauty of the mongoose's articulated design. Even if one set of appendages burns out, there are several left. Anyway, when we finally got it off, it exploded. It wouldn't have done much more than puncture the hull and open a single compartment to space, which would've been bad enough, but we had already cleared that section just in case. Sadly, the force of the explosion went into the mongoose instead, and now we're down to the backup."

"Poor Jo," Kate choked out before succumbing to more laughter, which set the other two off again.

Several minutes later, after he'd endured a wealth of technical conversation that he didn't understand, the three of them were interrupted as Kate's communicator sounded. She tapped her wrist to accept the signal, and Okoye's voice emerged. "Flynn, the Marines need an assist. Please go give them a hand in their regular quarters."

"Affirmative, Captain."

"Okoye out."

Kate stood. "It's been fun gentlemen, but duty calls."

Cross rose with her and said "I'm not busy. I'll go meet the Marines with you." She shrugged assent, and Jannik waved the both of them away, pouring himself another belt from the bottle hidden in the toolbox.

IT TOOK only minutes to reach the Marines' living quarters, where the members of the former *Toronto*'s Bravo Force were setting up shop. A full complement of Marines had gotten off the base and onto the *Washington*, meaning that all the rooms were filled to double occupancy, except for the officers who warranted singles. Cross and Kate walked down the hallway, seeing efficient Marines stowing their gear in some rooms, and others already asleep or playing cards together in others.

"One thing you've got to admire about the ground pounders is their ability to adapt to any situation." Crossed gestured as they passed a tall blond Marine who had laid out all the parts for his weapon on his bed and was meticulously cleaning each. "I'm guessing it comes from having limited brainpower." A sharp exhalation escaped when Kate backhanded him in the stomach.

"Behave, Cross."

They arrived at the end of the hallway to find two Marines in one of the officer's quarters, both sitting in desk chairs facing the door as if awaiting their arrival. When they saw that an extra person had come along, the female Marine stood up and spun her chair over to Kate, who caught it and sat with her stomach against the back. This earned her an approving smile, and the Marine introduced herself as Gunnery Sergeant Cynthia Miller.

"We have a small problem here aboard your fine vessel," she began, "and Gunnery Sergeant St. John and I have been brainstorming solutions for it. We've come up with a few, but since it's your ship, we thought you might have some better ideas." Her accent had hints of the southern part of what had been North America, Cross thought, but otherwise was as direct and forceful as one would expect a Marine's voice to be.

Her partner picked up as she finished, his formal British diction a decided counterpoint to Miller's delivery. "Our troops were originally assigned to the *Toronto*, which makes it very lucky we didn't make it on board. That said, we have no specific assignment right now, so we figure we are part of the *Washington* until someone tells us otherwise. With that in mind, we need to integrate ourselves into the ship's operations, and also find some opportunities for our people to train."

St. John turned his head toward Kate, displaying a smile that was all too perfect when combined with his striking blue eyes and his white-blond hair. The sharp lines and slight turn at the corner of his eyelids suggested some distant Asian or island ancestry, giving him an exotic look that Cross found irritating. "The captain told us that Lieutenant Commander Kate Flynn was our liaison for our time aboard the *Washington*. I presume that's you?"

She nodded and offered a smile in return. "Guilty as charged, Gunnery Sergeant St. John."

"Please, call me Rhys. No need to be quite so formal, is there?" Cross was sure that he had fluttered his damnably perfect eyelashes at Kate. *What sort of man fluttered his eyelashes?*

Kate smiled a little wider and said, "Formality is overrated, Rhys. You—you both—should call me Kate." She gave a backhanded gesture in his direction. "Allow me to introduce the ship's Executive Officer, Lieutenant Commander Anderson Cross. No one calls him Anderson."

Both Marines nodded and replied, "Lieutenant Commander," before turning back to Kate.

"So," St. John said, "how about we put our heads together on duty roster, supplies, and access for our people? Maybe over a cup of coffee?"

The tension that he'd released in engineering returned threefold as the Marine turned his masculine charm on Kate. A tiny part of Cross knew that she wasn't the sort to buy it, at least not for anything more than the entertainment value of some verbal sparring. The rest of him saw only that this moron was trying to make himself attractive to his girlfriend, or friend with benefits, or soulmate, or whatever it was that he and Kate were to one another these days.

He went still, pushing his emotions down low where they couldn't betray him, and said, "Wouldn't you all prefer to stay down here in Marine land?" He paused and gestured. "It seems like you have everything you need here, and you're not in the way of the working crew who is keeping you all alive."

They stared at him, and St. John raised an eyebrow. "Are you suggesting that Marines don't fall under the heading of working crew, Lieutenant Commander?"

"I'm more than suggesting it. While we're in transit, it's been my experience that you folks are next to useless, at best, and a hazard to everyone around you, at worst." Cross made a point of looking St. John in the eye. "I mean, what are you qualified for when there's no ground to pound?"

He could see the Marine's anger rise and knew that a counterassault was coming. He welcomed it, and braced himself. As St. John opened his mouth to speak, Kate interrupted, "Please excuse Cross. He's had a terrible time of it the last few days, and even at his best, his social skills rival those of a four-year-old. I'd be glad to have coffee with you and discuss how we can all work together. I'm afraid that Cross won't be able to come. He needs to hit the rack before he goes on shift, don't you, Cross?"

He stood up and showed the Marine his teeth, and said, "Yes, I guess I do at that. St. John, Miller." He left the room, refusing to meet Kate's eyes or say another word. He knew that Kate wasn't playing games with him, but was trying to do what was best for him, best for the Marines, and best for the ship. But that didn't make him want to punch the Marine, or the nearby walls, any less.

When he finally reached his quarters, he peeled off his uniform and stepped under the hot spray of the shower, scalding himself until the pain pushed him into an honorable retreat to his bed. He fell asleep to visions of Kate and St. John huddled together, that damned smile drawing her laughter as they talked about his failures, one after the other.

CHAPTER TWENTY-FOUR

After an effective, efficient, and pleasant cup of coffee with Rhys St. John, Kate wandered toward officer's country. The crew she passed gave her strange looks, but she barely noticed them. She was trapped in a conundrum and wasn't sure she saw a way out. On the one hand, someone needed to say something to Cross. His behavior was increasingly erratic over an extended period, and the most recent challenges seemed to have pushed him into a place where no one wanted their commanding officer to be. If his emotions overruled his logic at the wrong moment, he could get them all killed.

On the other hand, it was much more the captain's prerogative to advise about command. Kate didn't have the experience or the required knowledge of psychology to cover it. She feared she'd do more harm than good, and further undermine his already flagging confidence.

Kate leaned back against a bulkhead and banged her head softly on it. What she wanted to do was go to her quarters, sleep, and wake up the next day to find everything was back to normal. But normal would never come again, now that they had encountered the

Xroeshyn. Everyone would need to be at their best to deal with this new reality.

Since that included Cross, and since she was Cross's longest-tenured friend, she supposed the burden of getting him back on the right path to his best fell on her. She pushed herself into motion again and found herself at his door long before she was prepared to be there. Resigned to her fate, she keyed in the override to allow her to enter the room.

One of the many things that annoyed her about Cross was his ability to go from asleep to alert in the blink of an eye, while her brain refused to function without a hot shower and a dose of triple-strength coffee. He sat up as she entered, ready to fight. He must have recognized her silhouette, because he immediately lay back, put his hands over his eyes, and said "Kate, I'm sorry. I'm an idiot. I know it."

"It's not me you need to apologize to, Cross."

"I know. I'll do it. Soon. Just not right now."

She shrugged. "That seems fair. I don't imagine Rhys has any desire for a midnight visit from you, anyway."

Cross didn't quite growl, but Kate heard the rumble in his voice when he said, "I agree, he certainly doesn't seem interested in *me*."

She barked a disbelieving laugh. "You're being petty."

He sighed and said, "I know that, too."

Kate sat cross-legged on the floor next to his bed and looked up at him. When he tried to move toward her, she held up a hand to keep him in place. When he tried to speak, she waggled a finger to stop him.

"Cross, I'm going to make this simple for both of us. There's something wrong with you right now. It's messing up both your ability to lead the crew, and your ability to be a decent human being. Right now, you're not the Anderson Cross that I have always known. Would you like to tell me what's wrong?"

Kate knew what was wrong. As Cross had once said, they could read each other so well, it was scary. But it would be better coming from him, and there was always the possibility she hadn't quite figured out every single thing wrong with him on her extensive list. He sat up, crossing his legs on the bed and running a hand through his hair.

He took a preparatory breath, opened his mouth, and failed to speak. She watched as he marshaled his thoughts and tried again; "I can deal with the fact that I'm afraid. It's not that. Anyone who's been through what we have, would be, and there's no shame in it."

Kate nodded her agreement, and was glad he could see that much, at least.

A hoarse edge to his words, he continued "When we found ourselves pulled into the tunnel, I had no idea what to do when we reached the other side. The only thought in my head was to finish the battle against the *Gagarin*, so when we arrived, that's what I did. *I* created the situation we're in right now. I'm responsible. *Me.* Responsible for the deaths of everyone on the *Toronto*, for those who didn't make it off the starbase, for those on the other ships that were destroyed. And," he said, his voice shaking, "I'm responsible for all the deaths that are going to come."

Tears shined in the corners of his eyes, but they didn't fall. "Even worse, though, as if anything could be worse," he sniffed, blinking, breaking the flow of his words, "I almost got us all killed again during the battle at Starbase 14. I fell for that trap, and it's only dumb luck that I saw it coming before it closed on us. The best thing I could do for everyone right now, is to resign my commission. Maybe I could become a ground pounder too." He laughed, but it was full of sadness and self-recrimination.

"But I can't even bring myself to do that. It would mean abandoning the dream of commanding my own starship, and I've given too much to just walk away. So, I have to go through the motions, hide what I'm feeling, and hope it all works out." He took a deep breath, and Kate could almost see him willing himself to believe his plan was adequate. "On the upside, we destroyed something important of theirs, and they destroyed something important of ours. We're even now, right? Maybe they'll stay away, and no one else will have to die because of my mistake."

Cross had covered most of the things on her list, save one. His self-doubt was the thing most damaging to his ability to function. Again, she faced a choice, each option worse than the last. Kate could let him continue as he described and not risk their relationship or the potential damage her untrained counseling might cause. *Or*, she could tell him what he wanted to hear, which would strengthen their relationship and give him a boost of confidence without dealing with any of the underlying doubt. *Finally*, she could risk their relationship and his chances of continuing in command by forcing him to confront the root of the issue. At this moment, she wished the ship had someone on it who specialized in psychology.

Kate sighed, leaned over, and took his hand in hers. "Cross, look. I hope you won't take this the wrong way, but if you do, you do. You're right, it's fine to be afraid. I am too. But your problem has nothing to do with fear of the enemy. It has to do with you lying to yourself."

Cross opened his mouth to speak, and Kate covered it with her other hand. "Shut up and listen. I'm not going to give you platitudes. I'm not going to tell you things just to build you up or make you feel better. You don't understand the depth of the crisis you're actually in because you won't admit it to yourself or to anyone else." Her thumb stroked the back of his hand in comfort.

"There's a voice inside you, a tiny voice, that's working hard to convince you that everything you do is wrong. It says you were stupid for falling for that trap, and only luck saved you from it. It tells you attacking the *Gagarin* was wrong, even though it wasn't you that fired the first shots. It tells you trusting your instincts will only get you and those you love into trouble." He drew in a deep breath at her words.

She took her hand away from his mouth and pointed a finger at him. "There's only one word for that, Cross. Well, two. Total shite."

Kate stood up, suddenly angry, and her feet marked a figure eight into the carpet as she paced and spoke, never meeting his eyes. "You've been destined for command since the first day you set foot into the Academy. The hard classes were easy for you, and in the impossible ones you did exactly what a good commander should do: you sought help from those who knew better. You excelled in a ridiculous number of areas, making everyone around you—including me—envious of the breadth of your talent. Your ability to talk to people, no matter their background and no matter their station, made forbidden portions of the Academy open to you. Hell, you discovered the secret of the Suicide Run. Only three or four cadets in a year can say as much."

Cross attempted to interrupt, but at his indrawn breath Kate yelled at him. "Shut. Up. Cross." She pushed her long red hair away from her face, tossing her head as she started to walk again, continuing to punctuate each sentence with a gesture aimed at him or perhaps the universe as a whole. "When you entered your rotations, you accomplished just as much as you had at the Academy, putting yourself on the fast track for your own command. When tragedy struck the *Vancouver*, it was *you* who made the right choices at the right times. *You*, Cross."

She exhaled with force and sat back on the bed, not looking at him. "You have everything you need to be a great commander. You have the desire, you have the will, you have the smarts, and you have the courage. But for some reason, right now, in spite of every single piece of evidence to the contrary that your experience up to this moment has provided, you are listening to that one stupid voice telling you none of that matters."

Cross looked like he would try to speak again, and Kate glared at him until he thought better of it. "Maybe it's all come too easily for you, although I can't imagine how that could be, given the challenges you've faced. Maybe you just are really that good, and you've never faced this little voice before. There's no way for me to know what has brought you to this place. But I *can* tell you how to get out of it." Her voice went quiet, serious, in a tone she doubted he'd ever heard her speak in before.

"I will only say this once, and then I'm going to leave, and you're going to think long and hard before you offer me any response. Anderson Cross, you have taken the coward's path. You are hiding from the difficult truth that sometimes even *you* will fail. You tell yourself in your head that it's okay, everybody makes mistakes, and you just need to keep going. But in your heart, that little voice says you're supposed to be perfect, and you're arrogant enough to believe you can be. When reality shows you that you can't, because no one can be," she yelled, and forced her voice back down to a reasonable level, "you hide. You hide behind noble sacrifices, such as giving up your command, or enduring your suffering, so you may serve your crew. Two words, Cross. Total shite."

Kate stood, walked to the door, and turned before departing. "Do you know what the rest of us do when the world knocks us down, Cross? We stand tall, or we stand bent over, or we crawl up to our hands and knees. Then we look at whatever knocked us down and say, 'Is that all you've got?' Then we get back to doing our jobs." She waved a hand over the panel, and the door opened. "If you manage to get back up, you know where my quarters are. If you decide to keep lying to yourself, you'll do it alone. Goodnight, Cross."

Kate held back the tears until she made it to her own room. With the door locked behind her, she slid down the wall, sobbing. It was a long time before she dragged herself to her bed. Her dreams were filled with explosions and invisible traps that turned into black holes while she fell endlessly, unable to escape their pull.

CHAPTER TWENTY-FIVE

Kraada Tak again paced the aisle of his cathedral, gesturing broadly, delivering what had so far been a typical sermon. His congregation comprised the elites of all kinds, with everyone under the rank of emperor, who mattered seated somewhere in the congregation. The military stayed separate from the men of the cloth, and the bureaucrats and tradesmen gathered with their own. They needed something to unify them, to bring them all together in a common cause, to transcend the monotony that had been growing in the Xroeshyn for far too many years.

Far too many years without a challenge.

Far too many years without an enemy.

Far, far too many years without fulfilling the promise the gods had given them.

Today, that would all change.

Kraada stalked to the front of the room, ascended the altar, and picked up the *Dhadas Ve Xroe* in his hands. He waited, feeling its heft, the promises delivered, the promises still undelivered. He set it back down, reverently, but didn't open it. Instead, he stood in the center of the cathedral, his arms raised to the gods along the cathedral ceiling, the Holy Father above him, Vasoi's empty pedestal in front of him, and his patron goddess above and to the right, his mind filling in the image of her avatar and imagining the approval in her eyes.

He waited, one more beat, with the perfect timing of the accomplished showman.

"Brethren," he shouted, startling everyone in the congregation. "Listen well, for these are the words of our gods. In the *Dhadas*, they promised our ancestors will one day be delivered from the in-between into paradise. Imagine," he swept down from the altar and paced down the center aisle, spreading his arms wide to include them all. "Imagine, our ancestors, trapped forever in the nothingness of the in-between as they wait to be born again. We believe it is a place of neutrality, but do we really *know*? What if they are, in fact, in agony, awaiting the actions of their spoiled children to deliver them from this terrible fate? What if the waiting itself becomes agony, as year after year passes?"

"What have you done," he asked, pointing at a senior military leader. "Or you?" He pointed this time at an upper level priest. Striding, almost running down the center aisle, he pointed simultaneously at senior members of the bureaucracy and the trade guild, "And what have you done?" He gave them a contemptuous look, one that he turned on the higher-class individuals in the front of the congregation as well. "I know the answer. You have done *nothing*. Nothing but wait. Wait for the moment that everything is crystal clear, that everything is perfect, that every possible objection is conquered, instead of acting. Acting to free your ancestors. Acting for the glory of the Xroeshyn."

He marched again to the altar, where he stood dead center, in the shadow of the statue depicting the Holy Father, and let the room still —his hands clasped before him, his head down, his wings folded. He watched his congregation mastering their responses to his charges. Their faces radiated anger, some concern perhaps that their hierarch had lost his mind, and on some faces, contempt for the depths of his belief. *So be it.* Those who were contemptuous now would turncoat when the truth was revealed. *Spineless worms.*

"Brethren," he said again, "the time has arrived. Our moment of action is *now.* The gods have delivered upon their promise. The foretold enemy, the one that will open the gates of Paradise to our ancestors trapped in the in-between, has arisen. The one that will lead to the full ascendancy of the Xroeshyn people. The one that will make us worthy of all the great gifts the gods provide."

"As you have no doubt heard, only two eights ago, an alien species calling themselves 'humans' entered one of our holy places, and destroyed the relic contained there. The relic of Vasoi, mother of the gods, goddess of the in-between. She *demands* their destruction. The promise has been fulfilled, my brothers, my sisters. It is, finally, time."

"Brethren," he raised his arms once again to the icons of the gods above, closed his eyes, and spread his wings wide. "Today, I declare it. We shall war on behalf of our gods until either the human race or the Xroeshyn people are wiped from the universe. The promise of the gods will be fulfilled, and we will destroy this enemy that has dared desecrate our beliefs. That has dared damage the reliquary of our ancestors. That has dared affront the gods themselves." He dropped his face to look at his congregation, arms and wings still spread wide, and said in a whisper that could nonetheless be heard throughout the hall, "Holy war, to victory or destruction."

He dropped his arms into a prayerful position and folded his wings again behind him. Bowing his head to the gods above, he intoned, "So may it be."

The congregation responded—some shocked, some overwhelmed, some transformed by the delivery of something they'd been waiting for their entire lives, "So may it be."

AN HOUR LATER, Kraada finished his post-sermon ablutions, reappearing in his outer office to find Drovaa Jat waiting for him.

"What the hell was that, Kraada?"

The priest showed the marshal his teeth in a small smile and sat down to the tisane pot that had been laid out. He poured two cups, pushing the large sleeve of his vestments out of the way, and slid one over to the other man before replying, "I merely exercised the prerogative of my office, Drovaa. I know that you do not believe, but it may be that it's simply not given to you to believe. It is, however, given to me, by virtue of my meditations, by virtue of what the gods have shown me through them, and by virtue of my position. I know the humans are the promised enemy."

Drovaa shook his head and took a sip of his tisane before replying, "And if you are wrong, Kraada? Now that you have announced it to everyone, are you willing to pay the price, if this turns out to be a lie?"

"I would call it a mistake, rather than a lie. But to answer your question, yes, I am prepared to pay the price if needed. Let me ask you. Are you ready to reap the rewards if it is not?"

Drovaa frowned. "What do you mean?"

"There are two ways to proceed, my old friend. The first is to continue to walk the line, to do as you are asked as military leader, but only that and no more. No one would fault you, if this was your choice. But imagine... Imagine yourself, embracing the charge of this holy endeavor, taking the fight to our enemies clothed in the righteousness of the gods. Can you see it?"

Drovaa didn't reply, for a long time. Kraada understood he'd just presented the marshal with a possibility that hadn't occurred to him because it was simply not how the man thought. He was a good soldier, and loyal, mostly anyway. Kraada, though, could see possibilities for them both when the holy war was over, and they were wrapped in victory.

When Drovaa replied, Kraada could see that his suggestion had taken root, "That would be a beautiful picture, wouldn't it?"

"It would. And what's more, the populace would love it." Kraada smiled, and Drovaa joined him.

"Still, not giving me any warning wasn't the best way to treat a friend, or whatever we are."

"Friend is a good word. And you're correct, I could've given you a preview of what was coming. But I thought it would be better for you, among your people, to be able to write off that crazy hierarch. Your honest response will give you credibility."

Drovaa wasn't fooled. "Right, Kraada. That's what it was."

Kraada laughed out loud and leaned over to slap the marshal hard on the arm. "Whatever it was, my friend, it's over and done now. We must plot our path forward. If you want to hold it against me at a later date, I understand your desire to do so. Perhaps, wait until we have accomplished all we can with the situation before us, however."

"Just so." Drovaa finished his tisane and waggled the cup. "Anything stronger?"

"It's barely past midday."

"Your point?"

"None, I guess. After all, it's a day of celebration. Great tidings are at hand." One of the ever-listening attendants scurried into the room with a bottle of whiskey, depositing it and a pair of heavy, crystal glasses on the table beside Kraada. He poured and handed one to his guest.

"I noticed," Drovaa observed with complete nonchalance, "that the emperor was not in attendance today."

"You are correct. He was not."

"Strange. You would expect he would want to be present for such a momentous declaration."

"He no doubt would have, if he'd known about it. However, I didn't share that information with him, either. I didn't share that information with anybody." Kraada leaned back and watched Drovaa through half-lidded eyes.

"How very... disrespectful of you, Hierarch."

"That's one way of looking at it, I suppose."

"And now you suggest that I, and by extension you, should cover ourselves in glory from our efforts against these humans. Again, strange."

Kraada leaned forward, placing his elbows on his knees and holding his glass in front of him, staring into the brown liquid aglow from the light filtering through the room's windows. "Not strange at all, my friend, unless you assume the things I do are for the emperor's glory. Between you and me, the emperor has had plenty of glory already."

"And you are tired of basking in the reflected glow from it, preferring instead a more direct illumination?"

"Perhaps. Are you saying that you feel differently?"

"I am not."

"We are in accord then, my friend."

"We are."

"So, what will you do, Marshal?"

"I'm not sure, Kraada. You've given me a great deal to consider, and I need to spend a little time considering all the ramifications. This conversation shall remain between the two of us. And your attendant, of course. I've always been curious, how do you find the confidence to trust that these priests that serve you will not betray you?"

"Faith works wonders, my friend." Drovaa shot him a look that conveyed his disbelief. "Also, any of them that attempted betrayal and failed would face me within the lines of eight, and not a one of them has a chance of surviving such an encounter. They are, naturally, training for the opportunity, so I make time to train as well. Their best bet is to wait until age or the emperor claims my life and focus on defeating the others for the prize of my mantle."

Drovaa shook his head. "That would never work in the military. You would just wind up getting shot when you least expected it."

Kraada steepled his long fingers and peered over them at Drovaa. "In that case, I'd make sure I had the only functioning sidearm in the building, or shoot first if somebody looked at me wrong."

Drovaa laughed. "Good plan, my friend, good plan."

Kraada waved at him. "I'm sure you have places to be, Marshal, and I have tasks to which I must set myself. Shall I expect word on the departure of our attack force soon?"

Drovaa stood and stretched, unfurling his wings and then settling them back into place. "Yes, you should. The gods will not be well served by delay. Nor will we, for that matter."

The two men parted with smiles, gripping each other's forearms in a gesture of solidarity. Kraada knew Drovaa was aware of the new truth that stretched between them, that they were now more than friends. They were competitors as well. And perhaps they had always been.

CHAPTER TWENTY-SIX

The *Beijing* transitioned from tunnel space in the home sector of the Allied Asian Nations. Their exploration vector had taken them toward Teegarden's Star, and they had used the Epsilon Eridani system as their jumping off point for further discovery. Starbase Prime described a lazy rotation around the fourth planet in the system. It was the successor to the original Starbase One, which failed due to microfractures created by the system's strong radiation signature. Prime had much better shielding, and was also one of the new designs, vaguely resembling two children's toy tops connected by a long tube.

Spokes radiated outward from that central cylinder, extending to create the wheel that was the docking circle. Ships attached to hardpoints on the ring, and their personnel and cargo traveled down the spokes into the starbase itself. The biggest vessels in the fleet could dock at the top and bottom of the facility, but those positions were currently empty.

Dima had no need to involve himself in the docking process, leaving such things to his executive officer and his talented crew.

Instead, he was in his quarters wrapping up the ship's log for this stage of its ongoing voyage, and drinking a cup of lapsang souchong. Once he got aboard the starbase, the tea selection would be terrible. He picked up his private stock from a colony at the forward edge of their exploration where a sect of monks had cultivated varieties of teas thought lost to time. His patrol patterns coincidentally visited that settlement several times each year.

Dima heard and felt the clanking of the grapnels securing the *Beijing* to the outer ring. He could almost smell the fresher air of the starbase seeping through his ship as the connection was established. He checked his communicator and noted that he had some time before his meeting with the committee. Gathering up his materials, he decided to take a long, frustration-reducing walk on the way to the meeting.

An hour and a quarter later, he sat at a giant round table with twenty-three other senior officers. Along a consistent arc at one side were those holding the highest ranks, those in command of the Navy, the Marines, the ground forces, the exploration corps, the political officers, and the military liaison with the government. Admiral of the Fleet Victor Volkov called the meeting to order and offered his brusque congratulations to Dima.

"The reports we've had from the engagement between the UAL and the aliens are entirely satisfactory, Captain First Rank Petryaev. The crew of the *Beijing* acquitted itself well in gathering information about the battle while avoiding notice. This will give us a significant strategic advantage in the future."

The liaison smiled as if someone had given him a gift. "It's true, Captain, that you have performed very well. The vice president in fact has asked me to congratulate you on your success, and to encourage you to continue bringing back information that we can use to decimate our enemies."

Dima lifted both eyebrows as he caught the message behind their words. "You're referring to the information we discovered about the aliens' strengths and weaknesses, correct?" He knew what the answer would be, even as he feared hearing it.

"That, of course, Captain Petryaev," replied Admiral Yi Zemin in her high-pitched, raspy voice. "But, more importantly, you've given us several keys to use in future battles against those bastards in the Union. The wounded ship strategy that the aliens used drew off one of their ships most effectively, and that is something we can put into practice today."

Dima shook his head, masking his exasperation. "Ladies and gentlemen, while I desire victory over our historic enemy as much as anyone, the aliens pose a new and significant threat we cannot just ignore."

"Of course not," said the liaison through a mouthful of white teeth. "We wouldn't think of ignoring them completely. In fact, we look forward to monitoring further victories as they continue their battle against the Union forces."

Others around the table nodded in agreement, and the Fleet Admiral spoke for them all. "After careful consideration, it is the belief of this body, and of our scientists, that the aliens will focus their attacks on the UAL. They have no argument with us. We aren't the ones who launched torpedoes which destroyed their idol." Volkov said with almost a sneer, "We will revel in their efforts, as our enemies and destroy one another, and at the proper moment we'll sweep in and eliminate both of them."

"With all due respect," Dima began, shaking his head, "I don't believe we can afford to think this way. I join you in hoping for such a result. But we cannot predict the aliens' actions. It is possible they see all humans as one entity to be destroyed." He held up his hands and looked from one to the other. "How would an alien know that this differs from that? Perhaps all the aliens see is a species not their own that must be eradicated."

Volkov took immediate offense at Dima's words. "Captain Petryaev, in one breath you have rejected the opinions of your superiors, placed your own ideas above them, and suggested that we are identical to the United Atlantic League. Is that your intent?"

Dima stared at him. The man's skin had grown considerably thinner since he left the bridge of his own starship to command in the rear echelon. "Of course, Fleet Admiral, I do not suggest that my views are superior to those you have presented. I simply offer an alternative idea. One informed by my recent encounters with the Union forces *and* my observations of the alien ships." Inside, he fumed. The committee was too quick to make decisions, and too prone to do so on the basis of gut instinct and mob mentality, rather than a practical and systematic review of the situation.

He could see the other leaders falling in line behind the fleet admiral. Dima's strategies always involved moving out of the path of direct force instead of meeting it head on, so he gave in with a deliberate browbeaten expression. "No doubt you are correct though, and we will soon be able to celebrate the destruction of the Union at the hands of the alien threat." He took a moment to look down at his notes, centering his thoughts. "With that in mind, I'd like to suggest that a sizable force of ships, say at least a squadron of eight, better two squadrons, form a picket, to take position outside the projected landing points for the aliens' transport device."

Dima was interrupted by the admiral in charge of the AAN's science division, who held that position by virtue of his friendship with the president. "We've named it the wave drive, and we're certain they can only use it in the middle part of a sector. Our records of it, provided by the *Beijing*," the man gave him a nod, "show it building as it comes into the sector and then cresting near the midpoint when the ship appears on our scan. This evidence is reinforced by the positioning of the other ships as they awaited their last element."

Dima nodded back at the man, entirely unconvinced by the alleged science that the committee had undertaken. "With this in mind, we should place our vessels right at the outer edge of several sectors along the most likely invasion paths. In that position, they should be able to detect the aliens as they arrive and then tunnel to safety to get a message to us. Then a sizable reserve force stationed here can deploy to take advantage of any opportunity the aliens offer." *Or any threat they present.*

Dima was overwhelmed for a moment, reflecting bitterly upon a lifetime of having to circumvent the officers above him, rather than being able to trust them to do the correct thing. It was all he could do to bite down on the words threatening to escape from between his lips—challenging them to act for once in a manner appropriate to their ranks, instead of imitating a pack of children playing at toy soldiers. He tasted blood and discovered that he had bitten the inside of his lip. He touched it with his finger and regarded the blood as if he had never seen its likeness. This single drop would become liters, then buckets, then an endless cascade fountaining away the lives of the young people of the AAN.

Dima couldn't let that happen. He would make sure it didn't, starting right now. "Gentlemen, ladies," Dima said, "I'm ready to depart on this mission to seek the final destruction of our UAL enemies. I believe the plan I described gives us the best chance of striking while they are damaged, but I welcome any revisions or suggestions. As your fist, I will crush our enemy, and then I will crush the invaders in the name of the Central Committee of the Allied Asian Nations."

From their expressions, he figured he had fooled at least two thirds of them, and the ones that weren't convinced were willing to use him to their own ends. He was surprised, though, at the speed at which Admiral of the Fleet Victor Volkov responded, "You have your squadrons, Captain Petryaev, but they're under the command of Captain Ilyana Volokov of the *Moscow*. You're to report to Captain Volokov at 0800 tomorrow morning to receive your assignment. The *Beijing* will deploy, along with fifteen other ships, to act as our early warning network. Ready your crew and prepare to get underway as soon as your meeting is completed."

The entire committee stood as one, signaling the end of the audience. He knew this was the preordained result regardless of his words. It so happened that Ilyana was the daughter of the Fleet Admiral. As he left the room, Dima masked his fears behind a hard glare. Humanity was in a much more dangerous place now than it had been just twenty minutes before.

CHAPTER TWENTY-SEVEN

When the *Washington* emerged from tunnel space, they saw an unprecedented sight. A sizable majority of the UAL's fleet was gathered, and the sector was filled with vessels of every shape and size. Fighters performed exercises in a large defensive screen as small shuttles took people from one ship to another in a constant flow. Capital ships teamed up for simulated attack runs, heading to their positions as part of a layered grid of protection.

The remaining members of the admiralty had arranged a fleet-wide conference by video, since they lacked a starbase and were unwilling to risk their entire command on a single ship. Okoye and Cross sat on the disconcertingly comfortable couches in Okoye's quarters, a video connection allowing all the commanders to see one another. Kate was sitting in the captain's chair on the bridge with her earpiece plugged into the discussion.

Introductions were quickly made as the gathered officers identified themselves by rank, name, and posting. Not all the captains were present as those in charge of support vessels were resupplying ships that had been in combat and ensuring the rest were fully stocked before that critical moment arrived.

The admirals looked nervous. *Losing a large chunk of one's peers to an enemy they'd underestimated should have that effect,* Cross thought. He caught the captain's eye, and could tell he had noticed the same thing. He didn't appear at all positive about it. Hiding his mouth behind his hand, Cross whispered to Okoye, "They look afraid."

The captain made a cutting motion with his fist, but then answered using the gesture-language common among engineers. To the uninformed, it looked as if he was drawing an inverted V with three fingers. To an engineer, he was signaling the shorthand for 'affirmative, shut down.' Cross's eyes narrowed, then widened in appreciation of Okoye's mental powers as he realized the captain knew he'd recognize that language due to the connection he'd forged with Jannik. He shook his head, impressed that the captain walked the walk that he talked.

With a stammer, the admiral overseeing the logistics division called the conference to order. On the screen, Cross saw the various side conversations trail off, and all the participants turned forward to listen to the admiral. "Here's our situation, ladies and gentlemen. We have an existential threat from an alien species calling themselves the Xroeshyn. Due to an unavoidable series of circumstances," Cross felt a pang, but refused to give it the satisfaction of elevating it to a worry. Admiral Wesley Matthias continued, "We have come to the attention of these beings, and they intend, as demonstrated by their own words and actions, to destroy us. Their technology is notably different from ours, and our science team has been working on that problem. Admiral Sandoval will brief you on that matter shortly."

One captain interrupted, "What did we do to them?"

Matthias shook his head. "Irrelevant, Captain. Focus on what matters." Looking down at his notes, the admiral found his place again and resumed speaking. "Our plan, at this time, is to mount several roving patrols with overlapping check-in times, so we have maximum notice of the next incursion, when and if it comes."

"Oh, it'll come," Cross murmured into the space before Matthias spoke again.

"Once we have warning, either from the patrols or from the picket ships already dispatched to our outermost sectors, we'll converge with enough ships to give us at least a 1.5 to 1 advantage. If possible, we'll send more, but we will not commit our entire force to any battle. Instead, upon notice of enemy forces in our territory, squadrons will deploy from our rearward starbases to the starbase nearest the battle. Our picket ships will fall back to protect the next starbase in line, and we will leapfrog our ships backward as needed, defending each starbase, when and if the enemy reaches it."

Several of the captains' voices rang out at once.

"Why are we not taking the battle to them?"

"We will look like cowards."

"We should hammer them with all of our available forces and send them back to their part of the universe in pieces."

The admiral held up his hand to forestall anymore more outbursts. "The admiralty is well aware that this is a defensive-minded approach, and most of us would also prefer to take the fight to the enemy. But our limited information prohibits it. We'll get stronger with each engagement as we learn how to most effectively combat them. A fighting withdrawal that sacrifices time for empty space gives us the best chance to win a total victory."

A captain spoke directly to one of the people who'd made an outburst, "Of course, Charles, if you can defeat them all during the first engagement, that would be just fine. Go right ahead." Several others laughed, and Captain Charles Windham of the *Manchester* gave them a humorous growl.

Miguel Sandoval, the admiral representing the science division, took over the briefing. "So far, our best guess is that most of their weapons, their drive systems, and their defenses employ gravity in one way or another. We're still looking into the details but the evidence seems to support this assessment. We've seen their shields bend energy beams and appear to curve the paths of torpedoes. This would be consistent with a localized manipulation of gravity." He tapped a quick sequence on a handheld tablet, and his image was replaced by slow-motion replays of enemy ships arriving in the starbase sector.

"As you can see in these images, the wave seems to crash into the sector, leaving the ships behind. We feel this wave drive, for lack of a better term, is manipulating gravitic frequencies of the electromagnetic spectrum in a way we've never seen before. Our best minds are, well, at a loss, to be honest. All we know is that it works." He cleared his throat and reappeared on the screen. "We have some ideas on how to deal with their defenses using our existing loadouts, and how to modify our weapons to be more effective against them. We'll set up a conference with your sensor officers and your chief engineers after this one to discuss it. We've also discovered that overwhelming the shields is as effective against the aliens as it is against human ships, so anytime we can manage an advantage of two on one or better, we have a reasonable chance of getting through them."

"So, do that, Charles," the same captain quipped, gathering laughter again from the assembled officers. Even the admiral's lips quirked at the comment.

"Absolutely, absolutely," finished the science division's representative.

Next up was the supreme commander of the Navy, Admiral Anwen Davies, who had inherited the position when the previous fleet admiral died aboard the *Toronto*. "To facilitate these match ups, we'll designate wing ships for each vessel. Bigger ships, like the *Rio*, will have multiple wings. Think of it like your first day at the Academy, gentlemen and ladies, nobody goes anywhere alone. At the first sign of trouble, if both ships can tunnel, they will. If only one ship can tunnel, it will bring word of the incursion. If for some reason neither ship can tunnel, both ships will fight a delaying action until one can get away."

Davies looked into the camera, giving Cross the impression that she was looking straight at him. "Make no bones about it, people.

We're in a fight for our lives, but we're *always* in a fight for our lives. This time is different, though, because our very existence as a people is at stake. We cannot afford to screw it up, and that means each and every one of you needs to be at your best, one hundred percent of the time. I know you will be." She sat down again, and conferred with the officer next to her, their words unintelligible to those not in the room.

The logistics admiral stood up again and asked for questions. Cross opened his mouth to speak, but Okoye repeated the gesture for 'shut down,' and Cross obeyed. After several queries dealing with logistical matters, another commander spoke the words that had been in Cross's mind.

"Is it time to join forces with the AAN, Admiral? If not, are we still maintaining our defenses against them as we also defend against this alien threat?"

Matthias was clearly prepared for this question and paused hardly at all before offering the answer. "We cannot depend upon the Alliance. Too much is at stake. The aliens do not appear to have targeted them, but if we're lucky, perhaps they will. Even if they spent some time doing reconnaissance on the AAN forces, it would give us an opportunity to complete our defensive deployment. So, let's hope they notice our friends in the Allied Asian Nations. Next question."

Cross couldn't remain silent, despite seeing Captain Okoye raising his hand to stop him. He asked, "Should we at least warn them? Share information with them?"

The admiral looked exasperated. "Perhaps I'm not making myself clear, Lieutenant Commander Cross, is it? Our concern is not with the AAN. Our concern is with the technologically advanced alien species attempting to end our existence. Focus, please."

Cross bristled, but fortunately the session ended before his brain lost the battle with his mouth. Okoye turned to him, shaking his head, and said, "You are as predictable as the day is long, Cross."

"Are you saying I'm wrong, Captain?"

"There's the rub, as they say, Lieutenant Commander. I'm not saying you're wrong. I believe you are very right, and before this is over, we will need *all* the help we can get. However, as you are no doubt aware, you're part of a military organization, and that organization has an entrenched and respected hierarchy. Despite your occasional belief to the contrary, you're not at the top of this hierarchy. Popping your head up is a great way to get it cut off by those who are."

His frustration pushed him to his feet, and Cross walked a few steps before turning and facing the captain. "So, even though it's the wrong thing to do, we're going to stand by and let it happen? Is that what you're saying? For fear of getting my head figuratively chopped off, I should support a decision we both know is wrong?"

Okoye clapped his hands and bowed his head. "Cross, you're still seeing things in only two shades, when everything exists on a continuum. We cannot be sure it's the wrong decision until we have proof that it's the wrong decision. So, I guess the question is, do you want to be here where you might do some good, or do you want to be on a starbase filling out paperwork? Because ship captains who disagree in such an obvious fashion don't get to stay ship captains for very long."

The captain stood and made a shooing gesture at him. "Think on it Cross, think hard on it. But do it on the bridge where you can release Lieutenant Commander Flynn to take part in the science and engineering conference with Jannik."

Cross's ire had disappeared as Okoye spoke and possibilities presented themselves to him. Whenever he imagined he fully understood the captain, he found another layer of nuance he had missed completely. Taking the bridge watch would give him some necessary time to process this new information. As the captain intended, no doubt. "Sir, Yes, sir, Captain Okoye, sir."

Okoye smirked. "Dismissed, Lieutenant Commander."

CHAPTER TWENTY-EIGHT

Hierarch Kraada Tak strode along the street connecting the cathedral with the emperor's palace, the metal heels of his boots clicking a quick-time march. He could've taken other transport, but his mood was such that a long walk before meeting Emperor Enjaaran would be a good preventative measure. As was leaving his ceremonial mace at home. His hand itched for it, and he put the offending appendage into the pocket of his robe.

Two attendants hurried beside him, and he kept up a steady stream of instructions as they walked. Since the discovery of the humans, his workload had tripled, but the hours available in a day hadn't increased even a single eighth. "See that the proclamation of holy war against the humans is sent to all of our ships and is the central message of sermons in all of our churches for at least the next three eight-days."

"Yes, Hierarch."

"Verify that each vessel in the invasion force has a reliable religious officer on board. If there is anyone we doubt, reassign them to one not in the vanguard and replace them with someone we can trust. If we run out of trustworthy people, one of you eight will need to go.

Send Kiaan, he's an ambitious individual. Some time aboard a ship would be just the thing to take the edge off him."

"Yes, Hierarch." The attendants gave each other a grin behind his back. Anything that tore down one of the other aspirants elevated them by the same amount in their common quest to someday replace Kraada.

Work time ended as they crossed the threshold into the palace. Kraada turned to his attendants and gave them final commands. "Wait for me, this shouldn't take more than half the afternoon. If you run out of tasks," he moved closer to avoid the guards listening in, "see what you can learn about the mood of the palace. Carefully, brothers." They nodded to him, and he nodded in return.

He allowed himself to be led to the small meeting room beside the audience chamber.

"Welcome, Kraada Tak, did you have a nice walk to the palace?" The emperor, as always, projected a thin veneer of civility when greeting his subordinates. He was in his formal dress, complete with sheathed sword at his belt. Kraada indulged in a moment of fantasy that began with him having not left his mace behind and ended in grisly fashion.

"Good afternoon, Emperor, and thank you for asking. It is good to walk amongst the people and hear those things they may not intentionally bring to your attention."

The other man in the room spoke, "I couldn't agree more, Hierarch. Such information is always valuable, and the emperor is well served by those of us who gather it for him." Drovaa, too, was overdressed for the occasion, in the starship commander's uniform he was entitled to, but rarely wore in favor of his dress uniform. His holsters were empty, however. One did not wear weapons into the presence of the emperor.

Drovaa came over and clasped Kraada's forearm. He murmured softly, his voice carrying only across the distance between them, "Not my idea. Yours?" Kraada shifted his eyes left and right in response, as much of a gesture as he could keep hidden from the emperor. Both men turned to face their ruler.

"Where does our invasion stand, gentlemen?" Enjaaran Velt had taken him to task days before in a private meeting for declaring holy war without warning him first. Kraada had been conciliatory, but hadn't wavered where his primacy in religious matters was concerned. He *still* felt the residual tension from that conversation, and imagined he saw it also in the stiff way the emperor stood with his hand never far from the hilt of his sword, absentmindedly stroking it.

As if either of the two men in the room with the posturing idiot couldn't have ripped it from its sheath and run him through before he could cry out for his guards.

Drovaa's low baritone sounded. "We are ready to launch, Emperor. We have only to hear your will as to which target we should attack first."

The emperor frowned. "Multiple targets? Explain."

Drovaa clasped his hands behind his back, rearranging his wings to permit it. "Our initial sortie was against the group that calls itself the United Atlantic League. But you'll remember that when we first encountered the humans, two ships were fighting. We've learned that there are separate groups of these beings, and the other one calls itself the Alliance." He walked slowly as he spoke, maintaining a calm verbal flow.

"The mettle of this other group hasn't been tested. We know they were present and watching during the most recent battle, and we marked the ship that was doing so. We have not yet reconnoitered this Alliance, but can trace that ship's movements and current location. It's safe to assume that both groups of humans are attempting to identify strategies to thwart our armada, either separately or as a species." Drovaa turned to the Emperor and spread his feet into an at-ease position. "It's my recommendation we continue pushing along the already-established vector, attacking this League until it's defeated, and then turn our attention to the others."

The emperor looked thoughtful. He also seemed excited. Kraada remembered the man had behaved this way during a previous campaign. Kraada enjoyed the mental image of Enjaaran on board the bridge of the starship during combat, turning aside to avoid laughing out loud at the lunacy of the idea, then gathering himself.

Kraada adopted a pose similar to Drovaa's, and told the emperor, "I'm afraid I must disagree with the good marshal." Exasperation flickered across Drovaa's countenance, and he had to smother his own pleased reaction in response. "We have estimated the capabilities of the first set of humans and are confident they cannot stand against us for any substantial time. However, if we leave our flank exposed to the second group without assessing what technologies and strategies they might use, we engage in an unnecessary risk to the lives of our people."

Drovaa contradicted him. "The likelihood that the Alliance will possess better technology or tactics than the first group is negligible. The recording of their engagement within the asteroid belt shows these two groups to be far more alike than different. They are so similar, in fact, that we are best served considering them to be identical."

"And yet, if we destroy the first, but leave the other at full strength, we must then face the undamaged group. On the other hand," Kraada gestured with his hand and wing for emphasis, "if we keep them balanced and at each other's throats, we could reduce each to a lower level than if one is allowed to fly free while we attack the other."

The emperor and Drovaa both considered this idea for a moment before the marshal disagreed, "Better to claim victory over half than to permit both to remain on the board at partial strength. I stand by my original recommendation."

The emperor nodded. Kraada imagined the man appreciated decisive statements that didn't require him to think too much. Kraada also made a show of deliberating, of considering Drovaa's words, while he waited for the emperor to speak.

"Gentlemen, I'm convinced by the marshal's argument from a

tactical standpoint. From a strategic perspective, I see the benefits of the hierarch's position. Kraada, are there additional arguments you wish to bring to bear?"

"I do, Your Grace." Kraada took a steadying breath and launched into an oration. "The religious aspect of this matter must be considered. Will we define one half of the humans as our enemy? The *Dhadas* does mention a divided foe, but not a dual one. All of its references are to a pivotal campaign against a single opponent. This alone should encourage us to see them as a single people, rather than two separate groups, and to plan our strategy against them as a species."

As always when speaking in his religious role, his gestures and motions emphasized each point. It was completely unconscious and enthralling to those who watched him. Kraada pointed to the sky beyond the ceiling of the room.

"But the gods have told us more than this, even. In the *Dhadas*, we are enjoined to 'push the enemy back whence they came, and destroy that place that created such misbegotten demons.' This, too suggests a consistent movement across a wide front, rather than a deep strike on half, as the marshal favors."

He raised both palms in supplication to the eight. "It seems to me, that if we are to err, we should err on the side of the most direct interpretation of the will of the gods. I interpret that as engaging the entire species at once." He dropped his arms and looked at Drovaa. "I do not denounce the marshal or his strategy. It's completely viable, and in any other case, this would be as desirable as my own. However, where the gods are involved, we must defer to their words."

Kraada clasped his hands in front of him, and bowed his head, as if entering into a moment of silent prayer. In fact, he was doing as performers had done for eons before, awaiting the response of the audience to his monologue.

As he looked up again, he saw the emperor put his hand on Drovaa's shoulder. "Marshal Drovaa, I believe in this case the hierarch is correct. At this pivotal point in our history, we must not run the slightest risk of falling afoul of the gods' will."

Drovaa gave one sharp nod, and said, "Of course, Emperor Enjaaran."

"It is done, then," the emperor proclaimed with a clap of his hands. "Make it happen, gentlemen. Fulfill the promise of the gods and the destiny of our people. Destroy the humans and the accursed part of the universe that created them." He gestured them toward the door while calling for his seneschal to attend him, his mind already on to his next task. Which probably involved one or more of his concubines, as he'd had such a demanding day at work, thought Kraada with no small amount of scorn.

The leaders of the Xroeshyn military and church walked out together, the air between them crackling with distrust and individual priorities that were no longer in sync with one another.

"Either way," Drovaa said, "the result is the same. It's time to launch our assault. I'll send the squadrons today, targeted on the group we haven't yet engaged, so we may discover their vulnerabilities and exploit them."

Kraada nodded, letting the chance to twist the knife deeper pass unremarked. The men walked together in silence, until they reached the corner where their paths would diverge. Drovaa extended an arm and Kraada met him, gripping forearms yet again. They said goodbye, but as they moved to take their own separate ways, Drovaa turned back as if just remembering something.

"Indraat Vray is related to you, yes?"

"Indeed, she is my niece. Why do you ask?"

"The *Jade Breeze* has some equipment issues and will miss this sortie. The *Ruby Rain* will take the front position in the vanguard in its place. Hopefully there are no nasty surprises waiting for it against this new group of humans."

Drovaa turned and walked away, leaving Kraada's hands itching and clenched at the implied threat to his niece. *Next time, I'm bringing my mace.*

CHAPTER TWENTY-NINE

"They just don't get it," Cross said, tossing back his drink and wincing as it burned its way down to his already angry stomach. "An alien species with technology that's better than ours is knocking on the door, and the admirals are most concerned about defending against a surprise attack from the Alliance." His face showed his opinion of that small-mindedness. "What can they be thinking, Jannik?"

The older man shook his head in time with Cross. "I don't know, my boy. What I do know, is betting on the admiralty to act in a logical fashion is at best an even money proposition. Better to bet on whether some young upstart will break the rules. Way more chance of that."

Cross gave him a halfhearted obscene gesture in response. As much as time with Jannik was his most useful way to blow off steam, he just wasn't feeling it that day. His fingers strummed, his knee bounced. He was agitated and couldn't discern why. He watched as Jannik poured him another glass, knowing he should say no, but unwilling to make that concession to reality.

"Drink this and settle down, Cross. You're more wired than any three systems in engineering."

Cross sipped, aware he might be called to duty at any time. "It's the waiting," he said out loud, realizing it. "Normally you're going about your business, doing things, and the likelihood that some demon will jump out of the corner and attack you is pretty small. Right now, it feels like there are bogeymen everywhere, and I can't figure out why they're not attacking yet."

Jannik said, "You've hit the nail on the head there, no doubt. You should've been an engineer. No one ever tells us what's going on, we just hang out down here until someone yells they need more power, or until someone does something stupid and breaks my ship."

Cross laughed. "It may surprise you to learn this, but I was not the best engineer on either of my rotations in engineering."

"My boy, that doesn't shock me at all. You don't have what it takes to be one of us. I guess you'll need to be satisfied with being a lowly captain."

Cross laughed again and noted as an afterthought that his knee was no longer bouncing. He took a deep breath and tried to let more of the tension go, partially succeeding.

"You're a good man, Jannik."

"Don't I know it."

He was about to offer a riposte when Kate entered the room, puffing as if she'd run the length of the ship. Both men turned to her as she said, "We have a problem."

After she caught her breath, and fortified herself with a small sip from Cross's glass, Kate got a coherent, if hoarse, message out. "The captain asked me to monitor the command network while you were off the bridge. My channel must have been set up wrong because I connected to a private conversation between Okoye and the admiralty. It was already underway before I had a chance to turn it off, and when I heard the topic, I couldn't."

Cross leaned forward. Jannik mirrored him. They stared at Kate while she took another enabling sip.

"One of our early warning drones has sighted the aliens. Only they're not in our area, they've entered the outer reaches beyond

Alliance space. The drones were deployed to watch for the next expansion moves by the Alliance. This one has apparently been out there for over a year. It tunneled to Starbase 13, and the ship we left behind to keep an eye on things launched its own tunnel drone back to the fleet."

She paused, and Cross jumped into the gap. "Tell me we're going after them. Tell me this Kate. Please." He knew what the answer would be, but he had to ask.

"No. They're planning to send out several ships to record the battle, to learn what we can, but we won't intervene when the aliens attack into Alliance territory, which is what all indications suggest they're going to do. Or, are doing right now, given the delay in getting the message."

"Damn it," Cross yelled, standing up and kicking his chair across the room. He growled in frustration and stalked, muttering to himself. When he regained his composure, he came back to the table to rejoin Kate and Jannik, who'd been quietly talking.

Before he could speak, Jannik said it for him, "We need to tell them."

"We do," Kate confirmed.

Cross nodded, but his words didn't agree with his gesture. "What you're suggesting is treason, plain and simple. Court-martial for all of us if we're caught. Is it worth that risk?"

Jannik and Kate exchanged glances, and each paused before the older man spoke for them both. "Aye, it is," said Jannik.

Kate continued, "We can't just let them be taken by surprise. It's not right. When conscience and duty conflict—"

Cross finished for her, echoing their conversations at the Academy when they found themselves at odds with their professors over interpretations of historical situations, "—conscience must be our guide." The sad smile she gave him in response to that was beautiful, and it was all he could do not to tell her so.

"Right then," he said instead, "how?"

"I think I may have an answer to that," Jannik said. "If Kate here will give me an assist. You see, we paused a series of experiments involving our sensor modules due to all of this," he waved a hand at the air, "excitement that's been going on."

"Uh-huh," pressed Cross, to keep Jannik from departing on a tangent about young people and excitement and about how if engineers were in charge, things would be different and so on.

"Well, there's no reason not to continue those experiments while we are filling in the gaps between activities, right? Isn't that what an efficient crew would do?" He looked at Kate as he asked.

"It's certainly what I would do, and I've always considered myself to be efficient. How will this help us, though, oh wise one?"

"Well, you, young people wouldn't know this, but the original sensor design was built to include communication functionality in the low bands of the electromagnetic spectrum. Kind of like Morse code, but updated from the telegraph to interstellar relays. It would need special programming to bounce quietly from sensor array to sensor array, so would take time to get there, but encoded this way it would be well-nigh impossible to discover."

Kate tapped her chin, frowning, as she considered the possibilities. "Okay, it's easy to see how we'll get it encoded, and under the guise of testing the main sensor array I see how we can get it off the ship. But how we can we make sure that the Alliance receives it?"

"Petryaev," Cross said. "That's how. You two set up the technology, I'll take care of getting them to monitor the right frequency."

In his quarters, he composed the messages he wanted to send to Dima. The first read "Mutual friends incoming. Put out the welcome mat." That phrasing gave them at least face deniability with the admiralty since it didn't explicitly mention the alien threat. Cross knew it was thin, very thin, but he would do what he could, anyway. He was sure that Dima would understand it. Anyway, that message would be well-hidden within the activity of the sensors.

He signaled Kate to come by his room and gave her the first message. They would provide as little lingering evidence of their treachery as possible. He spent the next fifteen minutes figuring out how to convey the frequency information to Dima. When he was done, he leaned back and reviewed what he had written.

"Captain First Rank Petryaev. I have been told that you enjoy chess. Allow me to respond to your last message in kind. Queen to Bishop 4, Knight's pawn to Knight's pawn 3, Queen's Castle to Queen's Castle 4, King's Knight to King's Castle 3. I'm sure that the frequency of our moves will be low, but hopefully you are an accomplished enough player to sense my developing strategy."

Cross sighed. There was no easy way to communicate numbers and scientific terms in the open. Dima would be alerted by the existence of the message, so that would at least be something. He hand-delivered it to Jannik and Kate for approval before returning his to his quarters and recording it.

He cleared his throat and opened a channel to the bridge.

"Captain Okoye, sir? I request permission to send a message of a personal nature to AAN Captain First Rank Dima Petryaev. You may remember him, he's the one we met after the destruction of the *Gagarin*."

"I remember, Cross," the Captain said without inflection. "Content?"

"I've linked it to your tablet, sir. In essence, I am offering a response to his last message."

The channel carried a quiet hiss, and Cross guessed that the captain was reviewing it. "Interesting strategy, Lieutenant Commander."

"I thought so, sir."

"Fine," Okoye said, "you have my approval, although why you're bothering at a time like this is completely beyond me." Cross thought he might be laying it on a little thickly, but he was in no position to judge Okoye's skills in dissembling and secrecy.

"Also, Captain, I'm not sure if they mentioned it, but Kate and Jannik are ready to resume the work they were doing on our sensors before the unpleasantness with the *Gagarin*."

He pictured the captain shaking his head, and was pretty sure he heard it in his voice when he said, "Fine, Cross. Thank you for informing me. Now if there is no other vital and timely information you need to share, I'd like to get back to commanding my ship. If that's okay with you?"

"Absolutely, sir. Sorry to bother you."

"Sure, Cross, sure. Okoye out."

Cross smiled, his appreciation of Okoye's craftiness increasing with each passing day. He tapped the code into his communicator, and both Jannik and Kate received it as planned.

Just like that, they were traitors.

Just like that, they may have given the Alliance one chance in a hundred to survive the coming attack. Cross fell on his bunk to catch some much-needed sleep, but not before saying a small prayer to whatever gods might be listening to give him, just this once, that one percent.

CHAPTER THIRTY

It was a sight that he would never tire of, Dima thought. The Allied Asian Nations' most forward starbase hung in orbit over the planet next on the list for colonization. It glistened, white against the black sky—aglow as a beacon against the endless night that surrounded it. Alliance ships darted around the station like bees around a hive, docking, loading and unloading, then shooting off again.

The *Beijing* was in dock, though it was standard practice for Dima to keep at least two-thirds of his sailors on board. Other captains might let all of their crew members relax at once, leaving the ship with only a skeleton crew. Dima did not believe in skeleton crews. As far as his people knew, he didn't believe in shore leave, either. *If they'd known him when he was their age*, Dima thought, *they might have a different opinion.*

He had a feeling though—some would call it impending doom. However, Dima considered it a gut instinct. Long practice had taught him to listen to it, whatever it was.

"Helm, inform the starbase we will uncouple. Communication officer, please send a recall notice to our crew, shore leave is now canceled. If they don't get here by the time we undock, they can take a shuttle. Wing Commander, please launch shuttles as soon as we're at far enough away to do so. Also, once we're at an appropriate distance, deploy our fighter screen."

He rubbed his chin, realizing he'd been on shift so long that stubble was growing in. Keeping command while the younger officers sowed their wild oats was another tradition Dima kept—one he'd much appreciated when the opportunity was offered by his own captains in the past.

"Tactical, maximum safe sensors while we are still docked. I don't trust the base feed to tell us everything we need to know."

He frowned, sure he was forgetting something, then snapped his fingers as it hit him. "Michman," he said to the junior-most ranking member of the bridge crew. "Please have the galley deliver a fresh cup of tea. I seem to be out."

NINETY MINUTES LATER, Dima's instincts proved true. A wash of color fell over the sector, and where previously there were no ships, an invasion force stood. The new arrivals slid into motion, organizing into pairs and moving along separate vectors. Voices trampled over one another on the command channel heralding the aliens until the quiet voice of the starbase commander overrode all channels.

"Response plan Ichi. Execute."

Defenses spun up on ships that had been sitting dark, on those who were already under power, and on the starbase itself. Multiple options had been developed for an enemy arrival in various parts of the sector, and rather than accomplishing complete surprise, the invading aliens faced a force that had possessed at least a modicum of time to prepare for them.

Dima smiled as he watched the defensive strategy unfold. Cross's message had been convoluted, but it had put them on alert, even though it hadn't given any specifics. He hadn't expected the upstart

Lieutenant Commander to respond to his own warning. *His captain must be teaching him well,* Dima thought.

The forces settled into opposing positions, the defenders arrayed in a web with the starbase at its center, the attackers finishing their organization into two ship elements consistent with the approach he'd observed during the battle between the aliens and the UAL.

The view-screens on all the ships in the sector lit up with the image of a striking, tall, winged alien they hadn't seen before. It wore a uniform in black with shades of red and carried blades on its thighs. It seemed slightly smaller than the other. A translation, supplied as part of the signal, slid across the bottom of the transmission.

"Greetings, humans. I bring you joyous tidings in the name of the Xroeshyn people. You've been named in prophecy as the enemy that will deliver our ancestors from the in-between to paradise. You should be honored to die in the service of our gods, and perhaps you'll be rewarded with a chance to return as a higher form of life in the next turn of the wheel. We permit you a moment of prayer before we begin our attack. Use it to find whatever peace your false gods can provide to you." The being's wings twitched as it clasped its hands behind its back.

"I am Indraat Vray, commander of the *Ruby Rain*, and I will honor your sacrifice with clean, quick deaths. Fare well on your journey into the in-between." The screen reverted to an external view.

The command net lit up again with objections, boasts, and other nonsense, mainly from the younger commanders on the newer ships. Those who'd been around for a while dealt with their own fears in silence. The starbase cut through again, this time bearing a message spoken by the admiral in charge of the facility. "Prepare to defend the starbase. Those designated as attackers will begin assault at the enemy's first offensive move. Remember to overpower where possible. All ships, launch fighters now."

His tactical officer had already arranged the main display into Dima's favored breakdown, showing a real-time view from the forward part of the *Beijing* in one corner, standard battle schematic in another corner, and a smaller version of the battle schematic that included most of the sector. The final quarter showed data on his ship, including status of shields, armaments, and a tally of losses among his fighters. The countdown clock for the tunnel drive was at zero. They were ready.

"Communication officer, ship-wide channel please." He paused for execution of his command. "Comrades, once again we go into battle. This time, it's against an alien species, rather than those that we must now consider acknowledging as our brothers and sisters, because we come from the same planet and have a common enemy. Maintain your courage. Focus on your tasks. Do *not* give fear an entry. Together, we will overcome this challenge." He motioned for Zian to cut the channel.

Dima took a deep breath, exhaled, and drank the last dregs of his tea.

"You know what to do, people," he said to his bridge crew, now strapped into their stations and ready for combat. "As soon as the enemy ships move, act according to our preset strategy."

He waited, as did the entire AAN force, while both forces coasted into final positions as if they were two medieval armies awaiting the clarion call to charge.

WHEN THE ATTACK BEGAN, it bore little resemblance to the previous battle recorded in Dima's observational data. The eight pair of enemy ships joined into four sets of four, and all streaked low, attempting to overwhelm the forces arrayed to defend the bottom hemisphere of the starbase.

The admiral's voice came over the command channel, redirecting defenders from the upper section to curve down and intercept as the ships at the bottom reoriented their shields along the vectors of the incoming ships. Enemy ships fired at maximum range, launching salvos of torpedoes and blasts from energy weapons that were dispersed by the defenders' shields.

The *Beijing* weathered several of those strikes, and his tactical officer reported, "They're just testing, Captain. Those couldn't have been full force."

Dima nodded, having predicted that the aliens would try to get a sense of their defensive powers in the first pass. It was a standard opening move, one he hoped to blow up in their faces. He switched to his squadron's sub-channel and issued commands. "Attack squadron *Beijing*, deployment pattern San." The three other ships under his command surged forward along with the *Beijing*, dashing above the incoming vector of the alien ships. As they crossed the vertical plane of their target, the four ships in his squadron cut their main drives and used maneuvering thrusters to orient their weapons on a single foe. They formed a rough diamond, and the plasma beams they fired struck the enemy ship from four different angles, punishing its shields continuously as the AAN vessels reoriented themselves to chase the aliens as they streaked past.

Once they were pointing in the right direction, Dima gave the command to engage drives, and they followed the enemy ships in, maintaining the energy barrage on that single ship to negligible damage—when the beams did not bend away before impact, they failed to penetrate. When each of the four AAN ships fired a simultaneous salvo of torpedoes from their forward tubes, the results were far more pleasant. The missiles curved but still struck, and the enemy ship's shields overloaded. It exploded into its components parts, spraying the other three ships of its group with shrapnel. Dima informed the other squadron captains over the command channel of the success of his strategy.

Unfortunately for the defending forces, they didn't have the resources required to create positive matchups in all places. As Dima's squadron shifted toward its next target, he caught sight of an array of small objects cascading away from one of the alien ships. Depressing the button on his command chair that tied him into the squadron's fighter channel, he snapped, "Umbrella," the code word to defend their base from sharing the fate of the Union base. Individual fighters tracked the incoming mines and shot them down before they could adhere to the base's skin. The base released robots to detach the ones that survived the fighters from its hull.

The enemy ships, which so far had mainly evaded and ignored the defenders to focus on the starbase, reacted as one to the successful defense against the gravitic mines. With simultaneous symmetrical actions, they disengaged from combat and flew through a predetermined point, where they organized again into two ship units. They were down to fourteen, but the defending forces had lost twice as many and an unknown number of fighters. The Alliance maintained a numerical superiority, but it was thinner than Dima would have liked.

He ordered his own squadron back to a safe assembly point to await the aliens' next move. He scratched his cheek as he reviewed and discarded potential gambits to try. "What are you going to do now," he muttered to himself, attempting to fathom the enemy's strategy. He saw the opportunity just as the enemy ships moved again and rattled off quick commands to his forces.

"All ships, form up on the *Beijing* and stay in diamond formation. Helm, course 279, 41 high. Tactical, coordinate all of our squadron's missiles to operate from the same targeting laser. Lock us on the back ship in this pair," he said, marking one on his personal display. "Keep that designated, no matter what. All ships will fire all torpedoes when I call for it, set to hit that target 45 seconds after launch." He knew the tactical officers on all the ships would be racing to program the seeker heads of the projectiles, which had selectable targeting options. The computers would handle the initial time and distance calculations after launch but before releasing the missiles to autonomous control.

"All ships, prepare to send energy weapons into the lead ship of the pair, and launch torpedoes past it to the rearmost ship." He waited until they were within extreme range. "Fire energy weapons."

His star of four ships rained plasma and coherent energy into the shields of the forward ship, but with its shields balanced against them, it bent, absorbed, or evaded all the incoming beams.

"Continue energy barrage. Standby to launch torpedoes on my mark." He watched the display for several seconds, doing the calculations without conscious thought, then growled, "Mark." He felt the torpedoes leave the *Beijing* and saw on both battle displays the red traces showing the launches. They headed as if they would strike the primary ship in the pair, and it engaged its own countermeasures. A glistening rain of small particles shot out and propelled themselves toward the torpedoes. The defensive mines contacted and adhered to several of them. Once attached, they began to glow, shortly thereafter warping the structure of the torpedoes until they exploded or collapsed into a cone of fast-moving debris.

The defenses couldn't remove the threat entirely, and the torpedoes that survived smashed into the trailing ship. The bridge crew cheered as they overwhelmed the shields that hadn't been fully attuned forward. Logic suggested that the missiles were targeted at the advance ship, so the back one was focused on attacks from other directions. The exploding debris also ripped through the weakened rear shields of the lead ship and sent it pinwheeling away, at least momentarily out of the battle.

Dima guided his small squadron again to a safe spot from which to survey the entire battlefield. He realized they were losing. The enemy had been trading ships for strategic position, and he could already see how the endgame would play out. He conveyed this to the starbase admiral in a low tone, and the admiral agreed with his assessment, having arrived at the same conclusion on his own.

The command channel carried the admiral's order, "We've reached the point where we cannot hope to achieve victory in this battle. Initiate evacuation plan Hachi."

CHAPTER THIRTY-ONE

The command to evacuate called for new actions by all the AAN forces in the sector.

Larger ships, the *Beijing* among them, interposed themselves between the attacking forces and the base, absorbing what damage they could before rotating, bringing the next set of undamaged shields to bear. The defense fell back slowly, creating a rough cylinder around the starbase that gave ground, trading space for time.

Meanwhile, ships that weren't big enough to take the brunt of multiple enemies assaulting them at once rocketed to the base, transferring personnel from it as fast as they could run. As each ship reached capacity, it retreated to a safe distance and tunneled out of the sector to a waypoint, from which it would tunnel again to the AAN's nearest installation.

Dima thought the shift to a defensive posture was a good decision, but it had probably come too late. The remaining attacking ships, thirteen of them now, were adapting to the defenders' reorganization, and were turning the ship-to-ship combat numbers in their own favor.

As the *Beijing* rotated out of its blocking assignment to recharge its shields, Dima grudgingly accepted that the plan wouldn't work. They didn't have enough time, or enough space to trade, not to mention enough firepower in the sector, to pull off the evacuation. He keyed his connection to the command channel and said as much to the admiral. Naturally, the admiral disagreed.

Dima, frustrated, sought targets of opportunity and leapt to engage them. One enemy ship was apart from its fellows, skirting the battle and describing a large circle around the space. He ordered pursuit, and as they got closer, he noticed that it was shooting small objects in random directions. These were black instead of metallic, and did not seem intended to attack the base, so he alerted his sensor officer and filed them away to consider later.

Signaling to the captain of one of the other ships resting from its rotation in active defense, Dima requested a salvo of torpedoes launched at a certain moment, and the ship obliged with eight projectiles, all slaved to the *Beijing's* control once they were clear of their tubes.

Dima ordered the *Beijing* on an arcing path that would take it behind that solo ship, putting it between his weapons and the incoming rockets, forcing it to defend on two fronts. "Tactical officer, starboard torpedoes, fire on my mark." Dima watched the incoming missiles and timed his own launch to strike at the same time. "Mark." Immediately after the weapons left the ship, he ordered the helmsman to skew, bringing his other battery to bear.

"Tactical, single fire, five second intervals, port torpedoes. Launch when ready." The torpedoes formed a straight line, one after the other like ducklings in a pond, heading for the alien ship. Caught between both sets of incoming weapons, the enemy turned evasive and fired off countermeasures.

Lieutenant Yegorovich held the targeting laser on the enemy ship as it moved, and the defenses failed to distract the missiles from their singular goal. The initial strikes from the double set of torpedoes overloaded the shields for an instant, and the staccato punches of those driving in a line drilled deeply into the ship's structure before exploding it from within, hurling mechanical and once-living debris into the void.

There was no time to celebrate. The aliens were getting closer to the base, and it was the *Beijing's* turn to defend it. Firing his main drive and sliding deftly into position, the *Beijing's* forward shields caught an incoming barrage of missiles that would've done substantial damage to the starbase had they penetrated the defensive screen.

Dima again keyed access to the command channel and told the admiral and other captains, "We're running out of time. Unless you've got good ideas for how to turn this thing on its head, you have only minutes before station security will be compromised."

He was about to offer a suggestion on tactics when something he'd been seeing on the battle display suddenly made sense to him. "The aliens aren't trying to destroy the base," he said in sudden alarm. "They're planning to board it."

As if he had called it into being, the alien ships slid into a defensive posture around one of their larger vessels, pushing through the blocking screen toward the base. The large ship fired grapnels and pulled itself close to the starbase hull at the dorsal end. The admiral ordered his forces to attack the boarding operation, but the enemy wove a thick defense that none of the alliance vessels could break through. More than one was destroyed in the attempt.

"It seems as if the aliens are done comparing their weapons to ours, and have just decided to take what they came for," Dima said, his anger evident.

With a static crackle, the command network failed, the constant white noise from the starbase cutting off ominously.

Dima switched to the general battle channel and reached out to his fellow captains. "We must attempt to stop them from taking the station, and to do that we need to blast through their defenses. If we cannot do this," he made quick calculations in his head, "all surviving ships will have to fire all their weapons at the base. If we cannot dislodge them from it, we will at least try to deny them possession of it."

"The *Beijing* will—" he began, only to be cut off by his tactical officer with an uncharacteristic interruption.

"New ships entering the sector, Captain. Computer identifies them as Union."

"Open a channel," Dima said, turning to look at the display as if he could read the ship's names painted on the hulls from this distance.

"Hello, Captain Petryaev," came James Okoye's clipped accent. "May we be of assistance?"

Dima failed to quash the fierce predatory grin that stretched across his face at the arrival of reinforcements. "How many ships do you have?"

"We brought six. Several more may arrive within the hour, but from the look of things, that will be too late. Status update?"

"The aliens are boarding the base. I've given orders to dislodge them or destroy it, but we couldn't break through their defensive perimeter."

"I recommend you continue to try to scrape them off of your base. The *Washington* will attach at the midpoint and transfer our Marine contingent to help evacuate your people. We'll also set mines as we retreat as a backup plan to destroy it. Our ships will screen our boarders, but we would welcome your fighters to back us up. We brought none of our own."

"Affirmative," Dima replied. "Tell your Marines good hunting."

Dima watched as the Union forces swarmed to their destination, arranging themselves in a protective formation around the *Washington* and her boarding party. Her support ships flew in deliberate ellipses centered on the base—watching, prepared for incoming enemy weapons.

Dima switched back to the general battle channel, and informed his fellow officers that the Union ships were there to help, and that they would board the base to rescue the people trapped aboard. The inevitable protests materialized, accusing the UAL of entering to gather intelligence. They were more subdued than he had expected, and he didn't care in any case. It was beyond time to set aside old ways of thinking.

"Helm, let's make these uncivilized interlopers' lives difficult. Chart a trajectory that will put us out of weapons range for all but one of the enemy ships and send that point in space to our squadron. Tactical, make sure our defenses are balanced so they can take a few hits once we reach that position. Let's attempt to bring all of our energy weapons to bear on one ship and see if we can burn through his shields."

Dina returned to his executive officer, who had been feeding him information throughout the battle. "I do hope you're recording the results of all of these experiments."

The exec nodded and replied, "Of course, Captain. Someday, when you become an admiral, I plan to give my own executive officer such important tasks." The wry sarcasm brought the smile back to Dima's face, and he returned his gaze to the main screen.

Several moments later, all of his ships were in position, and they stabbed their foe with all of their energy weapons at once. The gravitic shields bent the beams at first, but as the multicolored lances stayed on target, the redirection diminished, until they all coalesced on one point, burning through the protective barrier and the ship behind it.

"Tactical, report," Dima snapped, his fingers working on his own display.

"We have nine ships remaining, Captain, and the enemy now has eleven. With the addition of the Union vessels, we outnumber them, but as we're operating as two disparate forces, this does us little good. One of ours has an engine leak, but otherwise we appear to be fully functional. The aliens also appear to be undamaged, but are focused on defending their boarding party."

Dima swore softly in Russian, his angst reaching only the ears of his exec, who was well acquainted with how Dima operated in battle. "It's a stalemate. We cannot stop them boarding, nor can they let down their guard to destroy us." He tapped a couple more icons on his display, highlighting two ships.

"Send the *Singapore* and the *Hanoi* to evacuate the lower part of the base. Send all remaining Alliance forces to defend the evacuation, even if that means leaving the aliens to their task. Have some of the fighters harass them, but only if they can do so without taking significant damage."

He keyed the communication channel that connected him to the *Washington* again. "Captain Okoye, we have reached a stalemate and are evacuating the bottom section. Your Marines can focus on the center and the top. We will plant our own scuttling charges and coordinate with you on discharging them."

"Affirmative," Okoye said. "We're working with your personnel to secure the airlock and will soon breach the station to evacuate your people. The *Washington* should be able to hold them all if our spies have given us truthful information about your bases."

Dima laughed. "I'm sure we told them to do so, since all your spies are really our spies."

He cut the channel and sat back in his command chair. "Keep a close eye on these alien barbarians, tactical. Until they do something, or until our evacuation is complete, all we can do is wait and watch."

CHAPTER THIRTY-TWO

Kate grabbed the side rails of the ladder, locked the sides of her feet against the outside of the railings, and allowed herself to slide down the three decks to the transfer level. The sleeves of her tunic protected her hands, and her boots were durable enough to absorb the friction and control her descent.

She landed with a bounce, turned, and took in the seeming chaos of the Marines as they prepared to board the Alliance base. Jumping to see over them, she looked over the milling crowd to find someone in charge. She spotted Cynthia Murphy and wove through traffic to get to her.

"Captain says you're coming with us," the Sergeant greeted her. "You're a little small for a Marine, but I think we've got a skell that'll fit you. Come right this way." Kate followed her to the far side of the room where several crates had been stacked and opened to reveal the Marines' gear.

"You'll need to put on the sensor suit," she said, looking at Kate with an expression that on anyone else she would've called sheepish. On the Marine, it just looked wrong. She nodded and peeled off her boots, tunic, and her uniform pants. She accepted the sensor suit and stepped into it, shrugged it into place, and allowed Murphy to seal her inside it. Her lack of modesty got her a nod of support from the gunnery sergeant.

"Over here," the Marine said to her, pulling her less lightly than she might have expected toward a standing exoskeleton. "Feet here, arms here, lock the braces around your forearms and your shins." She pointed out all the main parts, then walked away. Kate followed her orders, clambering into the skell by stepping into the foot rests and clasping the braces at shin, waist, chest, and arms.

The exoskeleton negotiated with the sensor suit in silence, and upon reaching agreement, powered up. She took several slow stomping experimental steps, and waved her arms around, careful not to remove the heads of any friendlies standing nearby.

"I could get used to this," she said as Murphy returned.

The Marine laughed and clapped her on the exoskeleton arm hard enough to rattle the entire frame. "We'll turn you into one of us yet, Flynn." She pointed across the room where the rest of Kate's gear awaited her.

The modular design of the Marines' armor was appropriate for a recon unit that would need maximum flexibility in loadouts for a variety of mission objectives. Pieces of gear could be easily swapped out among exoskeletons, and mission-critical components could be assigned to any team member.

The Marines had picked out modules for Kate, and Murphy assisted her in locking them onto the exoskeleton. Once in place, securing bolts extended and connected the armor plates as if they'd been welded together. Kate's modules included an upgraded sensor array and communication suite, located in her chestpiece and helmet, respectively.

As her heads-up display offered diagnostics, Kate reviewed those systems and the proper sequence of verbal commands and eye patterns necessary to trigger the suit to release her in case of malfunction or damage. She noted that her arm modules both had accessories, a targeting laser in the left and a grappling hook with a retraction motor in the right.

"Catch," Rhys St. John's voice jolted her out of her reverie.

Kate hadn't realized that he had joined them and was distracted for a moment. That plus the minuscule delay between desire and action in the armor almost caused her to miss the projectile, but she caught the Marine rifle without embarrassing herself. She received another nod of something like approval, and St. John launched into operation instructions.

"Since you're not fully trained on this equipment, you won't be able to use the sighting function as it's meant to be used, but that's okay. As long as you know which end to point toward the enemy, you'll be just fine." He pointed at the trigger guard, which had a strange scalloped design. "All four of your fingers have something to do. Your index finger pulls the trigger, your middle finger selects multi-shot by resting on the guard, your ring finger triggers the weapon's targeting laser the same way, and a flick of your pinky against that little nub on the bottom will launch a grenade."

Murphy grinned as she anticipated Kate's question. "We wouldn't want your thumb to get lonely or bored, so that's what you use to select the next target in your HUD. When the yellow overlay matches the red one, your aim is good and you can let it off the chain. Questions?"

Kate frowned. The gear she'd trained in during her Marine rotation (which was on a training base—they rarely put new naval officers into active ground combat during first rotations) had more features than this. "Ammo select? Grenade select?"

Murphy gave a short laugh. "You're my kind of mammal, Flynn. In this rig, those are controlled with eye movements or vocal commands. You have fire and frag grenades, and both standard and explosive rounds. Because we'll be on a space station, I recommend against using frag or explosives unless things are going bad in a hurry."

"Affirmative," Kate responded in a distracted tone, already trying to find the eye controls to select munitions. Her reverie was broken by St. John's voice over the communication system in her helmet.

"Form up, people. It's time to do that thing we do best."

As one, the Marines shouted, "Ooh-rah," in response. Kate shook her head and decreased the volume of the audio. The next sound emanated from a different part of her helmet, indicating a separate comm channel than that used for the entire squad.

"Flynn," St. John said, "you'll be our liaison with the *DC*." She felt a warmth from their use of the crew's affectionate name for their vessel. "If our orders change, or if new information about the tactical situation comes in, I expect you to communicate it to me and to Sinner. This channel is just the three of us. You can access it as comm six."

"Affirmative," Kate said again. "Report changes in orders and new information." He gave her the Marine hand gesture for understanding in return.

She got into line where the gunnery sergeant put her and used the next several moments while the Marines organized themselves to set up her connection with the *Washington*.

Okoye's voice came over the comm channel. "Forty-five seconds to hard dock. Standby to breach."

Kate took a deep breath, closed her eyes, and drew her awareness inward, focusing only on the moment. When she opened them again, she was ready.

WITH A LOUD CLANG, the *Washington* completed its connection to the base. The outer door opened, and the first two Marines in line fired grapnels and winched themselves across to the other side, assisted by a powerful jump from their exoskeleton legs. They were working to gain access even as the airlock sheath was extending to provide atmosphere.

By the time the airlocks were ready, so were the Marines, and the inner doors on both sides released. They moved in lines across the airlock, spreading out into a tactical deployment covering the entrances to the room they entered on the other side.

Each Marine had a wireframe map of the base overlaying their real-time view of the space, with their objective marked in green and a path toward it glowing in their augmented vision. She reported back to the *Washington* that they were safely in the airlock. After listening for a moment, she then activated comm channel six.

"The aliens are pushing for the command center. The estimate is that they will be there long before we can scuttle the base or get everyone evacuated. Alliance command is concerned that the data present in the facility may prove a significant vulnerability if the enemy takes it."

"Damned inconsiderate bunch of aliens, if you ask me," St. John said. "Okay people, now we have two priorities. Sinner, you and half of third squad evacuate the personnel according to our initial plan. Set limpets on your way back." She clicked an affirmative across the comm channel and organized her force. "The rest of third squad, deploy here and guard our exit. "First and second squads, including Flynn, you're with me. Let's go deny the command center to those bastards."

Kate heard the fuzz of people switching to different channels, and then the members of first squad moved off through the left entrance. "Kid, take point. Huge, you're second. I'm third. Flynn, behind me. Flame, stick to Flynn and make sure we don't have to explain how she got killed on our watch. That would seriously mess up my day—and yours." He pointed at her. "Keep yourself alive, Flynn."

"Red," she replied.

"Red it is. Second squad, same deployment in reverse to guard our backs. No one should feel the need to bring any ammo back. Now move."

KATE'S ROTATION among the Marines was a long time in the past, but she remembered the basics well enough. Stay with your unit, keep your head down, try not to get seen or killed. Destroy anything that tries to stop you from doing these things. She figured she could handle it.

As they moved through the base, she used her advanced sensors module to tap into the base's computer system. It required a great deal of conversation with her armor to hack the system's protocols, but she persisted and negotiated her way in. She called up the security interface, getting immediate access to hundreds of cameras showing nothing useful, since she was unsure of their locations.

Delving further into the system, she was able to overlay an infrared schematic atop her existing wireframe map, which enabled her to pinpoint the location of different bodies throughout the base. Clustered around the command center were several figures that were either humans with lethal levels of fever or alien beings with a higher natural body temperature.

Kate sketched what looked like the safest route from their current point to the objective and linked it to Sergeant St. John. He gave it a quick review, then clicked twice for affirmative across their communication link. He redistributed the signal to the squad, and the new trail appeared in each of their overlays.

As they advanced further into the base, Kate noticed that it was organized in an almost identical fashion to the Union bases that she'd visited. Although the exterior designs were different, the interiors suggested that the architects were working from the same plans all along. She sighed at the unnecessary waste that was the current state of human affairs.

The explosion came without warning and scattered the Marines like leaves in the breeze. Kate slammed into the upper part of the corridor wall and fell to land face-first on the floor, the armor and exoskeleton padding keeping her from harm. Her systems had reacted quickly enough to protect her hearing and sight. She took in the blasted remains of the hallway. The damage was significant, but didn't put the structure in danger.

She pushed herself to her feet as Sergeant St. John called for a comm check. One by one the members of teams two and three reported in by callsign. When all eight of them had finished, she added her own.

"Resume formation and advance," the gunnery sergeant said. His voice was somewhere on the continuum between determined, irritated, and bored.

She followed behind St. John, noting that all the Marines moved their weapons in a precise pattern, a choreographed routine that kept them focused and aware of their surroundings. The sergeant carried the same weapon as the team's point person, callsign Surfer. It was bigger than the rifle she held, with several round magazines attached to the underside that fed the grenade launcher below the barrel.

Hugo, the team's heavy gunner, lugged an absolute monolith of a gun—so big that it was mounted on a hardpoint at the waist of his power armor. A backpack fed the weapon through a pair of cables that snaked around his torso. This model was unknown to Kate, but she knew she was glad to be behind it, rather than in front of it.

They advanced, meeting no enemies until they were within a hundred meters of the command information center, then Surfer stopped them. Ahead was a maze of crisscrossing defensive traps, presumably set by the aliens, visible in their heads-up displays as a series of crimson lines shooting all over the hallway. She was sure that they could detect motion, sound, body temperature, and who knew what else.

St. John's voice resonated through her headset, "Looks bad, Red. Your opinion?"

"Standby," she replied, and toggled her communication to the *Washington*. A few moments later, she was speaking with Cross because the captain was busy coordinating battle operations for the

Union forces. She described the situation to him, and he responded, "We need it. You've got to get in there."

"Yeah, well, easy for you to say."

"True, but that's why the captain sent you. You're the smart one. I'm just the good-looking one."

Kate exhaled the tiniest of laughs at his stupid joke. Then she remembered a conversation they'd the last time they were together, and cut the link to him, connecting instead to the engineering section.

"Hey, Jannik," she said, "I have this idea. How many of those spiders do you have, anyway?"

CHAPTER THIRTY-THREE

Cross tapped commands to track the Marines' movements on the display built into the executive officer's chair. Using a pad in his other hand, he scrolled through a continuous data report on the status of the *Washington*. It was his task to maintain the ship's point defense and operations while Captain Okoye dealt with the overall tactical situation as commander of the Union forces in the system.

While the *Washington* was attached to the base, there was little to do. He drummed his fingers as the small dots that represented the Marines moved through the tiny map of the space station on his display and wished he could trade places with Kate.

To distract himself, he watched the forces fight for primacy on the main monitor, now given over to the battle schematic rather than any real-time view. The icons looked like pieces on the game board.

He fell into the strategy and tactics of the battle, except for the part of his brain that stayed focused on Kate and the *Washington's* dataflow, and the broad strategies of each force materialized. It was a mental challenge because there were three sides—the aliens, the AAN, and the UAL. His view showed the latter two weren't working well together against their common foe, even though he believed both Okoye and Dima wanted to.

The pattern developing in an upper corner of the screen demanded his attention. A pair of enemy ships traveled in a wide circuit of the sector. Three Alliance ships broke off to pursue them, seeing the opportunity for momentary superiority of numbers as an irresistible gift.

Cross felt it in the pit of his stomach, just the way he had when the aliens almost trapped the *Washington* during the last battle. He looked over at Okoye, but he was engrossed in coordinating the actions of their force, and not to be interrupted.

He banged his hands on the arms of his chair as the ships closed, hoping to be wrong but knowing he was right. With the captain unable to, he needed to act.

Cross stood and walked over to the communication officer, and whispered, "Ana, connect me to the *Beijing* right away." She nodded, and he picked up a headset sitting nearby, tucking the plug into his ear and positioning the mic near his mouth.

"Go, Cross," she said.

"*Beijing*, this is Lieutenant Commander Anderson Cross from the *Washington*. Take a look at your battle display. Those two ships in the upper left of the sector are leading your people into a trap."

Dima Petryaev's voice came back over the channel. "What are you saying?" Cross pictured him staring at the icons swimming like minnows on the screen, trying to make them speak to him the same way they did to Cross.

"The aliens did the same thing to me, Captain, in the last engagement. They show lesser strength, and the moment you commit, suddenly several quick ships close and flip the odds."

Dima grumbled in Russian, and the channel clicked off. Cross turned and walked back to his chair, then stood behind it and watched the trap unfold. As predicted, two more enemy pairs disengaged from their battle and rocketed toward the Alliance ships that had been drawn out of protective support range of their fellows.

The warning got there in time for the AAN forces to prepare for the incoming surprise, but too late for them to avoid it. Several other Alliance ships fired salvos of torpedoes that traveled far too slowly to make a difference in the unfolding battle.

The Alliance trio fought hard, and Cross rooted for them soundlessly as they took up defensive positions to combine the effects of their shields against the enemy that would soon swarm them on all sides at once. His fingers hurt from the way he gripped the top of the seat as he watched other ships reposition as if they could influence the outcome.

The six alien vessels created a rotating pattern around the triangle comprised of the three Alliance ships. The triangle was a strong defensive position that allowed their shields to focus on a 180° hemisphere rather than a full 360° sphere, giving them almost double the amount of protective power.

Cross couldn't help but be impressed by the symmetry and coordination of the aliens' flight path. Too unpredictable for their opponents to damage them with energy fire, it still kept all the alien ships engaged continuously with the target, pouring blasts into diminishing shields.

As the battle display showed the Alliance ships' defenses failing, it was clear the time left to them was drawing to a close.

The Alliance ships heading in that direction surprised Cross when they turned around to return to the main fracas, but his surprise lasted only a moment. The display lit up with the explosion of the three Alliance ships, a conflagration of overloaded engines.

Of the six ships engaged with them, five were converted to flaming debris, venting atmosphere and bodies into space. The sixth limped away, its reduced speed suggesting engine damage. Fighters from the *Beijing* and his brothers finally reached the area, swarming around and firing shots of frustration into the floating jetsam on their way to chasing down the escapee.

Their quarry fell to their guns, and Cross hissed in satisfaction despite the loss.

"Incoming transmission," Ana Fitzpatrick's low soprano tones spoke through his earpiece. He nodded at her and heard a raspy voice made thick with sorrow.

"Thank you for the warning, Lieutenant Commander Cross. Captain Zha was one of my trainees. The *Minsk* was his first command. It is," his emotions broke through in a slight change of tone, but he brought it back under control, "a great loss. But at least you gave them time to draw in the enemy ships, and they chose their death with honor."

CHAPTER THIRTY-FOUR

An ensign wearing a tunic in the hunter green of the engineering division ran through the cleared territory to reach Kate and handed her a satchel. "Chief put something extra in there for you. Sends his regards." Then he dashed away, his footsteps echoing as he retreated to the *Washington*.

She turned with a smile on her face and triggered the comm to her team. "I've got the solution to blowing those booby-traps before we reach them, but since we don't know what could happen, you might want to watch from a safe distance."

Gunnery Sergeant Rhys St. John came over to stand behind her and looked down at the object in her hands. "What do you have there?"

"Oh, you're gonna like these, Sergeant." Kate opened the satchel, pulled out the cylinder that rested inside it and clipped it to her belt. The handheld remote was next in line. She activated it and ran a quick diagnostic. Everything came up green, naturally—no piece of equipment would dare fail on Jannik's watch. She was sure that the Marines could hear the smile in her voice when she said, "These are some of our chief engineer's favorite toys. Take a look."

She upended the satchel, and a bunch of billiard-ball-sized metal objects fell out, clanking and rolling in the hallway. Kate interfaced with the remote, allowing her to use the suit's internal command structure to communicate with it. After tucking the remote away, she ordered the devices to a ready state. The spheres unfolded and long spindly legs extended until they resembled the arachnids that were their namesake.

Lance Corporal Hugo Galano, the biggest man on the team, noted conversationally, "I hate spiders."

The members of his squad laughed, and Kate joined in. "You're going to like what these ones can do," she promised. Another set of commands sent them skittering forward. They launched themselves at the origination points of the beams that crisscrossed their path. In several cases, the spiders managed to reach and disarm the devices. But in most cases, the spiders made the ultimate sacrifice, and explosions rang throughout the hallway, showering the Marines in dust and debris. When the cacophony had settled, they had a trap-free route to the command information center. A few of the little robots that made it through the destruction formed a line next to Kate, awaiting new orders.

"Good spiders," Kate said.

Galano didn't venture an opinion either way.

AS THEY REACHED the door to the command information center, the Marines took up defensive positions, protecting Kate as she interrogated the starbase's computer system.

"Dammit," she said, "suddenly the base won't talk to me."

Sergeant St. John's voice came over the comm. "Corporal Jameson, do you still have access to the base's computer?"

"Negative, sir."

"Dammit," echoed St. John. "All right, Flame, you're up."

"Make way," Private First-Class Moya Candella said, moving

forward and knocking Kate aside in her haste. She knelt in front of the door and dug a long roll of what looked like metal rope from a compartment in the right leg of her armor. She started at one corner of the door and worked her way up the side of the frame, pressing the cord into place. She repeated the process on the other side until she had fully outlined the door with the sticky substance, including a strip running down the middle. She retreated and nodded at the others.

St. John's voice spoke in her helmet, "Red, what's the situation inside the room?"

Kate checked and swallowed heavily. "Fifteen humanoid forms that are cooling, and eight that read as much warmer than you or I." She linked the positions of the heat blooms to her squad mates. A last-minute check of the map showed only this entrance into the CIC, unless they wanted to drill up or down from another deck, and she shared that option with the team.

"I know," he said, "it's a bad situation, no two ways about it. But bad situations are what we were born to handle. You've done your bit, move to the back, Red."

Kate didn't wait to be asked twice. Although she had a rifle and would use it if she needed to, she enjoyed the theory, tactics, and strategy of combat much more than the experience of it. A member of second squad tossed her a medical pack, and she reviewed the contents.

"We go in ten seconds. Flame, blow it on three." St. John began the countdown. At three seconds, the explosive ignited, and the door hurtled from its frame, cartwheeling in two pieces into the room. A second later, the Marines followed it in. Kate watched the action through the camera Surfer wore.

The first team entered and went both left and right. Hugo Galano used his heavy rifle to spray bolts of energy as he moved. Private Mark Miner and Corporal Jeffrey Baker fired standard projectiles, not caring one bit about whether they vented the room's atmosphere. Rhys St. John showed his own lack of concern about that matter by launching a fragmentation grenade that lanced shrapnel across three-fourths of the enemy combatants, who appeared to have been taken by surprise.

The second team entered immediately after, using projectile fire and energy bolts but refraining from adding more grenades to the mix. Ten seconds after they entered, the eight aliens were also on the ground, cooling as their sapphire blood stained the deck.

"All clear," came St. John's calm voice into her helmet speakers.

She was amazed to find any part of the room still intact as she crossed the threshold. The walls and equipment were scorched with energy discharge, and pitted with holes from shrapnel and bullets, or dented from the impact of body parts moving at high speed.

Kate crossed to a computer station that still appeared functional and connected the interface cable from her power armor to the system. "Downloading and erasing," she said, and pulled out several cables from the satchel, attaching them to the remote for the spiders. The mechanical arachnids followed her as she moved—obedient little pets awaiting a task.

Kate linked another device into the computer, and said, "This is a wireless repeater, and when we depart, if we don't have all of the data, this will keep feeding it to us."

Flame, who had been circling the room outside her view, stood in front of her and held up a control. "This is a wireless detonator, and when we depart, I'm going to blow the living daylights out of this place. So be sure to get all your data before we go, please."

"Going as fast as I can. You're awful pushy. Even for a Marine."

"Damn skippy, Freckles."

The comm channel was filled with the relieved laughter of warriors who had found a precious lull in the combat that made up their lives. It was short-lived, however.

"Flynn, this is the *Washington*. Be advised, you are running out of time. The base is speeding to pull itself apart, and there is another, much larger alien squad on its way to you as we speak."

"Affirmative, *Washington*. We're withdrawing." She retracted her cable and activated the repeater.

She passed the information on to Sergeant St. John, and he gave the orders to get them moving again. He took rear guard. Kate figured that grenades might be a bigger deterrent to pursuing aliens than standard ammunition and was glad for the switch.

They quick-marched in retreat along the path they'd used to reach the command center. The base shuddered around them.

"This is going to be a close one," Galano observed.

"No closer than that time on colony six," Baker responded.

That drew a chuckle from the rest of the squad.

"Colony six was a cluster—" began a voice, then stopped with a cough. "A mess, I mean."

"A mess it was," St. John said as they reached the entrance area again. He kept the channel open as he added another one to it, and said, "Sinner? Status?"

Cynthia Murphy responded as if she'd been waiting for the opportunity. "Evacuation complete, my people are pulling back, just setting the final mines. We've been in contact with the *Washington*, and you need to get your asses over here right now."

"Affirmative," St. John said. "Everyone out. I'm last. Red, you're first. Get over there, and let us know when we can blow this thing."

The Marines retreated along the gangway toward the ship, and as Sergeant St. John walked across it, it began to retract, leaving the base open to space on the opposite side.

Kate watched them cross, keeping one eye on St. John and the other on the display window she'd opened in her helmet when she left her remote behind. It was still feeding data at high velocity, but she could see it vibrating ever so slightly and knew the aliens must be closing in upon it.

The Marines had left them some presents, and the vibrations were from the explosions heralding the delivery of those gifts.

Finally, all the Marines were back, and the airlock door was secured again. Kate felt a slight lurching motion as the *Washington* pulled away from the base. Then, in that display screen, she saw an alien face, its strange scaled or feathered skin evident as it bent down to examine the device.

It was only a remote control, connected to the computer and feeding data, so it was no threat to them. However, the small cylinder she'd picked up out of the satchel that Jannik had sent her was a different matter entirely. Wedged under the base of the desk, it was just waiting for a trigger to set it off.

Kate regretted the necessity, but they needed to buy a little more time to finish the export. "Execute, execute, execute," she whispered. The device hummed for a second, then a crimson beam of coherent light extended through an arc of 180°, cutting a diagonal line into walls, chairs, and living flesh. She was happy that, at least, she was the only one to see the damage she'd wrought.

She watched the computer feed over the next several minutes as it drew to a close, and triggered her comm, "Bridge, Sensors, this is Flynn."

"Flores here, ma'am."

"Do you have a complete record of the data from the base?"

"Affirmative, Lieutenant Commander."

"Verify that the captain wants it linked to the Alliance forces, then see to it."

"Affirmative. Flores out."

Kate toggled her communication channel back to the unit and gave them the word. "We're good to go. Blow it."

Three seconds later, the feed from her remote went white, then disappeared.

She triggered her helmet release and removed it, setting it aside and running her hands through her sweaty hair to free it from the armor's tangling embrace. She popped the individual plates from her suit, adding them to the Marines' stash of items to be reviewed, repaired, and rearmed.

Finally, she tromped over to an exoskeleton bay and entered the appropriate codes on the frame. With a hiss of hydraulics and the metallic click of disengaging pieces, she stepped free of the skell that was now secured in its storage and transportation unit.

She found Sergeant Murphy, who was also taking off her gear, and gestured at the sensor suit. "I'm going to keep this until I can take it off in my own quarters, okay with you?"

She gave Kate a knowing smile. "Undressing in front of this lot gets old fast. Get it back to us when you can."

Sergeant St. John came over and put a hand on Murphy's shoulder. "Don't let Sinner fool you. She looks just as much as anybody."

Murphy laughed. "Well, it's true that there are some fine-looking people in this platoon, yourself included, Saint."

"Ooh-Rah, Gunny," he said with a grin, and turned to Kate.

"You're welcome to run with us anytime, Red. You kept your head and did a good job, and that's all we can ask of anyone."

Kate gave him a weak smile in reply, but it was clear that her heart wasn't in it. The parts of space that called to her were not the parts filled with anger, discord, and death. Her dreams were of exploration and new discoveries.

She sighed, and put those wishes back in the tiny box in her mind where they lived, where they awaited those moments when she needed to retrieve them to maintain her mental balance.

The ship lurched as it took a major hit, and atmosphere warning klaxons sounded. Kate ran for the ladder and climbed, knowing her proper place was with her fellow officers on the bridge.

CHAPTER THIRTY-FIVE

Cross was jolted in his chair as the *Washington's* shields absorbed simultaneous energy blasts and torpedo impacts from a pair of enemy ships. The tactical officer called out, "Several sections open to atmosphere, bulkheads closing to seal off the damage. No casualties."

He watched Captain Okoye as he dealt with the multiple streams of information flowing to him. As the senior commander in the zone, he was responsible for both the operation of the *Washington* and for choreographing the larger battle. The complexity of this position prevented effective coordination with the Alliance ships.

Cross's responsibility was to fight, freeing the captain to focus on the battlefield. The impact of the weapons and the damage to the *Washington* got him a glare from Okoye, but it was more a shared annoyance at their enemy than disappointment in his performance.

"What the hell is that?" Helm officer Zachary Lee was upset about something on the battle display, and Cross's eyes shifted up to see what it was. Three of the alien ships had a strange line connecting them, made of sparking energy. Where it intersected with other matter, that matter was cut as if by a laser. The two on the end were angling away from the center ship, allowing them to encompass more space with the devastating beams. The one in the middle headed straight for the *Washington*.

"Evasive," Okoye and Cross snapped together. The ship responded quickly despite her injuries, going low and fast to avoid the approaching energy net.

"They've just got all sorts of tricks up their sleeves, don't they," Okoye remarked with forced casualness.

"If they even have sleeves," Cross replied in the same tone.

"Good point, XO. No matter how good their technology might be, how impressive can they be if they don't have sleeves?" Small smiles were quickly stifled by the bridge crew, but Cross saw them before they disappeared.

"Sensors," Cross said, "analyze those ships and see if they differ from the others. It would be good to know whether all their ships can do this, or if we face two different classes of enemy."

"Aye, XO."

Okoye spoke next, "Lieutenant Fitzpatrick, please open a channel to Captain Petryaev."

"Ready." Cross made a motion for the communication officer to include him in the conversation, and she gave him an acknowledgment as she did so.

The Russian came through the headset accompanied by the sounds of his ship in battle. "Yes, Captain? We're a little busy at the moment." Cross heard him issuing commands, and Okoye waited to speak until his voice fell silent.

"Just wanted to give you a warning about the trio with the energy net. I'm sure you've seen them, but they seem to be trying to expand it, and we're concerned that more than those three have the capability. Probably best to stay out of the middle of them. Also, given that the base is evacuated, what are your intentions?"

They heard a loud crashing as the *Beijing* took fire from multiple opponents at once. "We still possess numerical superiority against the enemy, for all the good it seems to be doing us. My commanding admiral believes we can overcome these barbarians. I'm not as confident as he is."

"Admirals are all alike," Okoye responded. "We lost at least ten extra ships because of that attitude last time around."

The channel dropped, replaced with static, as the starbase blew apart.

THE SHOCK WAVE from the rending of the base pulsed outward in all directions, knocking ships aside like rowboats confronted with a hurricane. Unlike the Union starbase, which had been structurally torn asunder, the Marines' destruction combined with the stresses of the gravitic devices caused the power system to suffer a critical cooling failure. That allowed temperatures to increase, slagging all the safeguards that kept the nuclear reaction in check. The design of the system did its job, funneling the explosion outward instead of vertically into the living portions of the base, but secondary explosions were triggered, including the mines that the evacuation teams had left behind. A mere five seconds after the initial explosion, the entire starbase vaporized.

Anyone not buckled in on the *Washington* careened sideways and upward simultaneously as the ship was knocked in the opposite direction. It took only moments for the helm officer to right the vessel, but doing so caused further impacts as people fell to the deck. Alarms sounded at all stations, and when Lieutenant Jacobs reported one third of the ship's compartments were open to space to a greater or lesser degree. "Medical teams are en route to the worst injuries," he finished.

Protected by their command chairs, both Cross and Okoye watched the main display to see the results of the explosion. The toll was heaviest on the AAN ships, as they'd been closer to the base. Half their strength was suddenly gone. The *Beijing*, one of their most powerful vessels, was limping. "The *Beijing* is venting gasses from his engines," Sensors Officer Flores reported.

The enemy had lost multiple ships, including the energy net cluster. Cross pointed this out to Okoye, who responded with a grunt. "At least that's something, but it's certainly not much." The captain watched the display for a few minutes more and then turned to Cross. "Even strength."

"We can't win, Captain, not a fair fight and not now."

Okoye let out a sigh. "Dammit, Cross..." He began, but trailed off. Nonetheless, Cross heard the unintended and unspoken words echo in his soul. If he could travel back in time and undo the mistake that brought them to the enemy's attention, he would do it in a second, regardless of the cost to him. Instead of replying, he met the captain's gaze without flinching.

"It's time we were leaving this party," Okoye said, turning to face forward. "Helm, chart a tunnel jump in three steps so we don't lead them to our base. Tactical, bring our shields to full and if you see an opportunity for a shot as were getting out of here, take it. Communication, open a secure channel to all of our ships and whatever kind you can get to the Alliance forces."

A few moments passed, and then Fitzpatrick said, "Go when ready, Captain"

Okoye cleared his throat. "This is Captain James Okoye of the UAL *Washington, DC.* Our tactical situation here is unwinnable, and I am ordering all Union ships to leave the sector according to designated evacuation plans exactly sixty seconds from my mark. Alliance forces, I offer a temporary truce as we evacuate, and my sensor officer will provide routing information so you may retreat along our path with us. We can worry about settling our differences once we recover from this mess."

He paused, and Cross read the momentary sadness that flickered across his face. "We have all lost today, but we need not lose everything. Mark."

Fitzpatrick cut the channel, and Okoye turned back to Cross. "Last-minute recommendations, XO?"

"None, Captain. It's the right move." He laughed as if at a private joke. *You always make the right move, Captain*—the words he himself left unspoken also echoed in his soul. Okoye reached across and clapped him on the shoulder, not speaking, then turned back.

"Ten seconds to tunnel," Lieutenant Lee announced, and continued counting down from there. Cross was watching the battle display when he said one, expecting to see ships wink out as they did the same. The sound of the tunnel drive built to a crescendo and then failed to finish. Several seconds after they should have been safely away, they were still waiting for the drive to engage. A look at the battle display showed the problem was universal.

"What the—" Okoye said, as the communication officer announced, "All ships are reporting failure of tunnel drive."

Kate, newly arrived on the bridge, conferred with Flores. After several seconds, a new image appeared on the main monitor.

"Captain, watch this. This is the moment we should have entered the tunnel." On the screen, small pinpoints of light grew to an almost blinding level, then decreased, disappearing again among the blackness of space. "Our theory is that they somehow absorbed the energy that would have opened the tunnels. No way of telling whether this is permanent or single use, but we still need to wait for all of our drives to reset."

Okoye responded quickly, "Cross, share that information with all the other ships. Helm, go evasive but set up a defensive battle line at this location." He marked something on his display screen. "All ships with full shields and minimal injury make up the front rank. Those that sustained significant damage and need time to repair, hide behind it. Echo these orders to the *Beijing*. Hopefully the Alliance forces will join us, but if not, we'll do the best we can."

He swiveled in his chair to look at the weapons officer. "Walsh, I want you to keep them running, make it impossible for them to coordinate an attack. Lots of torpedoes, unpredictable fire rate, unpredictable targets. Get it done." The burly man got a happy look in his eyes, nodded once, and turned back to his controls.

"Chief Jannik to the bridge, please, Lieutenant Fitzpatrick." He turned to Kate. "Flynn, you two figure out a way for us to get out of the sector. I don't care what it is, but we need an exit strategy, and we need it fast. Our ability to defend against these bastards for an extended duration is minimal, and we can't outrun them in normal space."

Closing down his communication channel, Cross said, "The Alliance forces are searching for their own solutions to the tunnel problem, and will join us in a united defense. Captain Petryaev had the same idea to keep the enemy off balance, and the Alliance ships will work toward that goal." Okoye nodded.

The delaying tactics were effective, keeping the enemy focused on protecting themselves rather than making a coherent attack on the defensive position. Even so, a pair of ships, evading incoming fire, swooped in and destroyed one of the outermost defenders. Okoye reformed the line to fill in the gap, and sent them scurrying back with a full salvo of torpedoes on their tails, but the damage had been done. The enemies were chipping away at them, and there was no telling how long they could last.

Jannik stepped from the lift, and both Cross and Okoye pointed him over to Kate. Seeing the engineer on the bridge sparked a synapse in Cross's brain, and he turned to speak in a murmur to the Captain. "A beacon. We fire a beacon and see if it makes it out. That would at least tell us if these things are single use, or multi-use."

Okoye gave him a smile with something that resembled approval in it. "Good thinking. Make it happen."

Cross unbuckled and moved to the tactical station. In quiet tones, he told the officer what he wanted, and less than a minute later, the missile was jettisoned from the *Washington* and engaged its rocket drive to push it toward tunnel position. Cross, Okoye, and Jacobs all watched as it reached its terminal point and activated its tunnel drive. It failed to make the transition, defeated by more glowing pinpoints, and became just a dead hunk of metal traveling on inertial momentum.

Cross sent a message to Kate and Jannik, rather than disturbing their conversation, and returned to his seat. On the screen, ships fired weapons, other ships dived and dodged, and things looked bleaker by the moment for the defenders, whose ability to defend was being depleted with each torpedo spent.

Finally, Kate waved at the captain, and Cross joined him as they all gathered around the display at the sensor station.

"You're not going to like this," Jannik began. "Hell, I don't like it one bit myself, but it may be all we have."

Kate called up a display that showed a network of what looked like tubes connecting points in space. Cross recognized it from his time at the Academy.

"The wormhole network," he asked.

"Aye, LC, the wormhole network. The problem is, since the creation of the tunnel drive, only ships like the *DC* which were retro-fitted from wormhole drives can access it. The newer ships only have tunnel drives. There's no way of knowing how many of our ships and how many of the Alliance ships are wormhole capable."

"You're suggesting that we should probably abandon the majority of the ships here, Chief." Okoye's voice was iron.

"Aye, that I am, Captain."

"No other options?"

Kate and Jannik looked at one another, then back at Okoye. "No, sir," Kate said. The look on her face said everything she didn't put into words.

The silence that followed stretched until an incoming torpedo shattered it with devastating effect.

CHAPTER THIRTY-SIX

Cross picked himself up off the deck—bruised, battered, and bleeding from a cut over his left eye. His ears rang, and he couldn't remember how he'd gotten injured. He rose to his knees, and the ship spun around him. When it stopped spinning, he pulled himself all the way to his feet and fell into his chair. His vision stabilized, and he surveyed the smoking bridge of the *Washington*.

As his senses came back to him, he looked in a panic for Kate. She was fine, as was Jannik, although both had been sprayed with shards from the exploding displays. Fortunately, they were made of a glass designed to shatter in non-jagged fashion, leaving the deck littered with interlocking transparent octagons.

A commotion to his left caught his attention, and he turned to see the helm officer kneeling beside a prone body. Everything snapped back into real-time as he realized that it was Captain Okoye lying there motionless. He moved to assist, but was waved off by Lieutenant Lee, who was already calling for a medical team to come to the bridge. "Nothing you can do, XO. He needs a doctor."

Cross nodded and belatedly started to strap himself into his chair. Then it hit him, and he went blank for the tiniest moment before moving to the captain's chair. He reached up to trigger his headset only to discover that it had broken in two and pulled it from his head. "Fitzpatrick," he yelled over the sound of alarms and fire suppression systems. "Open a channel to Captain Petryaev."

Several seconds later, she replied, "Go for *Beijing.*"

"Dima," he said, "have you found a solution to the tunnel block yet?"

"Negative."

"We have one, but it's not great." As he was speaking, Cross reviewed the battle schematic, which showed the same standoff it had before the torpedoes' impacts. However, with each successful strike, their window of survival was closing. "How many of your ships can access the wormhole network?"

Dima laughed without humor. "I'm surprised a youngster like you even knows about that. I'd have to check to be sure but I imagine maybe half. More likely only a third."

Cross ran his hand through his hair, pushing it out of his face and streaking blood across his forehead. "About the same here. All the new ships have a single tunnel drive. Only old hawks, like the *Washington,* have both after a retrofit."

"Exactly. The *Beijing,* as well."

"We won't survive until the tunnel drives are reset to give it another try, according to our latest data." Cross looked over, and Kate gave him a nod. "I recommend all ships that can exit the system by the wormhole network should do so, and the rest of our forces fight a delaying action to protect their escape."

"To leave all those ships behind, though—" Dima began, but Cross cut him off.

"Honor be damned, Dima. We need every asset we can get to deal with the next attack that these bastards throw at us. And that includes you and the *Beijing.*"

"Why is it you telling me this, Cross? Where is Captain Okoye?"

"Injured. Status unknown. I'm in command of the *Washington,* and there's really no time to determine who's in charge of the Union forces at this point. I say we go. Do you agree?"

While he waited for an answer, he looked at the faces around the bridge, all of whom were staring at him. He didn't see support. He didn't see condemnation. He saw recognition that it was his duty to make the choices he was trying to make.

"I agree, Cross. We will do this thing."

"Very good. Let's regroup at one of our bases. I formally re-offer you a cessation of hostilities between the Alliance and the Union for at least the next fourteen days. That'll give us time to figure out what to do next."

"On behalf of the AAN forces deployed in the sector, I accept."

"Navigational data coming to you shortly. We move in one minute and thirty seconds from my mark." He paused to allow his tactical officer to set the timer and then said, "Mark. See you on the other side."

"Affirmative. *Beijing* out."

"Helm, plot a two-step transit to the forward-most UAL base. Then transmit that information to all our ships, and all Alliance ships. Fitzpatrick, give me a channel to all of our forces in the sector."

He waited a moment for the connection to be established, then took a deep breath and delivered the most painful message of his life.

"This is Lieutenant Commander Anderson Cross, acting captain of the *Washington, DC*. With our tunnel drives defeated, only one possibility remains for us. All ships that have the technology to use the wormhole network are instructed to follow the navigational orders that my helm officer has just transmitted to you. All ships without a wormhole drive, you must cover our retreat. If you succeed in defeating or evading the enemy, head to the nearest UAL starbase at your best speed. Possibly, when you get some distance, your tunnel drives will again be active." He grimaced. This was far from the glorious adventure he'd always hoped the captain's chair would bring.

"The Alliance forces that lack the wormhole drive will stand with you. Coordinate your actions where possible. Make the bastards pay as dearly as you can for what they have done here." He had no idea how to finish. Captain Okoye would have something inspirational to say at this moment that would carry the spirits of the sailors forward into the fight. Words failed to arrive, and he was left with only those that had been haunting him since the return from alien space.

"I, we, will do our best to be worthy of your efforts. *Washington* out."

He saw that the clock was at forty-five seconds, and looked around at the bridge crew, their eyes still locked on him. "Don't waste this. Do everything you can to deliver us home in one piece and I promise you—I swear to you—we will find a way to beat them." He paused, his nostrils flaring, his white knuckles gripping the arms of his chair. "Get to work."

Everyone turned to their controls and did as he asked. He was powerless to improve the situation, so he sat and watched and waited. When the timer counted down to zero, the ships with wormhole drives detached from the main force and reoriented to fly at full speed toward the opening. Unfamiliar sounds echoed through the ship as the machinery that made wormhole access possible spun up. Cross had never been a part of a wormhole transit, although they ran diagnostics on the equipment regularly to make sure it still reported as functional.

"Time to entry?"

"One minute, twenty-three seconds, sir," Lieutenant Lee replied.

"Jacobs, before we leave this system, I want every single torpedo we carry to be on its way toward an enemy ship. Relay that to all the wormhole ships."

"Affirmative."

"Jannik, do you need to get below?"

"No, my people can handle this. I'd like to stay and see it for myself. I've never been on the bridge for one."

"Well then, find somewhere to strap yourself in please." He looked at Kate. "Lieutenant Commander Flynn you are hereby assigned to the station of acting executive officer on the *Washington, DC*. Take your position." She nodded, and he gave her a sickly smile as she came over and strapped herself in slightly behind and to the left of him. He turned to her and beckoned for her to lean over.

In a whisper, he said, "What am I forgetting? What else can we do?"

She shook her head at him. "You've done all you can. We've done all we can. All that's left to us is to retreat, regroup, and find a new answer to these beings."

He leaned back with a sigh and rocked to fit into his seat. Strangely, it had always felt just fine to him when he was third in command.

As the timer clicked down to zero, he said, "Open it up."

On the main screen, an orifice in space appeared, triggered by the release of a specific frequency of energy from a trio of dishes mounted around the front of the ship. He took a deep breath and blew it out. "In we go. Execute."

FOUR DAYS LATER, the ships that had escaped the massacre were docked at Starbase 13. They had taken the wormhole transit to the next stop, then tunneled to the nearest base. Cross was sure that everyone breathed the same sigh of relief that he did when the tunnel drives functioned.

They'd gotten a day and a half of quality rest and relaxation, protected by the fleet elements stationed in the sector. All of the ships, Union and Alliance alike, were undergoing replenishment. Their crews were on shore leave with starbase personnel acting as skeleton commands aboard the Union ships. The Alliance ships preferred to maintain their own staff, but also rotated personnel onto the base for downtime.

Cross was in his most impressive dress uniform, and Kate was beside him in hers.

"How are they treating you down there," he said into his headset, which was connected to Captain James Okoye.

"Oh, you know, a hospital is a hospital is a hospital. These damned doctors aren't going to let me leave anytime soon though."

"Well, you broke your back and your brain," Kate commented. Even with the impressive technology available to the medical teams, brain trauma and a broken back were not things that healed quickly. For the time being, Okoye was a consultant, not a combatant.

"The former bothers me more than the latter," Okoye replied.

"A sure sign of brain damage, if I ever heard one," Cross quipped.

Cross and Kate fell silent as they walked through the doors into the meeting hall. It was identical to the space where they'd met the admirals the last time, just a little dingier and a bit more well-used. The same could be said of the admirals themselves.

"A very different bunch of uniforms here today, Captain" Cross murmured just loud enough for the microphone to pick it up. Only a third of the admirals that had been present at Starbase 14 had survived the attack and consequent explosion of the *Toronto*. A number of new admirals had been seated, and there were also several empty chairs.

This time the examination table had three seats behind it, and Cross's face broke into a guarded grin as he saw Dima Petryaev enter from the opposite set of doors. He and Kate walked over to the AAN officer and shook hands, accompanied by hard looks of shared commitment. In the back of his mind, Cross wondered what the admirals would make of that. They had not yet chosen to discuss the peace terms that first Okoye, and later Cross, had offered.

"Please be seated," the admiral in charge of the council said. The display screen on a side wall lit up, and an image of Captain Okoye appeared. He looked relatively dapper for a man with a broken back, and the dark blue bandage around his head kind of suited him, Cross thought. "We welcome Captain Okoye to these proceedings by remote, and also welcome Captain First Rank Dima Petryaev of the

Allied Asian Nations Navy." Both captains nodded as their names were mentioned.

"The purpose of this meeting is to ascertain the events of the recent debacle in which Captain Okoye and Lieutenant Commander Cross embroiled elements of our fleet. We will also determine our path going forward." Okoye's expression didn't change, but Cross jerked a little at the word "debacle."

"If I may be permitted to address this assembly," Dima Petryaev said, smoothly cutting in, "I believe I can answer some of the questions that you no doubt have. When I offered an early warning about the attack on your starbase, it came with conditions. I had your officers over a barrel, and they were forced to agree to return the favor if they discovered something. By doing so, they saved many lives in the attack on your base, and many lives in the attack on my base. It is a testament to the honor and bravery of your men—and women" he said, gesturing at Kate, "—that they fulfilled this agreement. Treating one another as allies, rather than perpetuating the enmity of decades of war, is necessarily the first step toward creating a united front against this alien menace." He looked each admiral in the eye after finishing, one by one, then sat without another word.

The admirals looked at each other, and then up at Okoye's image. "Is this true, Captain?"

"True enough."

"And you, Lieutenant Commander? Do you testify that this is true?"

"I do."

"Very well. Does anyone wish to ask further questions of the officers assembled before we declare this question closed?"

One of the admirals opened his mouth to speak, but quickly shut it again when his nearest comrade glared at him.

"On to the next issue, then. How shall we go forward to confront them?" He squinted at the small display screen in front of him. "Our experts, such as they are, suggest that the likelihood of a larger alien invasion is somewhere between probable and imminent. Would you all agree with this position?"

Kate put her arms on the table, folding her hands together. "I have had perhaps the greatest opportunity of anyone in the UAL to examine these aliens at close range. Although I wouldn't attempt to say that I understand how they think, it seems clear to me that they completed a probing attack against us, and a probing attack against the other dominant grouping of our species. In the reverse situation, it's very much what we would do prior to a full-scale invasion." She paused and swallowed hard. "It's my personal belief that they will be coming, they will be coming soon, and they will be coming in force."

CHAPTER THIRTY-SEVEN

"Would you characterize the battle as a success?"

Kraada Tak sat in a large comfortable chair made of the skin of some animal native to one of their conquered planets. A delicate glass full of amber liquid rested in his hand, and he swirled it while he waited for his answer.

"I would, Uncle," Indraat Vray responded. She, too, was seated in luxury and equipped with the burning liquor prized by the upper echelon of the Xroeshyn. She took a measured sip while waiting for her uncle's next query.

"I would hope for there to always be complete honesty between us, Niece. What I'm about to tell you should be kept strictly between the two of us." Indraat arched an eyebrow, as if to indicate that sharing any information she received wasn't even in the realm of possibility, and he should be aware of that already. At least that's how Kraada interpreted it.

"We lost more ships than I expected, and this has me concerned. Drovaa Jat, with the support of the emperor, has judged this enemy less dangerous than those we've faced in the past, and plans to commit a comparatively low number of resources to its destruction.

While I understand that his mandate includes the defense of all our people, and that we cannot predict who we might come up against in our explorations, I worry that his investment in this endeavor is not as strong as it could be."

Indraat shrugged. "And is that all that bothers you, Uncle?"

"You are very perceptive, Vray. There is one thing more. Drovaa has deliberately placed you and your ship on the front line, and shall continue to do so, to ensure you will be blamed for anything that goes wrong. You must protect yourself against this in every way possible, as it will have dangerous consequences for the both of us."

Indraat laughed, surprising Kraada. "As a member of your family, and as a woman in charge of a starship, I am *always* in that position, Uncle. This is nothing new." She leaned forward in her seat, placed her drink on the table, and rested her forearms on her knees, meeting his gaze. "Whether we succeed, or whether we fail, our family will emerge in a positive light. You can count on me for that."

Kraada gave her a thin smile in response. "That may require you to set aside your personal honor, Niece."

"What is personal honor compared to the honor of our family, and service to the gods?"

"You are truly my blood, Vray, and I'm proud to say it is so." He checked the clock on the wall and levered himself out of the all too comfortable chair. "It's time for me to battle my friendly foe yet again. I'll have a message for you before you leave. You should return to your ship and be ready to go, for events will move fast after this meeting."

A SHORT WHILE LATER, Kraada and Drovaa were once more in the small conference chamber beside the throne room, laying out their perspectives for the emperor that neither of them truly respected. "We've achieved a decisive victory against this enemy with minimal investment of resources," the marshal offered, "and this should be our plan going forward. I propose to allocate no more than two-eighths of our forces to this invasion."

Kraada was already shaking his head before Drovaa finished speaking. "This is our promised foe. We cannot afford to lose even a battle, much less the overall war. We should commit twice the resources we need, in order to guarantee a swift victory."

Drovaa faced him and raised his arms in disbelief. "And if we do, Hierarch, who will defend that which we have already claimed? Who will protect our home planet against invaders known and unknown? Would you leave our emperor, and our people, defenseless in the face of whatever enemies may appear?"

"Of course not," Kraada replied. "Our technological might and our superiority in tactics and strategy will carry us through any enemy that comes our way. We can easily commit at least half of our forces, endangering nothing we currently hold. You are too reticent to risk your ships, my friend. This is a holy war, ordained by the gods."

"Ordained by you, you mean," Drovaa said, accusation in his tone.

Kraada let the silence linger long enough to become uncomfortable. Then, softly, calmly, he offered a reply, "Yes, ordained by me. The chosen leader of our faith. The privilege and the responsibility are both mine, and I shirk neither. Can you say the same, Marshal?"

The emperor raised a hand and cleared his throat. "It will not do for the leaders of the church and the military to be divided. Let us not devolve into personal attacks. I am confident each of you is fulfilling your duties in as honest, true, and complete a fashion as you can." He turned to the marshal.

"DROVAA, realistically, what is the largest force available to commit to this invasion and still defend our people?"

The marshal sighed and took a moment to consider. "Your grace, I believe I could reallocate as much as three-eighths of our total ships to this endeavor, but no more. We have a large territory to protect, and it would be irresponsible in the extreme to leave our colonies, bases, and home system improperly defended."

The emperor turned to Kraada, "Will this meet your needs, Hierarch?"

He had reviewed all the potential results of this meeting ahead of time and had his answer close at hand. "I believe it will, if we include a fortress to act as our forward base." Drovaa's head snapped around, and he glared at Kraada.

"We do not have any fortresses available for this assault, Kraada."

"I don't agree that is the case, Drovaa. What about the *Sapphire Sky*?"

Drovaa's eyes narrowed, and the grimace that Kraada was sure lurked behind his lips failed to materialize, but only just barely. "*Sapphire Sky* is permanently detailed to the home system, you know that."

"I know it's convenient for it to be so, since you consider it your own command. However, I would suggest that everything you can accomplish on board that ship, you can accomplish on the ground, freeing it for the invasion. Alternately, I suppose, we could detail more ships to the invasion force, rather than bringing them to the home system to replace the fortress."

Drovaa's lips twisted in defeat. "Fine, Hierarch. You may have the *Sapphire Sky* for your invasion."

"And three-eighths of our ships."

"Yes," Drovaa forced out between gritted teeth.

"Well done, gentlemen," the emperor said, toasting them with the ever-present drink in his hand. "Everything is better when we can get along, isn't it?"

The leaders of church and military glared at each other. Kraada knew that he had shattered the fragile bonds that had connected them by usurping Drovaa's authority, and they were friends no longer.

MANY HOURS LATER, after the premature victory dinner the emperor demanded they suffer through, Kraada was safely ensconced in his own office, his priestly garments replaced with comfortable clothes for lounging. The remains of a small plate of fruit sat abandoned nearby, as he bent to his task.

He had retrieved his official stationery, a heavy parchment embossed with the seal of the church. He wrote in a flowing script, a letter of well wishes to his niece as she departed for war. Occasionally, he paused to check the book beside him, and then continued to write. Anyone intercepting this message would find it to be the blandest of communications.

Those who possessed the proper cipher, on the other hand, could read rather more into it. A simple word substitution code, it required both sender and recipient to have copies of the same book, and naturally, to know which book was being used. The key to the book was in the date—for the family had a text for each day of the month. The number of words in the first sentence, which was never part of the hidden meaning of the message, indicated the page on which to start.

In Indraat's case, since she was aboard ship, her copies were electronic. They had been carefully scanned from the original print versions, an affectation she'd been teased about more than once by fellow officers. Once decoded, it read:

"Remember your vow. Tensions are high. Sacrifice of opposing representative may be required. Act on own initiative. Full support."

The use of the family code, combined with the flowing script of his own hand, would be enough to authenticate the message when it reached his niece. After waiting a proper interval for the ink to dry, he rolled it, dripped wax upon it and impressed the signet of the hierarch. He then slid it carefully into a ceremonial tube and called for a courier.

When one arrived, Kraada was standing, staring into the fireplace. He turned and handed the junior priest the tube. "This goes from your hands to the hands of Indraat Vray, Commander of the *Ruby Rain*, at the spaceport. Deliver it as quickly as possible." He nodded and left, quick footsteps receding as he ran from the cathedral.

Kraada paced, worrying. He hadn't intended to push things so far with the marshal. It was important to Kraada's long-term strategy that Drovaa remain on the board, and he would've preferred he remain an ally. But no matter. The playing field was always influx, and only the bold emerged victorious. Armed with that thought, he retired to his bedroom to seek guidance in the *Dhadas*, and to consider his options three and four moves further along in this most vital of games.

CHAPTER THIRTY-EIGHT

The meeting space was dingy, almost deliberately low-technology. The AAN admirals conversed among themselves, standing around in groups of two or three, smoking cigarettes, cigars, pipes, and anything else that would help keep them awake and functional for just a few hours longer. Dima sipped his tea, sat in the corner, and waited for the start of the battle.

Several other first rank captains were present, and as they circulated, shaking hands and making sure the admirals knew who they were, each of them stopped by to greet Dima. He'd trained at least half of them. The rest respected him from the times their paths had crossed. Guarded looks transmitted silent questions, but he had no replies to offer. Not yet.

He had a feeling, though, that he would wind up doing things his superiors might not like, unless they rose above the collected actions of the admirals of the last century. He wasn't optimistic about this outcome.

Finally, the senior officers found their way to the rectangular table at the front of the room, and the captains took their seats in the audience with their staff members and other lower military rank officers.

"Comrades," a large man with bushy mutton chops and a matching shock of white hair on his head began, "we've received reports that the alien enemy discovered by the *Gagarin* has again entered human space. Our furthest pickets launched tunnel beacons, then retreated into adjoining sectors. They are taking it in turn to creep into maximum sensor range, then send us updates each half day."

Admiral Sergey Laskin folded his hands on the table in front of him. "Here's what we're sure of. They *are* here, and they are here in substantial force. Our first estimate is there are over 200 ships in that sector. If we were to scramble all of ours, we still couldn't meet them in a one-to-one basis."

Murmurs arose in the crowd, and the admiral held up a hand for quiet.

"We have two advantages here. First, we have a lot of space to trade for time. Earth is a long way away from their current position, and there are substantial defenses between here and there. Our newest ships are at our rearmost shipyards, being retrofitted with wormhole drives so we won't be blocked by that enemy tactic again. Vessels that can use the network are moving up, and will rally here within three days before deploying forward. We don't expect an attack anytime soon, which is our second advantage."

"Our pickets report the aliens appear to be orienting toward Union territory. It's our intelligence division's best guess that they will continue along that front, rather than dividing their forces and attacking both of us. This provides the opportunity to continue to retrofit our ships and to husband our resources until we see a moment to engage in a decisive strike against them, alone or in partnership with the Union."

"Per the provisions in our current nonaggression-treaty with the UAL, we are sharing information with them, and they are preparing their defensive strategies against the invaders. In the meantime, we will bring ourselves to maximum effectiveness for when the enemy turns to us."

Another admiral took over, "Each of you should be sure your ship is fully provisioned and rearmed. Resources will be shifted back from our forward bases, and transports are already delivering supplies and personnel away from the front. We don't plan to abandon those installations, but they will have the minimum number of people necessary to fight, and not a single person more." She gestured, and a display screen lit up in the far side of the room. "From a tactical viewpoint, there isn't much more we *can* do. We recommend those of you with fighters recalibrate their sensors to find the small projectiles that the enemy has been using. Obviously, those that attached to the bases are gravitic in nature, and it's probably safe to assume the ones that defeated our tunnel drives are as well. A sensor update has been issued to improve detection of gravity-related anomalies."

The first admiral spoke up again, "We will now take questions."

Dima stood at attention, his hands clasped behind him. "Respectfully, admirals, are we really going to just stand back and watch as the enemy takes on the Union forces?"

Mutton chops blew through his mustache and gave Dima a look that had probably withered many a young officer over the years. "Captain First Rank Petryaev, everyone in this room well knows your experience and success, and your opinion is heard and respected. However, each division of the military has come to the same conclusion. Adding our forces to theirs right now will be far less effective than biding our time in preparation, waiting for an opening to exploit."

"The prudent thing isn't always the right choice, sir," Dima's voice cast a chill in the room.

"Nonetheless, Captain, we will do that prudent thing and protect the lives of our people for as long as possible. We will not invite our own destruction. We will, instead, gather data and try to find a different route to victory."

"And if the Union should be destroyed by the enemy before we discover it, so much the better, right?"

"What are you implying, Captain?"

"I'm implying nothing, sir. I am stating, for the record, that our decision not to support the other half of humanity at this moment in our history is myopic, ill-advised, and cowardly."

The admirals rose as one and Laskin spoke a final time, "This meeting is over. You, Captain Petryaev, are dismissed. Return to your ship and do *not* let us see you again anytime soon."

Dima stood unbowed, his eyes locked on the admirals as they left the room.

"DO YOU BELIEVE THAT NONSENSE?" Captain Ikumi Shoda of the *Osaka* asked her fellow captains over the comm channel. This virtual gathering of Dima and those officers who'd served under him and were now in their own commands was inevitable, given the state position of the AAN leadership.

"It's insanity," Captain Do Dae Han replied. His ship, the *Busan*, was a match to the *Beijing*, and was one of the last ships commissioned with a wormhole drive. "We're abandoning our only opportunity to overwhelm them with superior numbers."

Dima cleared his throat, and the chatter fell silent. "Gentlemen, ladies, we're at a moment of decision. Our admirals have made their opinions clear. I, for one, do *not* agree with them. Despite what has gone before, we are now allies with the United Atlantic League, and standing by while they're attacked is not what an ally does."

"To do anything other than stand by would be treason, would it not?"

"Hiroji, as you well know, there's treason, and then there's treason. I have enough influence with the staff in the admirals' office to arrange a patrol schedule that would concentrate those of us who are of, shall we say, like minds, near the area where the next battle will most likely be fought. However, it's true we could be held account-able as traitors if the admiralty chose to do so."

There was a jumble of crosstalk on the channel, and Dima took a bracing sip of the tea he'd spiked with spicy liquor. If ever there was a moment for spirits, this was it.

Finally, the chatter died down, and Captain Shoda spoke into the quiet. "Even if we're in the right place, at the right time, do you think we can be of benefit? We're only a couple dozen ships, at best."

Dima let slip an involuntary growl of frustration. "I don't know. I really do not. We are in uncharted territory here. What I am positive of, though, is that we abandon our honor if we abandon our allies. It's a fine distinction, and the admiralty would say we abandon our honor by not following orders. I—"

Dima's voice was drowned out by laughter from across the chan-nel. Captain Do spoke for them all when he said, "And we're all aware of how you feel about orders you haven't personally given, Captain Petryaev."

Dima joined in the mirth and spoke again when it subsided, "Fair enough, although all of you should be far politer to your elders. As I was saying, I believe it's the right thing to do, and I *will* do this thing. Will you do it with me?"

They agreed, every single one of them.

Much later, in the hours where night turned to morning, Dima sat alone in his cabin, behind the ebony pieces of a meticulously carved chessboard. The opponent's forces were arranged in a classic mid-game formation in which black was heavily outnumbered. He leaned back in his chair and let his mind explore how to deal with his opponent's numerical superiority. A smile grew as he saw an oppor-tunity, and he moved pieces around the board, running through moves and countermoves at a fast pace. When the field was clear, and only white was left standing, he stood, sighed, and refilled his tea.

"It's going to be a long night," he muttered to himself as he reset the pieces to try a different solution, knowing the right one was lurking in the dark and quiet part of his mind, and only relentless effort would bring it into the light.

CHAPTER THIRTY-NINE

Cross shook Petryaev's hand as he entered through the *Washington's* airlock. "Welcome to my ship, Captain"

"Please, call me Dima. I think we are beyond most formalities here, are we not?"

"Do you mean because we are both technically traitors at this moment?"

"Exactly," Dima said, inclining his head.

"Well, then, you should continue to call me Cross. Everyone does." He gestured toward the hallway leading off to the left. "I thought we'd keep things informal and meet in engineering. Our chief engineer and my executive officer await us."

A short time later they were seated, drinks in hand. Jannik took a sip of his and grimaced.

"Listen, I'm all for a nice cup of tea, but if ever a moment called for a stiff drink, this is it." As an icebreaker, it shattered the tension as everyone engaged in a somewhat rueful round of laughter.

"Cross, Chief, Lieutenant Commander—"

"Kate, please."

Dima nodded and continued, "Those above me have decided that we should only preserve our own people, while awaiting an advantageous position to strike during your battle with the alien invasion. Several of my captains and I are in agreement that this is shortsighted and believe it's possible to influence matters enough to put us near the incursion point so we can act in support. I cannot, however, promise how many ships we'll be able to provide, or when they may arrive."

Cross drummed his fingers and sighed quietly. "I must admit, I hoped the news you were bringing would be full of a few more ships than that," he said. "Say, your entire fleet, maybe."

Dima shrugged. "I'm sure it's the same in your service as it is in mine. The higher you go up, the less open your mind becomes."

"Amen," said Jannik. "That's why I've never made it past chief. Too smart. Not like the lieutenant commander there."

Cross gave him a long-suffering glare and turned to Kate. "What's the latest?"

"Pickets are patrolling all the likely incursion areas, spread in an arc that should give us the most response time regardless of the vector they come in upon. That assumes a great deal, but we can't defend all of space, either."

Dima agreed. "We face a similar challenge in considering how to best respond to this alien threat. Until we understand how their technology works, it's almost impossible to predict what they'll do. However, they have provided a few clues."

"Do tell, Dima," Cross said, pushing his sudden hopefulness down deep where no one could see it.

"Just as we can analyze one another by examining strategies and tactics through the lens of a common frame of experience, like a chessboard, I've been trying to do the same with our alien friends. Ignoring for a second the advantages of technology, and their motivations which we cannot even guess at, there are several important factors we must take into account."

Dima stood and walked over to a display surface covered with notes in Jannik's scraggly handwriting. He looked over for permission, and the chief engineer gave him a brief nod. Dima cleared the screen and sketched out each point as he made it.

"First, let's assume that the two attacks so far were testing strikes. In the first, they sent a minor force in to test our response to their tactics and one particular technology, the gravitic mines. They succeeded in this effort, by suffering fewer losses than you did and destroying the starbase. In that battle, they arranged their forces in subgroups to support one another, and laid a sophisticated trap that almost peeled off one of your own defensive ships." He didn't look at Cross, but he shrunk in his chair anyway and looked up through half-lidded eyes. Dima continued to write, never releasing his military bearing or perfect posture.

"In the second, they dispensed with pairs and worked with larger groups, to lesser effect. They brought more decks, and tried a different tactic, boarding the starbase before destroying it. In so doing, they tested our Marines as well as our ships. They also deployed a new surprise, no doubt based upon their analysis of our own technology, defeating our tunnel drives."

Jannik interrupted, "You think they whipped those up in response to what they saw from us? That seems awfully quick."

Dima turned to face him and shrugged. "There's no real way to tell whether they had an existing tool they could repurpose, if they've seen the tunnel drive before and already had a defense built against it, or if they were working from zero. We can't make assumptions about that."

Jannik nodded, satisfied by the other man's logic.

The Russian's deep voice began again, "Closer analysis shows that there were two ships hanging back during the second attack, coordinating the actions of larger groups. When we examine the numbers of both battles, we discovered that the enemy most likely thinks in sets of eight. Two command ships overseeing squadrons of eight ships each. If they are true to their escalation, the next advance should have thirty-two ships, and we would expect at least one ship to coordinate the actions of four sub-command vessels. As there are over two hundred decks in their staging area, by our estimates, this wouldn't be a difficult force for them to commit."

Cross snorted out a sharp laugh. "No offense, Dima but there's a lot of assumption going on there."

"Too true. But what else do we have at this point?" Dima sat again in his seat at the table. "At the very least, we should consider two plans, one for if they bring thirty-two ships, and one for if they bring sixty-four ships."

"And if they bring more, what then," Kate asked.

Cross supplied the only logical answer, "Retreat, as fast as we can."

AN HOUR LATER, they'd moved on to what Jannik considered real drinks, and they dug into the options for dealing with the potential invasion forces. Dima had taken off his jacket and loosened his tie, and the other officers had achieved similar levels of comfort with their own attires.

Dima pointed at Cross. "You're basing your plans on surprise. There's no way we can gain that against the alien threat. They're the invaders. They'll know what's coming. Improvisational tactics won't suffice as they did in the previous battles, given their numerical superiority."

"Dammit." Cross smacked his hand on the table. "You're right, I know. Why do you have to be right? Is there no way to get more of your people to join us?"

Dima shook his head. "I can only rely on those that I trained. In this area, there are only eight."

Cross looked over at Kate, who shook her head as well. "We'll have twenty, maybe twenty-four if the enemy waits long enough. After that, though, expect at least two weeks before the first ships being refitted are ready for battle. Until then, they can only serve as our defense force for a retreat."

"Jannik. Something in your bag of tricks to help us here?"

"We can apply the sensor upgrades to all the ships in the fleet. I can also provide a copy to you, Dima, if you agree to keep it only among those you're bringing." Dima gestured his agreement. Jannik reached up to scratch his skin through his beard. "That really only gives an advantage against their smaller mines and tunnel drive blockers, though. I don't have anything to help with their shields, or to make ours more effective against their weapons. On the offensive side, I have something in mind, but I can't promise it will work. My people are designing it right now. It's not ready for sharing."

Cross knew better than to push his chief engineer. "Okay, okay. So, there are several things we must accomplish. First, we need to blunt their initial attack and hold them in the engagement sector. We can't let them run about our systems in force, which means we need to engage as many of them as possible. Second, we have to figure out a way to not die while doing it." He banged his forehead on the table. "Well, that's simple. We've got this all figured out."

This drew a few laughs, and a teasing comment from Kate, "You're in charge now, Cross. You have to maintain your image for the troops. No putting your head down on the table."

Dima looked up, clearly thinking about something. "That's *it*, Kate. The leaders. That's the one thing we don't know, how the aliens will act in the absence of those ships coordinating the battle. If we lost most of our commanders, we would retreat and regroup."

"We would do the same," Cross said thoughtfully. "But they'll be at the rear. So how do we dive into them without getting ripped to pieces on the way?"

They looked at one another and found no answers lurking in the space between.

"WELL, we've made good progress, anyway," Dima said, standing. "It's time for the *Beijing* to get to his designated post before my admirals discover that I'm not where I ought to be." He shook hands around the table, and then asked, "Would you like to see my ship before we go, Cross?"

"Of course, Captain Petryaev."

As the two men entered the *Beijing*, Dima's executive officer came up to them carrying a small rectangular object. Dima nodded, and the officer opened the equipment case, displaying the contents. An array of computer chips and blocky devices lay inside. She closed the case, set it down at their feet, saluted Dima, and departed.

"There are so many things, Cross, that we don't know about one another. However, I believe in my heart that this is a time for open honesty and trust. In here are the specifications for every equipment system where we estimate we have an advantage over your forces. Provide it to your chief engineer, and he should be able to make improvements to your ship immediately. Also included is a decoding device that will allow us to communicate together, and you to communicate with the other ships in my group."

"I propose that going forward, if an attack is in your space, you will coordinate our combined efforts. If it is in our space, I will coordinate our combined efforts. Wherever possible, we will collaborate to determine strategy and tactics."

Cross nodded and extended his hand. "Regardless of what our higher-ups say, truce until all of this is over?"

Dima shook it, hard, and gripped Cross's forearm with his other hand. "And longer, if we can make it stick."

"That's a goal worth surviving for, Captain. Together, we'll give these bastards some surprises."

"That we will, Lieutenant Commander, that we will."

CHAPTER FORTY

"Dammit," Kate said, putting her face down on the table display in front of her. "Our survey maps are the worst. Who did they assign to do this? Academy freshman? Anyone with half a brain would've done a much more systematic job."

Jannik's expression was turned away from her, but Kate was pretty sure he was smiling or quietly laughing at her. To be honest, her histrionics were more theater than anything. The frustration, though, was real.

He spoke, "Well, my girl, we only have what we have, so it'll have to do."

Kate sighed and lifted her head from the table. "You're right. I know you're right. But still, if we could travel back in time and tell these people to do a better job, that would be a lovely thing. Why were we so bad at this?"

Jannik looked thoughtful and scratched his chin. "Well, since you ask, we never developed the skill. Most of our maps were, shall we say, 'creatively licensed' from the Alliance."

"What?" Kate stared at him. "Are you serious?"

"Of course. What officer worth his salt wouldn't find a better option than sending probe after probe out into distant space if it could be avoided? One of our early ships liberated the exploration records from an Alliance ship before he was scuttled. That data formed the basis of our exploration plans, so we sent out far fewer probes and survey teams than you might think. We were looking for colony spaces, not exploring the universe the way the Alliance was."

Kate's words resonated with forced casualness, "Hey, Jannik. I know it would've been unethical to do so, but I don't suppose we saved a copy of the data we pulled from the AAN starbase before we handed it over to them? You know, just for the sake of curiosity."

"For general edification, you mean, something like that?"

"Yes, that's a good word. Edification. You know, to understand how other people think, or the things they've seen, that sort of thing?"

"Well, as you mentioned, it would be absolutely unethical, so it's not something I would've ever done on purpose." Jannik reached out and hit several buttons on the display, then pressed his thumbprint into a reader that appeared on the glass. "However, our standard practice is to hold data in a safety buffer, so it can't get into our computer system until we've vetted it. I suppose it's possible something might have lingered in there, as we don't always remember to clear the information until we need the space again."

Before Kate's eyes, a complex file structure flowed across the display, one not organized in the same way their own files were. "Jannik, you, beautiful bastard."

Dramatically offended, he said, "Such language, from such a lovely girl. It's like you're my own daughter."

Kate heard him, but paid no attention, her fingers busy manipulating the system to dive into the data before her. In moments, she'd found her way into the navigational records, and then into their maps. With a tap to select and a sliding motion to indicate what she wanted, she threw up a gigantic representation of the frontier up on the walls in engineering, every one of which was a display surface. She stood and walked around the room, peering at the various images.

Jannik rose and moved to stand beside her. "What are we looking for?"

"We want to get behind them. We have a fairly good idea of where they'll come in, at least within a few sectors. So, what we need is a wormhole that ends in a sector close enough for us to transit to the battle in time, but far enough away that it won't be affected by those bloody tunnel drive defeaters."

Jenna gave a small laugh. "Is that the technical term?"

"Shut up and find me a wormhole."

Forty minutes later, the search was still in progress. Through several layers of digital refinement, they had removed most of the things on the maps that were not gravitational anomalies, and were working to differentiate the ones that remained. The wormhole drive exploited such gravitational anomalies to enable transit.

"All we need to do is find the right one," Kate growled. "Why does it have to be so difficult to do?"

Jannik was hunched over the display table, adjusting filters to make finding their quarry easier. He looked up and said, "You know, I have a thought."

"First time?"

"Did anyone ever tell you that you're hilarious? No, I imagine they haven't. Anyway, as I said, I have a thought. All of our technologies are based upon an understanding of gravity we've had forever. We know what it does, we know how it works, we know what frequencies to use to detect it." He stood and stretched his back with a groan. "But these bird things use gravity in a way that's completely different. The color display when they enter a sector suggests they're using frequencies at the border of, and maybe beyond, those we can see."

"So, what you're thinking is, there may be more wormholes than we've seen before, but they're hiding at a different threshold?"

"You should've been an engineer," he replied, tapping commands into the system. "These maps are sufficiently detailed, and carry enough sensor data, that we might be able to run some tests to see if they *are* present."

Kate frowned. "That's all well and good, but even if we find them, do we have a chance of opening them at that new frequency?"

"Of course, we do. Luckily for us, I made the correct career choice. Unlike you."

FOUR HOURS LATER, they had a plan. It involved a tunnel jump into a far sector, then required the *Washington* to open a wormhole at a higher frequency than they'd ever attempted before. The transit would deposit them behind the enemy where they could make an attempt on the commanders of the alien force. Fortunately, there was a universal relationship between the frequencies of portals to a single wormhole, so they were able to identify the entrance and exit to this one without too much difficulty.

The problem was, the plan would take them out of the main assault, and there was no guarantee of how long they'd spend in transit. If they went too early, they risked showing up before everyone was positioned properly. If they started too late, the battle might be over before they arrived.

"It's risky, no doubt." Jannik stood with his arms folded, staring at the solution that was now running through its sixth test, as if the five previous results were not definitive.

"Risky in the timing," Kate replied, "but not in the actual technology, right?"

"Oh, the tech is fine. There are always unknowns going into an untraveled wormhole, but chances are good it will work as intended."

"So, you're saying it's time to inform Cross."

"Aye."

"You should tell him."

"Not I, my girl. This one is all yours."

"Bastard."

"Guilty."

A SHORT LIFT RIDE LATER, Kate was on the bridge, settling into the XO chair behind Cross. He swiveled toward her in response to her gesture for conversation. "We've got it figured out. It uses existing technology. We can share the engine tweaks with the other ships, no problem."

His face lit up, and her stomach twisted as she followed with the bad news. "The timing is a variable. We don't know how long we'll be in the wormhole. We estimate, based on similar wormholes, that transit time should be less than thirty minutes. But there's just no way to tell until we've tested it."

"Could we send in a probe?" Cross's question was logical, but one Kate and Jannik had discarded early on.

"Only at the risk of showing our cards if it arrives while the enemy is watching the sector."

"Damn."

"Exactly."

"Okay, are there any other options for getting behind them?"

"None that we could figure out. I take it you all didn't find one either?"

Cross shook his head before replying. "No. We've been working the problem from all angles, but there are just too many unknowns."

"Exactly."

"So, alright then. We know what the situation is. We know what our options are. You and Jannik should get some rest. There's bound to be some excitement ahead."

She nodded and stood to leave the bridge. Cross touched her arm, gentle as a feather. "Thank you, Kate. It will be enough of an edge to make a difference."

She smiled down at him and brushed his hand. It felt like a good-bye. "Don't let me sleep through the fireworks."

"I'd never go into battle without you, Red."

"Always the charmer, Ace."

She turned for the lift and heard him issue the commands that would ready them for tunnel and wormhole transit. Soon they would again face the implacable enemy that wanted all humans, and their ship in particular, reduced to interstellar dust.

CHAPTER FORTY-ONE

The *Beijing* just happened to be the closest ship in the patrol rotation when the color wave washed the alien ships back into real-space. Using the communication equipment he'd given to Cross, Dima sent an immediate message giving the coordinates and likely positions of the Xroeshyn forces. He knew the *Washington* was waiting for this word before jumping into the wormhole, so as not to arrive prematurely.

The Union had set up a sizable force in defense, twenty-two ships strong, all they had capable of using the known wormhole to retreat if needed. The rest were either being retrofitted or were occupying fallback protection positions at nearby starbases.

His crew was quiet and calm, going about their duties in the most professional manner possible. They knew that they were operating outside the boundaries of the admiralty's desires, but none of them showed a single concern about doing what Dima asked them to do.

He was, as always, proud of them.

"Tactical, full sector view on main screen please. Designate Union ships as allies, alien ships as enemies." Yegorovich overrode the native preferences of the display and the colors changed before him.

Dima leaned forward as something unexpected caught his eye. "There's only twenty-seven of them. That makes no sense."

His executive officer looked at him with a question on her face and said, "Sir?"

Dima gritted his teeth, thinking hard, staring at the screen. "Everything we've seen from them is based on multiples of eight, or at worst, even numbers. It's against precedent that they would bring twenty-seven. There's something unaccounted for."

He tapped his fingers on the arm of his chair and took a sip of his tea, still staring as if the display would reveal its secrets to him any second.

"Communication officer, send this information on to the *Washington, DC*." He frowned. "Also, distribute to all of our ships, and just in case Cross is already in the wormhole and can't receive it, copy the message to the lead ship of the Union fleet. I believe it's the big one over there."

"The *Anchorage*, sir. You are correct."

He waved an acknowledgment. On the display, the forces took positions opposite one another. The enemy seemed to be taking a good long time to divide into pairs, and pairs of pairs, and to arrange themselves in response to the waiting defensive forces. Two hung back, and Dima made an educated guess that those were the command ships. "Tactical, tag those two at the rear and send to our ships. When Cross arrives, we'll join him in the attack on the commanders, as planned." His eyes rapidly scanned the screen, taking in every detail and strategizing.

"Weapons, ready all. Get the pilots into their fighters. Have the computer run simulations on expected moves and counters, and route them to my personal display." He watched out of the corner of his eye as possible battle results spewed from the processors hidden deep within the core of the ship. Few turned out well for the Union and Alliance forces.

"Now we wait and watch."

TWO CUPS OF TEA LATER, the sector was still at rest. The alien ships had settled into pairs, with the one extra ship standing alone between the front lines and what they'd identified as the command ships. The Union had chosen a cluster defense, using four ships to support one another in five diamonds, with two singles behind in reserve. Dima wasn't sure what the aliens were waiting for, but the tension was as thick and heavy as a slab of newsteel. Perhaps that was the point. To let fear worm its way into the defenders.

The main display twitched as his communication officer routed a message to it. The first alien they'd ever seen was on the screen again. An arrogant confidence exuded from him as he spoke.

"Demons. Defilers. Your time has come. By the grace of our gods have you been delivered to us, and by the grace of our gods' promise, we will deliver you to the in-between, where your presence will free our ancestors to journey on to paradise. The Xroeshyn offer all of you a quick, clean death—except for one. The ship that trespassed upon our holy ground and defiled the creche of Vasoi will suffer torments unimaginable on its way to the in-between, as will anyone who stands up to defend them. They're now the chattel of our gods. We grant you several moments in which to make peace with those that you worship, and to say farewell to those around you." He opened his mouth to speak again, but suddenly vanished.

"Enough of that noise, I thought," explained the communication officer. A ripple of laughter circled the bridge.

"Well said, Loh, well said." Dima stood and inspected each station, exuding a quiet confidence that eclipsed what they'd just seen on the screen. "My friends, we have been here before. We have fought battles. We have been bloodied. We have reveled in victory. We have consoled each other in loss. Our task is clear, and we no longer fight only for our beliefs and our way of life. We also battle for the very survival of all the children of Earth. I know you'll each do your best. Take heart knowing that not one of us will fail the other in effort, in courage, or in execution. We will prevail, or we will scratch and claw to survive and fight again."

He sat and buckled himself into the chair. "Set highest alert throughout the ship." Klaxons sounded, and those who were previously required to be near their stations were now required to be at their stations, strapped in and ready. Three additional officers reported to the bridge, to serve as supplements or replacements at any of the stations. Dima pointed to their chairs, and they secured themselves not a moment too soon.

On the battle display, the outermost pair of alien ships and the single ship in the second row moved, the front ones arcing outward to come at the clusters from the rear, the one in the back climbing in what projected as a long arc. The defenders didn't move, but the largest vessel in each cluster disgorged fighters, which organized and shot out toward the aliens.

"Enemy ships are ejecting projectiles," reported the sensor officer, highlighting them on the display. "Our sensors indicate that they're likely the ones that prohibit tunneling into or out of the space."

Dima nodded. It was a logical guess since there was no starbase for them to adhere to. However, he wouldn't put it past the aliens to be using a third type of projectile that did the same thing to individual vessels. He shuddered at the thought. His desire to launch his own fighters just in case was high, but their hiding place had been chosen for a reason and he didn't want to reveal his forces early.

Before any of the defenders could engage, the entire alien line moved, sending five ships after each cluster of four, leading with torpedoes fired from a range the humans couldn't match. Countermeasures eliminated most of them, and daring fighter runs picked off a majority of the rest. Of those that made it through, none penetrated the focused and overlapping defenses of the cluster.

"They're using the same tactics that the ancient Spartans did.

Each ship overlaps its shields to protect the others. Apparently, our alien friends didn't expect that," observed the executive officer.

"Very true, Exec," Dima said. "It works well until one falls, at which time chaos ensues. Let's hope, we don't get to see that." He preferred to keep his ships on the move and only rely upon coordinated defenses when absolutely necessary.

The defenders set their clusters into rotation. The synchronization of the giant machines moving as a unit was impressive to watch. As each broadside came to bear, the ship fired then rolled in space to bring the next broadside in line. In this way, they constantly fired energy and projectiles at the incoming aliens. The alien shields deflected, redirected, or absorbed the damage without issue.

At the periphery of the battle, Dima saw a squadron of UAL fighters flying behind the solo ship, destroying the devices it was distributing throughout the sector. Unfortunately, Dima also saw other ships releasing the travel blockers.

He felt something strange in the bottom of his stomach, as if the world had lurched. Then he saw a wash of color appear behind the line of defending clusters. "Damn them to hell, that's what they were doing!" Five alien ships appeared as the waves departed, and the solo ship adjusted its vector to join them. Within moments of their arrival, they were releasing torpedoes and energy weapons at the under-protected rear of the clusters. The defenders made the only choice they could, which Dima agreed was the right one even as he regretted the necessity of it.

The mutual defense clusters vanished as each of the members split off on a separate vector, now responsible for its own defense and significantly more vulnerable than when grouped. Dima drummed his fingers again and was silent until he saw one of the biggest vessels overwhelmed by four enemy ships working together. As it vaporized from its position upon the intersection of sixteen energy weapons, Dima saw how the battle would play out. One or two more big losses and it would turn into a rout of the Union forces.

"Communication officer, signal all our ships. We advance at

13:50." That was two and a half minutes away, and Dima was sure that the message could be received and acted upon in that amount of time. "Tactical, designate the command ships as the targets for four of us, two each, including the *Beijing*." He looked back at the screen where another Union ship was reduced to its component atoms. At least this one did significant damage to its attacker, who was now limping toward the protection of its fellows. "Send the other four after the damaged target, then split them to support each remaining cluster."

His officers made preparations for the advance, while Dima watched the continuing battle. The Union had gathered into a strategic arrangement again, but it was defensive, their chance for offense lost with the appearance of the additional aliens. A grim smile creased his features. His forces would tilt the board in an unexpected direction.

With one minute to go, he addressed the seven other commanders in his battle group. "You are all free agents now. You have your tasks. Do them to the best of your abilities. If a better opportunity presents itself, take it. If you need to retreat and regroup, do so. It's imperative that we strike fast, strike hard, and fade away. We will not win this war in a day, and we must conserve our resources as we can. If today is your day to embark on the final voyage, do your best to take some of the bastards with you. I'm proud of each and every one of your accomplishments as if you were my own children. I know I will be proud of you today. Petryaev out."

When the clock reached the appointed time, eight ships streaked in from the enemy's port side, slipping from the shadows of the asteroids they'd been anchored to, a full salvo of torpedoes from each ship leading the way into battle.

CHAPTER FORTY-TWO

The *Washington* and her unexpected escort, the *Belize*, tore out of the wormhole into the battle sector. Cross let out an undignified whoop as they reverted to real-space at a much greater velocity than their engines could produce on their own.

The ship had vibrated during transit as if she was ready to fly apart, and Cross was happy to be out of the wormhole. A glance around the bridge showed matching relief on several faces.

"Combat view, full defenses, engines full when our speed drops to a reasonable rate."

Cross stared at the battle display, which filled in as quickly as the sensors could populate it, and far too slowly for his peace of mind. Data from Dima's message appeared seconds later, as the communication officer reviewed it and deemed it unnecessary to share the actual words.

"All right, all right. It looks like the *Beijing* has entered the game early and is shaking up the other side of the formation. Perfect. Message to Captain Labranche: We'll take the closer one. The other one is yours."

Ana Fitzpatrick nodded, and Cross turned back to the screen.

"Status?"

"All weapons and defenses ready to go, Commander."

"Well, let's do it then. Fire forward torpedoes as soon as we're in range and broadsides when the opportunity presents itself. Our goal is to harass that ship until it runs or dies, while trying not to let it or anyone else kill us. So... you know... make that happen."

The bridge crew gave him the laugh he needed, despite their nerves.

"Helm, loop a little to port so we get some separation from the *Belize*."

"Aye, sir."

The mad rush into the sector had clearly taken the command ships by surprise, judging by the delayed reactions to the new additions. When they responded, their strategy was the same he would have used, splitting up and running for the safety of nearby allies.

"Oh no, you don't," Cross said. "Message to Captain Petryaev: Block 'em."

The main display was now split. One half presented a real-time image from the front of the ship, showing them closing on the enemy vessel, which glinted in shades of metallic scarlet that hurt the eyes. The other gave the battle schematic overhead view, as if on a sand table, with ships color-coded for relative depth and status as friend or foe.

"Tactical, watch that ship two levels down. It's angling for a shot at our belly."

"Aye."

There was chatter from bridge officer to bridge officer, which Cross relegated to the back part of his mind, tracking it but not concentrating on it. He trusted his people to keep the ship running and to deal with any ordinary problems that might appear while he worked on the overall strategy for their attack. He felt the vibrations as the forward torpedoes launched, and realized he needed to get his head a little further down out of the clouds.

"Battle display to plus-25." The field-of-view shrank, showing the

Washington and the one-quarter area of the sector surrounding her. "Message to Captain Labranche: Next launch we switch targets, then return to original target. Tactical, make that happen on our end." Another vibration a minute later as the salvo of torpedoes leapt from their tubes, this time taking the longer path to the enemy vessel designated as the *Belize's* foe. "That will give them something to think about, anyway."

Cross focused on the enemy growing larger in his display. They would be within full weapons range in less than two minutes. Out of the corner of his eye, he caught Dima's forces blocking the direct path of the command ships, both of which changed heading and kicked up to high-speed. He ran through the geometry of it and grinned. "Oh, that was a mistake. New orders. We'll use our target as a shield, so that the other one doesn't see us coming. Prepare to defend against a full salvo from ours as we go by. When we're clear of it, unload everything at the other ship and keep firing until it's down or we're past it."

"Helm, I need all the speed you can give when we're by this enemy. Do what you need to do to avoid incoming blasts and such, but when the far ship spots us, light them up."

As they bore in on their target, it fired from an unexpected distance and added weapons to the barrage as they closed. The *Washington's* countermeasures deployed, and fireworks filled the space between them. Point defense cannons accelerated devastating balls of metal at the incoming projectiles, and the helm officer wove the ship through the lances of coherent light that sought to destroy her. It was impossible to avoid them all, and the *Washington* shook and creaked, and in some places even cracked under the strain.

Cross dared a quick look at his tactical officer. Jacobs had his head down in his displays, his fingers flying as he worked the countermeasures. Lieutenant Marcas Walsh fired enough weapons to not give the game away while reserving the majority of the blasts for when they were past their attacker.

When the torpedo got through their defenses, it was a surprise to everyone except the tactical officer who had barely enough time to yell, "Brace." The ship lurched as internal gravity fluctuated for a moment.

"We good?" He spoke louder than he wanted to and took a breath.

Kate responded, "Weapons green. Shields holding. Alien bastards will have to try harder than that."

Cross turned to the display in time to watch the *Washington* speed along the length of the enemy vessel and loop over her top. The other command ship was shockingly close, a definite mistake on somebody's part.

"Weapons free. Fire them all."

The helm officer, weapons officer, and tactical officer had worked out multiple options before they ever entered the wormhole. Jacobs called out "Echo," and Lee killed thrust from the main engine. He used positioning boosters to spin the ship along its X-axis. This allowed all the ship's arms to fire in sequence, except for those that required a held position. Two broadsides, forward and rear torpedoes, and energy sloughing across its length combined to ravage its shields. The defenses were strong enough to reroute the first three sets of missiles on different headings, but the starboard broadside punched through, as did the lasers and plasma blasts that followed.

They flashed by too fast to see the impacts, but Lee brought them back around unbidden to review the results of their handiwork. The damage was barely short of catastrophic. While the ship was still moving, and probably hadn't vented all of its atmosphere, it trailed a cloud of debris, and explosions and electrical discharges wreathed it as it sputtered away.

"Kill it," yelled Cross, and Walsh sent another wave of torpedoes and energy flying toward the vessel. Just when he thought they had it, when he was savoring that impending moment of impact, the red ship flashed in between and absorbed the barrage, firing one of its own at the *Washington*.

"Evasive! Bloody hell and damnation," Cross yelled, punctuating each word with a soft rap of his fist on the arm of his chair. "Stupid,

stupid, stupid." He'd been battle-blind before and knew the symptoms. Hooray for hindsight.

"Tactical, select nearest target, head toward it. Put some distance between us and the command ships please." On the battle display, the alien forces were falling back while still mixing it up with the Alliance and Union forces. A quick count showed that they had knocked out about a fourth of the enemy's number, at a cost of about half of theirs, and none of Dima's.

"Comm, voice channel to the *Beijing*."

"What can I do for you, Lieutenant Commander Cross?" Petryaev's tone was as calm as if he was sailing through smooth space.

"The command ships seem to be pulling back, is it possible we broke them?"

"Anything is possible, but based upon what we've seen, it is fair to assume they have another trick or two awaiting us."

"Yeah. I thought so too. Suggestions?"

Cross could almost hear Dima shrugging across the channel. "Don't be tricked. Play it safe. Stay in groups. Take care not to overreach."

He laughed. "You sound like one of my Academy instructors."

"He must have been a very smart individual."

Cross shook his head with a smile. "Indeed, he was. Stay safe. Cross out."

The UAL battle net came to life before he could give another command. "All ships, this is Admiral Valentina Ferro of the *Anchorage*. The enemy is in retreat. Damaged vessels, withdraw to the rear of the sector and begin evacuation back to the rally point. The rest of you, form up into groups, clustered around the *Medellin* and the *Cartagena*. Let's show these things what happens when we go on the offensive."

"That," Cross said to no one in particular, "is a really bad idea."

CHAPTER FORTY-THREE

The battle display told the tale, and Cross could see why the Admiral had chosen to attack. One third of the remaining UAL ships headed for the rally point, too damaged to continue. The rest organized into two separate forces. The enemy appeared to be retreating at random, strung out at various distances as they raced for safety. It made perfect sense.

It made no sense.

Prior experience suggested retreat was unlikely, and uncoordinated movements less so. Even accepting for the moment that they had unsettled the alien leaders, one of the two command ships remained uninjured and the second still lived. The enemy had no reason to be acting headless.

Which meant it was a trap. And the admiral had ordered them into it.

Cross said, "Let's hope they're aware of what they're doing, asking us to put our heads in the noose like this."

Kate nodded in agreement. "What are the odds?"

"It depends on whether they are capable of learning or not. I would like to think, after the disaster at Starbase 14, they have gained a greater respect for our enemy's intelligence."

"It's a nice thought."

"It is. All we can do is follow orders and be prepared to improvise. Helm, keep an evasive pattern ready and a course plotted straight to the nearest wormhole out of this place. Tactical, a quiet word to your counterparts on the other ships sharing the possibility of a trap would not go amiss." Lieutenant Jacobs dropped his gaze to his controls as he got to work doing so.

The command to advance came over the battle net and was reflected on the battle display. The *Washington* joined cluster Alpha, congregated around the Pulsar-class cruiser *Medellin*. Their mission was to arc to high port at top speed and then slash down across the enemy's line of retreat. Cluster Bravo would do the opposite from high starboard, so they wouldn't risk a crossfire. Ship-to-ship automatic communication would prevent them from colliding.

"Well, that sucks," observed the helm officer.

"Understatement of the year, Lieutenant Lee. I don't like giving over command of piloting the *Washington* to the computer any more than you do. Just keep your fingers close to the controls and be ready to take over."

"Aye."

Cross leaned forward in his seat and ran his hand through his hair. He peered at the display as if the intensity of his gaze would reveal the enemy's secrets to him. "What are we missing, XO?"

Kate matched his pose, staring hard at the main screen. It showed a textbook case of a disorderly retreat, with each vessel seeming to do its own thing and following its own vector. The only commonality was that they were all moving away from the human forces at high speed.

She reached down and touched her own display, and a single target glowed on the main screen. "Sensors, is there anything wrong with this ship?"

Flores peered down at his displays for several seconds, then replied in the negative. "Seems to be unharmed. The computer has no record of it taking damage."

"Then why is it so much slower than the others?" Kate's question hung in the air.

The admiral's voice commanded them to move. "Cluster alpha, commence attack run."

The six ships curved and dove as one, coming in from above the retreating aliens. Beams of energy and torpedoes shot out, concentrating for a moment on each of the targets in their path before moving on to the next. Computers controlled the whole process, synchronizing their actions across the Union's tactical network. The combined force destroyed the outermost ship before the others knew they were under attack.

The aliens were quick to respond, and missiles tracked back toward cluster Alpha, forcing them to redirect energy and attention on their own defense. Cluster Bravo attacked in that interval and took out another two alien ships before they were engaged. Cross watched it all and saw that lone ship falling further and further behind the others. The vibration in his armrest indicated an incoming communication. A glance down at Dima's message confirmed his fears.

"Trap. Sacrifice play. Retreat."

Cross took a deep breath, knowing he might very well be throwing his career away with his next actions. Time stretched as he thought about it, considered all he'd fought his way through to reach this point, only to risk it all.

To risk it all in order to do what he knew was right. Not a decision at all, but something he couldn't not do.

"Jacobs, mark and link that ship." He activated the battle net and used one of the override codes commanders carried for moments like this. "This is Lieutenant Commander Anderson Cross, of the *Washington DC*. Apache, Apache, Apache. Repeat. Apache, Apache, Apache. All ships break off and head to rally point at top speed. Apache bogey is marked on display."

The announcement was shorthand for ambush and covered a

variety of possible enemy actions. The response happened without thought. On every Union ship, the helm officer tapped in the triple-apache code, and the computers took over. The battle display showed all the Union ships in the sector break off their attacks and accelerate to highest speed on a path away from the marked target and toward an extraction point. The computers pushed the ships to their tolerance in velocity and maneuverability, then routed the shields to defend against detected enemies and the purported ambush ship.

For several moments, nothing happened on the enemy's side, and the admiral's voice piped in over the battle net, "Lieutenant Commander Cross, what the hell—"

The force of the alien ship's explosion was greater than anything they could have expected from something that size. He guessed it was at least ten times as powerful as any they'd seen from an enemy ship, including the ones that had been destroyed with a single salvo. Worse, it spewed damage of multiple kinds throughout the sector. Communication systems were knocked out by a frequency overload that popped the protection circuits. Ships were thrown off course by a gravitic wave that spread out in all directions. Finally, small metal projectiles flew in an expanding sphere, peppering shields and on occasion breaking through and venting inhabited compartments to space.

Had any of them been closer, the explosion would have been catastrophic. Even with the warning, half of the escaping ships took significant physical damage.

"Status," Cross snapped.

Jacobs responded, "Weapons green. Shields green. Several sections compromised. No casualties. Light injuries."

He exhaled and leaned back in his chair. He only noticed the sweat covering his forehead when he ran his hand through his hair again.

On the main display, a communication arrived from the aliens. This one was smaller than the last, with different radiant hues reflecting from the scales that made up its skin. "I am Commander

Indraat Vray of the *Ruby Rain*. You fought bravely, as we would expect of the implacable enemy promised in our prophecy. Understand this, though. Testing is complete. We know your strengths, futile as they are. We know your weaknesses, which are as abundant as the stars. When we meet again, you *will* meet your end. And a special message to the commander of the *Washington, DC*. You and your ship live today by my will. I could have removed you from the board after your foolish attack on the *Jade Breeze*, but I prefer to wait until we can battle with honor, rather than with tricks. Your deaths are delayed, but still certain." The communication cut off, and the Xroeshyn forces disappeared from the sector in a wave of color.

"They seem like very intelligent beings, if you get past the fact they want to kill us all for no apparent reason," Cross mused.

"Aye," said several of the bridge officers.

"Intelligent and determined," pointed out Kate. "Besides, they have a reason. They've met you. Everyone who knows you wants to kill you."

The crew laughed at her words. Cross gave her a nod. They were discovering the secrets of this command thing.

Several of the ships, including the *Washington*, looped around to escort the more damaged of their comrades to the rally point. Cross stared at the display of the emptying sector. In one part of his mind, he feared the next meeting with the aliens, for all the pain and death it would bring.

In another part, he relished the opportunity to test himself against them, and by so doing protect the people who were not so well-equipped to go toe-to-toe with them. He imagined that Captain Okoye would tell him this was the burden, and the privilege, of command. He looked forward to talking with the old man again.

With one last look at the main display screen, Cross gave the order. "Helm, take us to the rally point." The engines spun up, the perimeter of the wormhole appeared, and the *Washington* blasted into it.

CHAPTER FORTY-FOUR

News of the battle had reached him days before, but Kraada hadn't acted on the reports from his niece. He preferred to debrief her in person before going up against Marshal Drovaa and whatever ideas the emperor might put together in his copious spare time. In the interim, he'd focused on his duties—leading services, reassuring the people, ensuring the loyalty of those under him for the day he would need to call upon it.

He feared that day was coming sooner, rather than later.

The doors opened, and Indraat Vray hurried to his side, dropping to a knee beside his chair. "Hierarch, I apologize—"

"Quiet, Niece. There's nothing to apologize for. We followed the marshal's strategy, and we reaped the rewards of that choice. How many did we lose?"

"One eight."

Kraada made a sound somewhere between negation and amusement. "That's all? I thought from your report it would be something far more dire. The loss of eight ships is easily accommodated, especially with the *Sapphire Sky* projected to be in range soon." He stood, drawing her to her feet, and gestured her to a sideboard where a light meal waited. "Please, sit and eat. In between bites, you can tell me what transpired."

Indraat filled her plate and sat down at the table across from her uncle. She ate methodically, filling in bits and pieces of the battle for him as she went along. By the time the food was finished, she had completed the tale.

"So, what are you not telling me?" Kraada had a talent for reading people, and Indraat Vray was definitely carrying a secret.

She gave a short laugh. "It's that obvious, is it?"

"Only to me. This is, after all, what I do."

Indraat pushed back from the table and paced while she apparently searched for the words she needed. Finally, she turned to her uncle, placed her hands on the chair, and said, "It was incompetence. Plain and simple."

Kraada nodded, unsurprised. "On whose part?"

"The *Jade Breeze*. Upon taking damage, the captain signaled a retreat to all of our forces. We were in an advantageous position, and if we'd pressed, we would've defeated them. In the worst case, we would've drawn more of them in to be eliminated by the sacrifice. I myself was forced to let the trespassers' ship fly free from under my guns in order to support the *Jade Breeze*. But for that cowardly command, we would've had the first part of our revenge."

"That is an incendiary accusation, Niece."

"Yes. But it doesn't make it any less true."

"I had deduced he was a fool, but hoped he was sufficient in a military capacity. Apparently not?"

"Definitely not." Indraat leaned forward on the chair to better meet his gaze. "The destruction of at least four ships was the direct result of his incompetence."

"Somehow, I doubt he'll accept responsibility for this, am I correct?"

She laughed. "He's like fresh-forged armor plate, nothing sticks to him. His former religious officer wasn't in the wrong, regardless of the fate the gods chose for him within the lines."

Kraada sighed and leaned back in his chair. "The messages I've had from Radith, the religious officer on that ship, echo your opinion. This is a conundrum, and no doubt. The emperor will look for someone to hang this supposed failure upon, and as the designated second-in-command, Marshal Drovaa may attempt to make sure that rope wraps around you." He paused, thinking. "Of course, the truth is, that doing so would damage him as well, since he appointed you to that position. In front of Enjaaran, at least, perhaps the play is to maintain that all the decisions during the battle were tactically sound, and we simply overstepped in our haste to serve the gods."

Indraat sat again and gave him a look.

"What, Niece? Speak freely."

"It seems as if you are always several moves ahead, Uncle. I can achieve the same thing on the battlefield, but to be able to do it in the arena of politics...." Her voice trailed off, and she raised a hand in surrender.

"The one is no different than the other, my dear. The playing field just has more layers, and more pieces. The strategies and tactics are the same."

A distant bell rang, the chime of someone at the entrance to the cathedral. "Unless I miss my guess, further conversation will need to wait. I believe we're being summoned." One of his eight came in a moment later to confirm an immediate appointment with the emperor.

KRAADA AND INDRAAT changed into appropriate costumes for the audience, then set off to the palace. Upon their arrival, they were led into the main throne room, rather than being diverted into the smaller, more intimate space from before. The emperor sat on his throne in full regalia, crown atop the long draping feathers that substituted for hair in the ruling family.

Before they got close enough to be overheard, Kraada whispered, "If I had known it would be in this room, I would've worn my armor."

She nodded and said, "And I would've hidden a few more weapons."

He gave her an inquiring look, and she inclined her head ever so slightly. *Interesting. Bold.*

Kraada ruffled his wings and spread his arms wide. "My emperor, may your servants approach?"

Enjaaran waved them on, not interested in yelling across the distance that separated them, and they continued to walk forward. Their progress cleared blocking pillars from their view, revealing that Marshal Drovaa and the captain of the *Jade Breeze* were both in attendance, and had gotten there before them. That had the potential to be a problem, but it was too early to worry about it.

Kraada gave Drovaa a guarded nod and received the same in return. Captain Traan Aras, on the other hand, bristled at Indraat, his eyes boring into her like lasers. Kraada noticed this in time to see her meet his optical assault with a toothy grin.

Finally, they reached the steps leading up to the emperor's throne, and stopped there. Only members of the royal family and one hereditary servant could ever ascend the dais.

"Marshal, Hierarch, Captain, Commander. I've heard the reports of the war against those who call themselves humans. I am unimpressed. You assured me that this would be a simple task, and yet we've lost eight ships in a battle that can at best be called a draw, and might more appropriately be called a defeat. Would you care to explain yourselves?"

Kraada stepped into the center of the space before the dais, looking up at the emperor. He spread his wings and took a steadying breath, then folded both wings and hands prior to speaking.

"Who can know the will of the gods, Your Grace? The marshal and I could offer you a plethora of excuses explaining why the battle was not a decisive victory. These could include everything from the humans unexpectedly sensing the traps we'd laid for them to our decision to attack before the fortress was in position to support the assault. It could be attributed to the strategies concocted beforehand," he looked pointedly at Drovaa as he said this, "or the tactics of the commander in that battle." His gaze shifted to Captain Traan Aras, who didn't back down. Kraada gave him a nod of acknowledgment.

"In any case, Your Grace, it is but a small setback on the way to a great victory. We have gathered important data about the enemy, including the fact that the two factions worked together to repulse our first wave. That alone is of enough strategic value to warrant the minimal losses we incurred during the battle."

Kraada lifted his gaze up to the high ceiling of the palace as if he was seeking inspiration. In fact, he was leading the eyes of those assembled up to the mural on that distant surface. "The gods watch us here, as they do in my cathedral, as they do everywhere in our systems. They know our hearts, and they know our purpose is pure. That they have given us additional challenges in our path is a reward, not a punishment. The stronger this promised enemy is, the greater shall be our victory when we overcome them." His eyes drifted back down to meet the emperor's.

"Your Grace, I find this development to be entirely in keeping with the holy word, with prophecy, and with our expectations for the conquest of this new species."

The emperor gave a grunt in return for Kraada's bellicosity. "Marshal?"

Kraada yielded the center position to Drovaa, who stepped forward to claim it. This was the pivotal moment. He had two openings ahead of him, and which he chose would be quite instructive.

"I must agree with the Hierarch, your Eminence. This is but a transitory setback. If anything, it is a reminder we should not regard the enemy too lightly, but should focus on purity of strategy above all else, as we've done in campaigns past." He gestured to take in both ship captains. "We have the right people, we have the right ideas. We will wait until all our forces are assembled, and then we'll attack and not turn back until the humans are no more."

The emperor nodded. "Gentlemen, this goes without saying, but I'll say it, anyway. You've taken us far out on the wire, and the purchase beneath our feet is uncertain. If I'm forced to appease the masses after a defeat, it will be the two of you, and any surviving commanders tainted by this failure, who will be fed to that beast. Is that understood?"

Both men spoke together, "Yes, Your Grace."

"Good. Get out of my sight and do not presume to return until you have something worth sharing."

HOURS LATER, Kraada was hosting Drovaa to an elegant meal. Indraat was nearby, unseen but listening in with Kraada's attendants. "I thought for a moment you would choose the other path, my friend."

Drovaa looked up, all innocence. "I'm sure I don't know what you mean." He took a bite, chewing slowly and clearly savoring the taste.

"I'm sure you do. I left you one opening that would result in mutual support, and one opening that would require you to take an opposing position to mine. You stayed allied. I say that was a good decision."

Drovaa shook his head. "It is always wheels within wheels within wheels with you."

"Are you suggesting that it is not the same with you?" Kraada leaned back, glass in hand, and awaited the other man's response.

"I believe that we play the game differently." Drovaa Jat looked thoughtful for a moment, then continued, "Your strategy is secrecy, misdirection, influence, and stealth. My approach is more direct, overwhelming force applied judiciously."

"Fair enough, fair enough. That is what makes us such complementary leaders, I guess. We think in similar directions, but we take different journeys to reach them."

"True, true." Drovaa stood and stretched his arms wide, his wings fanning out. "There is a great deal of planning to finish before we can restart the invasion. It's best that I go get started on the overwhelming force part."

"And I shall resume my nefarious efforts," Kraada said with a laugh as he stood and gripped the other man's forearm. He looked him in the eyes and held his gaze. "Before you depart, be aware that a debt might be owed. If it is, it is *not* my niece who will pay it."

Drovaa didn't flinch, and his only response was a quiet statement. "We shall see what the future brings, Hierarch."

"So may it be, Marshal."

CHAPTER FORTY-FIVE

Starbase 9—long underappreciated due to its spot in the middle of the UAL's chain of installations—was experiencing a new renaissance. Dry docks floated in space around it, and technicians poured over the vessels inside them, retrofitting wormhole drives onto the newer vessels of the Union fleet. Traffic in the system was intense, with additional personnel delegated to routing it hither and yonder to avoid collisions.

Although, there were many ships still out defending other starbases, patrolling, and on picket duty in the forward sectors, a disproportionate number had gathered here. This would be the center of the defense movement for as long as it lasted, with starbase 3 ready to pick up that task should nine become imperiled.

The *Washington, DC* had docked several days earlier, and her crew had rotated out for shore leave, shift by shift. Only a skeleton staff drawn from the starbase personnel was aboard, overseeing the ship's upgrades and repairs.

Captain James Okoye, Lieutenant Commander Anderson Cross, and Lieutenant Commander Kate Flynn waited together in a nondescript room next to a large auditorium. Each was in full dress, black-on-black uniforms with shining *DC* badges at their sleeve tops, rank insignias on the shoulders, and in Okoye's case, combat ribbons marching toward his wrists.

"What I wouldn't give for a cup of coffee," Okoye said with a sigh. This drew a small laugh out of both Cross and Kate, who well knew their captain's prodigious appetite for the Navy's legal stimulant.

"So, what's the deal, here, Captain?" They hadn't been given the reason behind the order to come to this location.

"Oh, just a little pomp and circumstance," Okoye replied with the grin that told Cross he knew more than he was saying.

They ran out of time to discuss it, as an ensign opened the door and beckoned them forward. Okoye stood and grabbed the polished black cane with the chrome handle he was using to help him get around. While mostly recovered from his injuries, and at a speed much greater than that of any ordinary human, Cross thought, the captain still needed a little more rehabilitation before he would be shipshape. In the meantime, Cross hoped to be allowed to continue commanding the *Washington*.

Okoye led, and his two junior officers followed behind.

Cross blinked at the lights that bore down upon the stage in the otherwise dimly lit auditorium. Ahead of him, he saw all the admirals present at the base in full uniform, standing at attention. Admiral Anwen Davies was at a lectern in the center of the stage, facing out toward the audience. Cross raised a hand to shield his eyes and saw that the venue was filled with officers from each of the ships in the sector.

The senior admiral spoke, "We are gathered here today for several reasons. First, to discuss the important changes in strategy and tactics we will undertake in light of the existential threat we face from the Xroeshyn. Second, to discuss the new timetable for combat patrols and rotations, and the reasoning behind them, so that when your crews complain, you'll have something useful to tell them."

That got a chuckle from all the members of the audience, and the people on the stage, as well. There was nothing more tenacious than an unanswered question on a starship. It would burrow its way into every conversation, into every thought, into every action, until the answer was revealed.

As the laughter subsided, Davies continued speaking. "Third, we're here to recognize the actions of some particular individuals in service to the United Atlantic League. Captain James Okoye, please step forward."

Captain Okoye complied, tapping the floor with his cane in a dignified manner as he advanced to the podium and stood at ease next to it. The admiral turned to face him and intoned, "Captain James Okoye. For valor in battle, you are awarded the combat star twice over in recognition of your leadership in the defense of Starbase 14 and the AAN starbase." She paused as applause rang out from the gathered officers. "Further, you are hereby promoted to admiral." She pinned the stars on Okoye's epaulets, while he maintained an appropriately neutral gaze looking out over the auditorium. Cross could read the pride in the set of his head, and in the further straightening of his already rigid spine.

"Admiral Okoye, please step back." Okoye executed a smart about-face, and walked to stand next to Kate, leaving Cross nearest to the podium among the three.

"Lieutenant Commander Cross, please step forward." Cross did it without embarrassing himself, but certainly with less dignity and formality than Okoye had showed. In moments, he stood beside the podium as the admiral began to speak again.

"For your brave actions in the most recent battle with the Xroeshyn, where your timely decision-making and willingness to override the orders of those above you," again she paused for audience reaction, this time a knowing laughter, "preserved the lives of many of our people, you are awarded the Naval Shield." This medal, given only to those whose actions directly save others, resembled a kite shield from deep in Earth's history, engraved with the date of the battle. As she pinned it on his jacket, Davies whispered so that only he could hear her, "Excellent work, sailor."

Turning again to the microphone, she continued speaking. "Lieutenant Commander Cross, upon the recommendation of Admiral James Okoye and with the support of the admirals assembled here, you are hereby promoted to Commander. In addition, until command officers of a higher rank are available, you retain command of the *Washington, DC*. Congratulations, Commander."

Cross broke into a grin, smartly turned about, and walked back to his place in line on the other side of Okoye. He'd gotten what he wanted, command of the *Washington*. The medal and the boost in rank were bonuses. His face hurt as he tried to confine his expression into one appropriate for this event. Still, the edges of his mouth quirked beyond his ability to control them.

"Lieutenant Commander Kate Flynn, please step forward." The admiral turned to watch her glide into place, then faced the audience again. "You are receiving two decorations today, Lieutenant Commander Flynn, for two very different accomplishments. First, for your bravery in accompanying a unit of Marines into an enemy starbase to retrieve vital data, you are awarded the Marine Commendation Ribbon. Gunnery Sergeant Cynthia Murphy will pin it upon you."

Sinner walked forward in full Marine dress uniform and smiled as she pinned the ribbon on to Kate's sleeve. She stepped back and offered Kate a salute that was returned with appropriate decorum. The Marine leaned down and whispered in Kate's ear, slapped her on the shoulder, and then walked away laughing to herself. Cross would've given cash money to know what she'd said to put that embarrassed look on Kate's face.

"Lieutenant Commander Flynn, for your scientific work in analyzing the aliens, in isolating several new wormholes to add to the network, and assistance in the creation of the technology to make that possible, you are awarded the Naval Commendation Medal with a science cluster." The admiral pinned this one on Kate's uniform jacket and then returned to the podium.

"Finally, Lieutenant Commander Kate Flynn, you are hereby promoted to the rank of Commander. Congratulations."

The assembled officers broke into applause for Kate, and for the three of them once she'd rejoined them. Despite the positivity of the moment, Cross was unhappy that Kate was again the same rank as he was. Traditionally, the command hierarchy on a ship the size of the *Washington* had a threefold reduction in rank: Captain, Executive Officer of Commander rank, and second shift Captain of Lieutenant Commander rank. He had hoped Kate would be able to remain with him aboard the *Washington*.

"Admiral, Commanders. You are dismissed. You should head out for an evening of entertainment, secure in the knowledge that your food and bar tab will be picked up by Admiral Matthias." Matthias looked shocked, but then laughed and nodded in agreement.

LATER THAT NIGHT, the three officers were ensconced in a quiet corner of a darkened restaurant, bottles of wine and liquor joining the debris of an excellent meal in the center of their table.

"Where do we go from here?" Cross asked. Kate shook her head and pointed at Okoye, ceding the response to him.

"We go forward, just like always. I join the admiralty and try to make them see sense a little more often. Every now and again, when I'm bored, maybe I'll take the *Rio* out for a spin." The thought of what that would do to the pretentious leader of the *Rio* was good for one more round of laughter. "Cross, you'll go back to being a steadily improving commander in charge of the *DC*."

Cross wisely did not respond, but raised his glass in a toast to his mentor.

"Kate, have they told you what you will be doing?"

Kate, more than a little tipsy, pointed at Okoye. "Shouldn't you already know that, sir, Admiral, sir?" Another round of laughter ensued as she made the universal sign for zipping her lips.

"Fair enough, Kate, fair enough. Now a toast to the two of you: sail safely until our voyages bring us together again."

"Aye to that, sir," Kate said. Cross grinned and toasted. At this moment, despite the mistakes he'd made and the looming threat of alien invasion, he was exactly where he wanted to be.

CHAPTER FORTY-SIX

A week later, Cross walked onto the bridge of the *Washington, DC* for the first time as its official commander. It had taken all his willpower to stay away, but he would've just been in the way of the repair crews, and didn't want to start his tenure by being a pain in the ass. He meandered through the space, watching the crew—his crew—work through their checklists to verify that their stations were ready for departure. His circle eventually brought him to the captain's chair, and he sat down in it, toying with the displays built into the arms, assessing the upgrades that had been made to the venerable ship.

"Commander," the communication officer said, "starbase traffic control sends their compliments. We are cleared to launch in ninety minutes on our assigned vector."

"Thank you, Fitzpatrick. It'll be good to get underway. Too much shore leave is... detrimental to one's health." The bridge crew laughed, having heard the stories of an intoxicated Cross picking a fight with a Marine gunnery sergeant. No charges were filed, and the combatants shook hands and shared a drink in the end, but for a while there it seemed pretty vicious. Or so the bystanders said.

To Cross, it had been just one more night of good clean fun. He was confident his opponent felt the same.

The normal flow of his work was broken some time later. "Incoming message from Captain Dima Petryaev, Commander."

"On screen."

Dima appeared on the display, his ever-present cup of tea in hand, and the bridge of his ship looking undamaged behind him. "Commander Cross, congratulations on your promotion."

"Thank you, Captain."

"You will be happy to know the AAN admiralty has agreed with our assessment, and has decided in its infinite wisdom that perhaps a truce between our peoples would be in order, at least until the alien threat is dealt with."

Cross laughed. "Who did you have to blackmail to make that happen?"

Dima beamed in return. "Only about forty percent of them. The rest either saw the rationale behind it, or realized they could somehow increase their own power by making that decision."

Cross shook his head. "Our people have more in common than I thought, Dima."

"Indeed, Commander, they certainly do."

"Is that a new piece of insignia on your collar, sir?"

Dima looked theatrically shocked and peered down to check. "Oh, that. They added to my burden of command by giving me twelve ships to control, rather than just the one."

"Congratulations are in order for you, then, as well."

"I figure this is my penance for escaping the confines of my carefully crafted orders."

"Whatever it is, Captain, your people couldn't have a finer man in charge of them. I wish them and you very well."

"And I the same to you and yours, Commander Cross. Petryaev out."

Finally, the time was at hand. His crew was at their stations, and Cross gave the commands to uncouple from the station and back out of their berth. As he felt the ship move under him, the reality of it hit him. He had finally gotten everything he wanted, command of the *Washington*, and—

His executive officer burst out of the lift, walked over, and buckled in. Leaning forward, Commander Kate Flynn said the scariest thing he'd ever heard her say, "Probes have found the what looks like the main Xroeshyn fleet in the sector that the AAN suggested we reconnoiter. There's a lot of them. And they've started moving."

THIS IS the end of Trespassers. The Chaos Shift Cycle continues in Book 2, Defenders, available October 2017.

Thank you for reading! Please consider leaving a review and check out the next page to discover how to get more of Cross and Kate for free!

Want More Fantastic Science Fiction Action and Adventure for Free? Join the Readers' Group and get *Suicide Run* as a thank you!

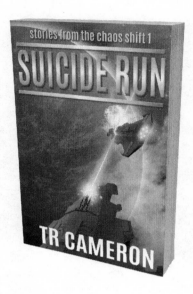

Visit www.trcameron.com/Trespassers to download it for free!

THOM'S TRESPASSERS NOTES: 22 AUGUST 2017

Thank you for buying this book. Thank you for reading this book. Thank you for reading these notes. Seriously. Thank you.

It's taken a little over a year to get this from concept to completion. I'm not going to lie and say it was easy, or that it was always fun. But in the aggregate? It was an amazing experience.

I started an entirely different book, then took a left turn when I heard Cross, Kate, Dima, and Kraada whispering at me. Kate and Kraada, in particular, became favorites as I was writing.

I had several of the story's events planned, but the tunnel blockers came out of nowhere, as did the spiders and Jo the mongoose. I think my favorite bits just happened. Which is too cool.

Books 2 and 3 are already written, and will be ready, assuming my fantastic editors meet their deadlines, in October and November. I'm hoping 4 and 5 will hit in December and January, but I have some extra demands on my time with the school year beginning, so i'm not confident guaranteeing it.

I encourage you to join the reader's group mentioned on the page before this. *Suicide Run* is big fun, and I hope to provide more exclusive content and opportunities to those who join me for the rest of this wild ride.

If Books 1-5 of this series prove popular, I have another 3-5 that are banging around trying to get out of my head. If they don't, I've got an awesome Urban Fantasy Thriller series burbling in the background.

Please, please, please: if you enjoyed this book and have read this far, would you take another couple of minutes and leave a quick review on Amazon? It can literally mean the difference between success or failure of the series.

Finally, I'd love to connect with you! You can find me on Facebook and Twitter. Be sure to mention me on Twitter to catch my attention - that feed goes by ludicrously quickly.

My daughter Dylan has been quoting Jojo Siwa at me lately, so i'll leave you with that quote, which sums up my author journey so far:

"Dream. Believe. Achieve."

Peace, Joy, and Good Fortune to you - So may it be. TRC.

ACKNOWLEDGMENTS

Family, friends, and coworkers: thank you for bearing with me during this process. You are appreciated.

Most memorable comment, from Todd: "It ended and I still wanted more, so that was irritating." It's good to know that I can always count on my friends for support.

Editing: Tracey and Charlotte, you do great work.

Cover: Deranged Doctor Designs, who have been fantastic at dealing with a clueless new author.

Parting comment:

Dylan: "Is your book like Harry Potter?"

Me: "No."

Dylan: "I probably won't read it then."

Thanks, kid.

ABOUT THE AUTHOR

TR Cameron is an emerging author of Science Fiction Adventure. By day, he teaches things to people. By night, he writes and edits and tries to be a decent partner and parent.

Once upon a time, he played World of Warcraft far too much, and remembers the days when Molten Core was everything. When he finds time to play now, story-heavy games are always at the top of his list.

His personal favorite authors range from Douglas Adams to David Weber, Anne Bishop to Jacqueline Carey to CJ Cherryh, Matthew Woodring Stover to Stephen R. Donaldson.

You can find him here:

www.trcameron.com

troacameron@gmail.com

ALSO BY TR CAMERON